HAMMOND PUBLIC LIBRARY

3 1161 00880 5072

P9-BZS-319

Pyper, Andrew.
The demonologist
FICTION PYPER

HPL

AUG 0 1 2013

FEB 2014 HPL

Withdrawn by the
Hammond Public Library

Hammond Public Library
Hammond, Ind.

ALSO BY ANDREW PYPER

The Guardians
The Killing Circle
The Wildfire Season
The Trade Mission
Lost Girls
Kiss Me [*Stories*]

THE DEMONOLOGIST

ANDREW PYPER

Simon & Schuster
New York ✦ London ✦ Toronto ✦ Sydney ✦ New Delhi

Hammond Public Library
Hammond, Ind.

Simon & Schuster
1230 Avenue of the Americas
New York, NY 10020

This book is a work of fiction. Names, characters, places, and incidents
either are products of the author's imagination or are used fictitiously.
Any resemblance to actual events or locales or persons, living or dead,
is entirely coincidental.

Copyright © 2013 by Andrew Pyper Enterprises, Inc.

All rights reserved, including the right to reproduce this book
or portions thereof in any form whatsoever. For information, address
Simon & Schuster Subsidiary Rights Department,
1230 Avenue of the Americas, New York, NY 10020.

First Simon & Schuster hardcover edition March 2013

SIMON & SCHUSTER and colophon are
registered trademarks of Simon & Schuster, Inc.

For information about special discounts for bulk purchases,
please contact Simon & Schuster Special Sales at 1-866-506-1949
or business@simonandschuster.com.

The Simon & Schuster Speakers Bureau can bring authors
to your live event. For more information or to book an event, contact
the Simon & Schuster Speakers Bureau at 1-866-248-3049
or visit our website at www.simonspeakers.com.

Design by Esther Paradelo

Manufactured in the United States of America

10 9 8 7 6 5 4 3 2 1

Library of Congress Cataloging-in-Publication Data
Pyper, Andrew.
The demonologist / Andrew Pyper.—1st Simon & Schuster
hardcover ed.
    p. cm.
1. College teachers—New York (N.Y.)—Fiction. 2. Adult children
of alcoholics—Fiction. 3. Psychic trauma—Fiction. 4. Demonology—Fiction.
5. Psychological fiction. I. Title.
PR9199.3.P96D46 2013
813'.54—dc22 2012025715
ISBN 978-1-4516-9741-4
ISBN 978-1-4516-9743-8 (ebook)

Raymond Public Library
Raymond, Ind

FICTION
PYPER

For Maude

Millions of spiritual creatures walk the earth
Unseen, both when we wake, and when we sleep

JOHN MILTON
Paradise Lost

Last night I had the dream again. Except it's not a dream. I know because when it comes for me, I'm still awake.

There's my desk. The map on the wall. The stuffed animals I don't play with anymore but don't want to hurt Dad's feelings by sticking in the closet. I might be in bed. I might be just standing there, looking for a missing sock. Then I'm gone.

It doesn't just show me something this time. It takes me from here to THERE.

Standing on the bank of a river of fire. A thousand wasps in my head. Fighting and dying inside my skull, their bodies piling up against the backs of my eyes. Stinging and stinging.

Dad's voice. Somewhere across the river. Calling my name.

I've never heard him sound like that before. He's so frightened he can't hide it, even though he tries (he ALWAYS tries).

The dead boy floats by.

Facedown. So I wait for his head to pop up, show the holes where his eyes used to be, say something with his blue lips. One of the terrible things it might make him do. But he just passes like a chunk of wood.

I've never been here before, but I know it's real.

The river is the line between this place and the Other Place. And I'm on the wrong side.

There's a dark forest behind me but that's not what it is.

I try to get to where Dad is. My toes touch the river and it sings with pain.

Then there's arms pulling me back. Dragging me into the trees. They feel like a man's arms but it's not a man that sticks its fingers into my mouth. Nails that scratch the back of my throat. Skin that tastes like dirt.

But just before that, before I'm back in my room with my missing sock in my hand, I realize I've been calling out to Dad just like he's been calling out to me. Telling him the same thing the whole time. Not words from my mouth through the air, but from my heart through the earth, so only the two of us could hear it.

FIND ME

UNCREATED NIGHT

THE ROWS OF FACES. YOUNGER AND YOUNGER EACH TERM. OF course, this is only me getting older among the freshmen who come and go, an illusion, like looking out the rear window of a car and seeing the landscape run away from you instead of you running from it.

I've been delivering this lecture long enough to play around with thoughts like these while speaking aloud to two hundred students at the same time. It's time to sum things up. One last attempt to sell at least a few of the laptop ticklers before me on the magnificence of a poem I have more or less devoted my working life to.

"And here we come to the end," I tell them, and pause. Wait for the fingers to lift from the keyboards. Take a full breath of the lecture hall's undercirculated air and feel, as I always do, the devastating sadness that comes at reciting the poem's closing lines.

Some natural tears they dropped, but wiped them soon;
The world was all before them, where to choose
Their place of rest, and Providence their guide:

They hand in hand with wand'ring steps and slow,
Through Eden took their solitary way.

With these words I feel my daughter next to me. Since she was born—and even before that, as the mere idea of the child I wished to one day have—it is Tess whom I invariably imagine walking out of the garden with, hand in hand.

"Loneliness," I go on. "That is what this entire work really comes down to. Not good versus evil, not a campaign to 'justify the ways of God to men.' It is the most convincing case we have—more convincing than any in the Bible itself—that hell is real. Not as a fiery pit, not a place above or below but *in* us, a place in the mind. To know ourselves and, in turn, to endure the perpetual reminder of our solitude. To be cast out. To wander alone. What is the real fruit of original sin? Selfhood! *That* is where our poor newlyweds are left, together but in the solitude of self-consciousness. Where can they wander now? 'Anywhere!' the serpent says. 'The whole world is theirs!' And yet they are condemned to choose their own 'solitary way.' It is a fearful, even terrifying, journey. But it is one all of us must face, as much now as then."

Here I take another, even longer, pause. Long enough that there is a risk I will be taken as being finished, and someone might stand, or slap her laptop shut, or bark out a cough. But they never do.

"Ask yourselves," I say, tightening my hold on Tess's imagined hand. "Where will you go now that Eden has been left behind?"

An arm almost instantly shoots up. A kid near the back I've never called on, never even noticed, before now.

"Yes?"

"Is that question going to be on the exam?"

MY NAME IS DAVID ULLMAN. I TEACH IN THE ENGLISH DEPARTment at Columbia University in Manhattan, a specialist in mythology and Judeo-Christian religious narrative, though my meal ticket, the text upon which my critical study has justified my tenure in the

Ivy League and invitations to various academic boondoggles around the world, has been Milton's *Paradise Lost*. Fallen angels, the temptations by the serpent, Adam and Eve and original sin. A seventeenth-century epic poem that retells biblical events but with a crafty slant, a perspective that arguably lends sympathy to Satan, the leader of the rebel angels who became fed up with a grumpy, authoritarian God and broke out on his own in a career of making trouble in the lives of humans.

It's been a funny (the devout might even say hypocritical) way to make a living: I have spent my life teaching about things I don't believe in. An atheist biblical scholar. A demon expert who believes evil to be a manmade invention. I have written essays about miracles—healed lepers, water into wine, exorcisms—but have never seen a magician's trick I couldn't figure out. My justification for these apparent contradictions is that there are some things that bear meaning, culturally speaking, without actually existing. The Devil, angels. Heaven. Hell. They are part of our lives even if we never have and never will see them, touch them, prove them to be real. Things that go bump in the brain.

> *The mind is its own place, and in it self*
> *Can make a heaven of hell, a hell of heaven.*

That is John Milton, speaking through Satan, his most brilliant fiction. And I happen to believe the old fellow—*both* old fellows—have got it right.

THE AIR OF COLUMBIA'S MORNINGSIDE CAMPUS IS DAMP WITH EXAM stress and the only-partial cleansing of a New York rain. I've just finished delivering my final lecture of the spring term, an occasion that always brings a bittersweet relief, the knowledge that another year is done (the class prep and office hours and evaluations almost finished) but also that another year has passed (and with it, another distressing click on the personal odometer). Nevertheless, unlike many of the coddled grumblers who surround me at faculty functions and fuss over pointless points-of-order at departmental committee meetings, I still like teaching, still like the students who are encountering grown-up literature for the first time. Yes, most of them are only here as pre–Something That Will Make Serious Money—pre-med, pre-law, pre–marrying rich—but most of them are not yet wholly beyond reach. If not my reach, then poetry's.

It's just past three. Time to walk across the tiled quad to my office in Philosophy Hall, drop off the clutch of late term papers guiltily piled on my desk at the front of the lecture hall, then head downtown to Grand Central to meet Elaine O'Brien for our annual end-of-term drink at the Oyster Bar.

Though Elaine teaches in the Psychology Department, I'm closer to her than anyone in English. Indeed, I'm closer to her than anyone I know in New York. She is the same age as me—a trim, squash court and half-marathoned forty-three—though a widow, her husband claimed by an out-of-nowhere stroke four years ago, the same year I arrived at Columbia. I liked her at once. Possessed of what I have come to think of as a serious sense of humor: She tells few jokes, but observes the world's absurdities with a wit that is somehow hopeful and withering at the same time. A quietly beautiful woman too, I would say, though I am a married man—as of today, at any rate—and acknowledging this kind of admiration for a female colleague and occasional drinking buddy may be, as the University Code of Conduct likes to designate virtually all human interaction, "inappropriate."

Yet there has been nothing remotely inappropriate between O'Brien and me. Not a single stolen kiss before she boards her train on the New Haven line, not one flirty speculation over what might happen if we were to scuttle up to a room at some Midtown hotel and see what we'd be like, just once, in the sack. It's not repression that prevents us—I don't think it is, anyway—and it's not entirely our mutual honoring of my marital vows (given that we both know my wife threw hers out the window for that smug prick in Physics, the smirky string theorist, Will Junger, a year ago). I believe O'Brien and I (she is "Elaine" only after a third martini) haven't nudged things in that direction because we fear it might befoul what we already have. And what do we have? A profound if sexless intimacy of a kind I've never known with either man or woman since childhood, and perhaps not even then.

Still, I suppose O'Brien and I have been carrying on an affair of sorts for the better part of the time we've been friends. When we get together, we talk about things I haven't talked about with Diane for some time. For O'Brien, it is the dilemma of her future: fearing the prospect of single old age while recognizing she's become used to being on her own, indulgent of her habits. A woman "increasingly un-marryable," as she puts it.

For me, it is the dark cloud of depression. Or, I should say, what I reluctantly feel obliged to call depression, just as half the world has diagnosed itself, though it doesn't seem to precisely fit my case. All my life I have been pursued by the black dogs of unaccountable gloom, despite the good luck of my career, the initially promising marriage, and the greatest fortune of all, my only child: a bright and tender-hearted daughter, who was born following a pregnancy all the doctors said would never come to term, the only miracle I am prepared to concede as real. After Tess arrived, the black dogs went away for a little while. But as she graduated from toddlerhood to chattering school age, they returned, hungrier than before. Even my love for Tess, even her whispered bedtime wishes of *Daddy, don't be sad* could not hold them at bay.

There has always been a sense that there's something *not quite right* with me. Nothing you'd notice on the outside—I'm nothing if not "polished," as Diane described me with pride when we first started dating, and now uses the same term in a tone that bears scathing connotations. Even on the inside I am honestly free of self-pity or frustrated ambition, an atypical state for a tenure-track academic. No, my shadows issue from a more elusive source than the textbooks would have it. And as for my symptoms, I can tick few if any checkmarks beside the list of warning signs on the mental health public service announcements plastered above the doors of subway cars. Irritability or aggression? Only when I watch the news. Lost appetite? Nope.

I've been unsuccessfully trying to lose ten pounds since I left college. Trouble concentrating? I read Dead White Guy poems and under-grad papers for a living—concentration is my business.

My malady is more an indefinable presence than pleasure-draining absence. The sense that I have an unseen companion following me through my days, waiting to seize an opportunity, to find a closer rela-tionship than the one it already enjoys. In childhood, I vainly tried to ascribe a personality to it, treat it as an "imaginary friend" of the kind I'd heard other children sometimes conjured. But my follower only followed—it did not play or protect or console. Its sole interest lay—and still lies—in providing dark company, malicious in its silence.

Professorial semantics, maybe, but it feels more like melancholy to me than anything as clinical as the chemical imbalances of depression. What Robert Burton called in his *Anatomy of Melancholy* (published four hundred years ago, back when Milton was first sketching his Satan) a "vexation of spirit." It's as though my very life has been haunted.

O'Brien has almost given up suggesting I should see a shrink. She's grown too used to my reply: "Why should I when I have you?"

I'm allowing myself a smile at this when it is instantly wiped away by the sight of Will Junger coming down the Low Library's stone steps. Waving my way as though we are friends. As though his fucking my wife for the last ten months is a fact that has momentarily escaped his mind.

"David! A word?"

What does this man look like? Something sly and surprisingly car-nivorous. Something with claws.

"Another year," he says once he stands in front of me, stagily breathless.

He squints at me, shows his teeth. It's expressions like these, I suppose, that counted as "charming" in his first post–yoga class coffees with Diane. This was the word she used when I asked the always first, always useless, question of the cuckold: *Why him?* She shrugged, as though she didn't require a reason, and was surprised that I might. "He's *charming*," she said finally, landing on the word as a butterfly decides which flower to rest on.

10

"Listen, I don't want this to be difficult," Will begins. "I'm just sorry for the way things have turned out."

"And how is that?"

"Sorry?"

"How have things turned out?"

He rolls out his lower lip in a gesture of hurt. String theory. That's what he teaches, what he talks to Diane about, presumably, after he's rolled off her. How all matter, if you peel it down to the essentials, is bound by impossibly tiny strings. I don't know about matter, but I could believe that this is all Will Junger is made of. Invisible strands that lift his eyebrows and the corners of his mouth, an expertly rendered puppet.

"I'm just trying to be a grown-up here," he says.

"You have any kids, Will?"

"Kids? No."

"Of course you don't. And you never will, you selfish child," I say, heaving myself full of damp air. *Trying to be a grown-up here*? Fuck you. You think this is a scene in some indie drama you take my wife to in the Village, some pack of lies the guy at the *Times* said was so naturalistically performed. But in *real life*? We're bad actors. We're slobs who actually hurt. *You* don't feel it, *you* couldn't, but the pain you're causing us—causing my family—it's destroying our lives, what we have together. What we had."

"Listen, David. I—"

"I have a daughter," I go on, steamrolling him. "A little girl who knows something is wrong, and she's slipping into this dark place I don't know how to pull her out of. Do you know what it is to watch your child, your everything, come apart? Of course you don't. You're empty. A *summa cum laude* sociopath who talks about literally nothing for a living. Invisible strings! You're a nothing specialist. A walking, talking vacancy."

I didn't expect to say all this, but I'm glad I have. Later, I'll wish I could hop in a time machine and return to this moment to deliver a better-crafted insult. But for now, it feels pretty good.

"It's funny you say that about me," he says.

"Funny?"

"Ironic. Perhaps that's the better term."

"*Ironic* is never the better term."

"This was Diane's idea, by the way. That we talk."

"You're lying. She knows what I think of you."

"But do you know what *she* thinks of *you*?"

The puppet strings are lifted. Will Junger smiles an unexpected smile of triumph.

"'You're not here,'" he says. "That's what she says. 'David? How would *I* know how David feels? *He's not here.*'"

There's no reply to this. Because it's true. That's been the death sentence of our marriage, and I have been powerless to correct the fault. It's not workaholism, not the distractions of a lover or obsessive hobby, not the distance to which men tend to retreat as they drag their feet into middle age. Part of me—the part Diane needs—simply isn't here anymore. Lately I can be in the same room, the same bed, and she reaches for me, but it is like trying to grasp the moon. What I'd like to know, what I'd pray to be told if I thought praying might work, is where the missing piece is. What did I leave behind? What did I never have to start with? What name is to be given the parasite that has fed on me without me noticing?

The sun comes out and all at once the city is bathed in steam, the library steps glinting. Will Junger wrinkles his nose. He is a cat. I see that now, far too late. A black cat that's crossed my path.

"Gonna be a hot one," he says and starts away into the new light.

I HEAD PAST THE BRONZE OF RODIN'S *The Thinker* ("HE LOOKS LIKE he has a toothache," Tess once rightly said of him) and into Philosophy Hall. My office is on the third floor, and I take the stairs clinging to the handrail, drained by the sudden heat.

When I reach my floor and make the corner I'm hit by a sensation of vertigo so intense I scramble to the wall and cling to the brick. I've had, now and then, panic attacks of the sort that leave you momentarily breathless, what my mother would call "dizzy spells." But this is something else altogether. A distinct sensation of falling. Not from a height but *into* a borderless space. An abyss that swallows me, the building, the world in a single, merciless gulp.

Then it's gone. Leaving me glad that nobody witnessed my spontaneous wall hugging.

Nobody but the woman sitting on the chair outside my office door.

Too old to be a student. Too well-dressed to be an academic. I put her in her mid-thirties at first, but as I approach, she seems older, her bones overly pronounced, the premature aging of the eating disordered. She looks to be starving, in fact. A brittleness her tailored suit and long, dyed black hair cannot hide.

"Professor Ullman?"

Her accent is European, but generically so. It could be an American-flavored French, German, or Czech. An accent that hides one's origins rather than reveals them.

"I'm not holding office hours today."

"Of course. I read the card on your door."

"Are you here about a student? Is your child in my class?"

I am used to this scene: the helicopter parent, having taken out a third mortgage to put her kid into a fancy college, making a plea on behalf of her B-student Great Hope. Yet even as I ask this woman if this is the case, I know it isn't. She's here for me.

"No, no," she answers, pulling a stray strand of hair from her lips. "I am here to deliver an invitation."

"My mailbox is downstairs. You can leave anything addressed to me with the porter."

"A *verbal* invitation."

She stands. Taller than I expected. And though she is as worryingly thin as she appeared while seated, there is no apparent weakness in her frame. She holds the balls of her shoulders wide, her sharp chin pointed at the ceiling.

"I have an appointment downtown," I say, though I am already reaching for the handle to open the door. And she is already shuffling close to follow me in.

13

"Only a moment, professor," she says. "I promise not to make you late."

MY OFFICE IS NOT LARGE, AND THE STUFFED BOOKSHELVES AND stacked papers shrink the space even more. I've always felt this lends the room a coziness, a scholarly nest. This afternoon, however, even after I fall into the chair behind my desk and the Thin Woman sits on the antique bench where my students ask for extensions or beg for higher grades, it is suffocating. The air thin, as though we have been transported to a higher altitude.

The woman smoothes her skirt. Her fingers too long. The only jewelry she wears is a gold band on her thumb. So loosely fitting it spins whenever she moves her hand.

"An introduction would be customary at this point," I say, surprised by the crisp aggression of my tone. It doesn't come from a position of strength, I realize, but self-defense. A smaller animal puffing up to create the illusion of ferocity before a predator.

"My real name is information I cannot provide, unfortunately," she says. "Of course I could offer something false—an alias—but lies of any sort make me uncomfortable. Even the harmless lies of social convenience."

"This puts you at an advantage."

"An advantage? But this isn't a *contest*, professor. We are on the same side."

"What side is that?"

She laughs at this. The sickly rattle of a barely controlled cough. Both hands flying up to cover her mouth.

"Your accent. I can't quite place it," I say when she has settled and the thumb ring has stopped spinning.

"I have lived in many places."

"A traveler."

"A wanderer. Perhaps that is the way to put it."

"Wandering implies an absence of purpose."

"Does it? But that cannot be. For it has brought me here."

She slides herself forward so that she is perched on the bench's edge, a movement of perhaps two or three inches. Yet it's as though she has come to sit upon my desk, the space between us impolitely close. I can smell her now. A vaguely barnyard whiff of straw, of close-quartered livestock. There is a second when I feel like I may not be able to take another breath without some visible show of disgust. And then she begins. Her voice not wholly disguising the scent, but somehow quieting its intensity.

"I represent a client who demands discretion above all. And in this particular case, as you will no doubt appreciate, this requirement limits me to only relating the most necessary information to you."

"A need-to-know basis."

"Yes," she says, and cocks her head, as though she's never heard the phrase before. "Only what you need to know."

"Which is what?"

"Your expertise is required to assist my client in understanding an ongoing case of primary interest. Which is why I am here. To invite you, as a consultant, to provide your professional insight, observations, whatever you may feel to be of relevance in clarifying our understanding of the—" She stops here, seeming to choose from a list of possible words in her mind, and finally settling on the best of an inadequate selection. "The phenomenon."

"Phenomenon?"

"If you will forgive my generality."

"It all sounds very mysterious."

"Necessarily so. As I mentioned."

She continues to look at me. As if I have come to *her* with questions. As if it is she who waits for me to move us forward. So I do.

"You refer to a 'case.' What does it involve, precisely?"

"Precisely? That is beyond what I am able to say."

"Because it's a secret? Or because you don't understand it yourself?"

"The question is fair. But to answer it would be a betrayal of what I have been charged to disclose."

"You're not giving me much."

"At the risk of overstepping my instructed limits of conversation, let me say that there isn't much for me to give. You are the expert, professor, not me. I have come to you seeking answers, your point of view. I have neither."

"Have you yourself seen this phenomenon?"

She swallows. The skin of her neck stretched so tight I can see it move down her throat like a mouse under a bedsheet.

"I have, yes," she says.

"And what is your opinion of it?"

"Opinion?"

"How would you describe it? Not professionally, not as an expert, but you personally. What do you think it is?"

"Oh, that I couldn't say," she says, shaking her head, eyes down, as though I am flirting with her and the attention is cause for embarrassment.

"Why not?"

She raises her eyes to me. "Because there is no name for it I could give," she says.

I should ask her to go. Whatever curiosity I held about her when I first spotted her outside the office door is gone. This exchange can go nowhere now but into some revelation of deeper strangeness, and not of the amusing anecdote variety, not something about a crazy woman's proposal I might later repeat at dinner parties. Because she's not crazy. Because the usual veil of protection one feels while experiencing brief intersections with the harmlessly eccentric has been lifted, and I feel exposed.

"Why do you need me?" I find myself saying instead. "There are a lot of English profs out there."

"But few demonologists."

"That's not how I would describe myself."

"No?" She grins. A show of giddy humor that is meant to distract from how clearly serious she is. "You are a renowned expert on religious narrative, mythology, and the like, are you not? In particular, the recorded occurrences of biblical mention of the Adversary? Apocryphal documentation of demonic activity in the ancient world? Is my research in error?"

"All that you say is true. But I don't know anything about demons or inventions of that kind outside of those texts."

"Of course! We didn't expect you to have firsthand experience."

"Who would?"

"Who would indeed! No, professor, it is only your academic qualifications that we seek."

"I'm not sure you understand. I don't *believe*."

She merely frowns at this in apparent lack of comprehension.

"I'm not a cleric. Not a theologian either, for that matter. I don't accept the existence of demons any more than that of Santa Claus," I go on. "I don't go to church. I don't see the events in the Bible or any other holy document as having actually occurred, particularly not as they pertain to the supernatural. You want a demonologist, I suggest you contact the Vatican. Maybe there are some there who still take that stuff seriously."

"Yes." She grins again. "I assure you there are."

"You work for the Church?"

"I work for an agency that has been endowed with a substantial budget and wide-ranging responsibilities."

"I'll take that as a yes."

She leans forward. Her blunt elbows audibly meeting her knees. "I know you have an appointment. You currently still have time to travel to Grand Central to make it. So may I now deliver you my client's proposal?"

"Wait. I didn't tell you I was going to Grand Central."

"No. You did not."

She doesn't move. Her stillness a point of emphasis.

"May I?" she asks again, after what feels like a full minute.

I lean back, gesturing for her to continue. There is no more pretending I have a choice in the matter. She has, in just the last moments, enlarged her presence in the room so that she now blocks the door as effectively as a nightclub bouncer.

"We will fly you to Venice at your earliest convenience. Tomorrow, preferably. You will be accommodated at one of the old city's finest hotels—my personal favorite, if I may add. Once there, you will attend at an address to be provided. No written document or report of any kind will be required. In fact, we ask that you *not* acknowledge your observations to anyone other than the individuals attending on-site. That is all. Of course, all expenses will be paid. Business class flight. Along with a consulting fee we hope you will feel is reasonable."

At this she stands. Takes the single step required to reach my desk, picks a pen out of a coffee mug, and scribbles a figure onto the memo pad next to the phone. It is a sum just over a third my annual salary.

"You'll pay me this to go to Venice and visit somebody's house? Turn around and fly back? That's it?"

"In essence."

"It's a hell of a story."

"You doubt my sincerity?"

"I hope you're not hurt."

"Not at all. I sometimes forget that, for some, verification is required."

She reaches into the inside pocket of her jacket. Lays a white business envelope on my desk. Unaddressed.

"What's this?"

"Aircraft voucher. Prepaid hotel reservation. Certified check for a quarter of your payment, the remainder to be paid upon your return. And the address at which you are to be in attendance."

I let my hand hover over the envelope, as though touching it would concede a crucial point.

"Naturally, you are welcome to bring your family with you," she says. "You have a wife? A daughter?"

"A daughter, yes. I'm less certain about the wife."

She looks up at the ceiling, closes her eyes. Then recites:

Hail wedded love, mysterious law, true source
Of human offspring, sole propriety
In Paradise of all things common else.

"You're a Milton scholar, too?" I ask when she's opened her eyes again.

18

"Not of your rank, professor. I am an admirer only."

"Not many casual admirers have him memorized."

"Learned knowledge. It is a gift of mine. Though I have never experienced what the poet describes. *Human offspring*. I am childless."

This last confession is surprising. After all the elusiveness, she offers this most personal fact freely, almost sadly.

"Milton was right about the joy of offspring," I say. "But trust me, he was way off about marriage as being common with paradise."

She nods, though seemingly not at my remark. Something else has been confirmed for her. Or perhaps she has merely delivered all that she was meant to, and is awaiting my reply. So I give it to her.

"My answer is no. Whatever this is about, it's intriguing, but quite beyond my scope. There's no way I could accept."

"You misunderstand. I am not here to hear your answer, professor. I am here to deliver an invitation, that is all."

"Fine. But I'm afraid your client will be disappointed."

"That is rarely the case."

In a single motion, she turns. Steps out of the room. I expect a cordial acknowledgment of some kind, a *Good day, professor* or wave of her bony hand, but she only starts clipping down the hall toward the stairs.

By the time I lift myself out of my chair and poke my head out the door to look after her, she's already gone.

2

𝕴 GATHER SOME WORK THINGS INTO MY SATCHEL AND MAKE MY way back out into the heat to the subway. The air is more wretched down here, vacuum-sealed and sweetened by garbage. This, along with the human scents, each relating a small tragedy of enslavement or frustrated desire as they pass.

On the ride downtown I try to summon the Thin Woman, to recall the physical details of her person, so vividly present only minutes earlier. But whether it is the unsettling events of the day or some corner of my short-term memory gone on the fritz, she returns to me only as an idea, not as a person. And the idea is more unnatural, more frightening, in recollection than she struck me at the time. To think of her now is like the difference between experiencing a nightmare and telling someone in the bright safety of the morning about its meandering, foolish plot.

At Grand Central I rise up the escalator and tunnels that feed into the station's main concourse. Rush hour. It feels more like panic than purposeful travel. And nobody is more lost-looking than the tourists, who have come to witness the thrill of bustling New York but now stand merely stricken, clinging to their spouses and children.

O'Brien stands by the information kiosk beneath the gold clock at the center of the floor, our traditional meeting place. She looks pale. Possibly irritated, rightly, by my lateness.

She's looking the other way when I sidle up next to her. A tap on her shoulder and she jumps.

"Didn't know it was you," she apologizes. "Though I should have, shouldn't I? This is our place."

I like that more than I perhaps ought to—the notion of "our place"—but write it off as merely an accident of words.

"Sorry I'm late."

"You are forgiven."

"Remind me again," I say. *"Why* is this our place? Is it a Hitchcock thing? *North by Northwest?"*

"And you are my Cary Grant? A self-flattering notion. Not that the casting is so far off, so don't pout. But the truth is I like meeting here precisely for all that makes it so *uncivilized.* The crush. The masks of greed and desperation. The pandemonium. Organized chaos."

"Pandemonium," I repeat absently, though too quietly for O'Brien to hear amid the hubbub.

"What'd you say?"

"It's the name Satan gives the fortress he builds for himself and his followers after being cast out of heaven."

"You're not the only one who's read Milton, David."

"Of course. You were way ahead of me."

O'Brien takes a step to look directly up at me. "What's up? You look all wobbly."

I think of telling her about the Thin Woman, the strange proposal delivered to me at my office. But there is a sense that this would be sharing a secret I was meant to keep—more than a "sense," a physical warning, my chest tightening and a distinct squeezing around my windpipe, as though invisible fingers have passed through my flesh to silence me. I find myself murmuring something about the heat, my need for a stiff drink.

22

"That's what we're here for, isn't it?" O'Brien replies, taking me by the arm and leading me through the mob on the terminal floor. Her hand on my elbow a patch of cool on my suddenly burning skin.

The Oyster Bar is underground. A windowless cavern beneath the station floor that, for whatever reason, lends itself to the eating of raw seafood and the drinking of cold vodka. O'Brien and I have spent our time here mulling over the state of our careers (mine hitting the top of its game, enjoying "leading world expert" status at almost every mention, and O'Brien's writing on the psychological underpinnings of faith healing lending her recent semi-fame). Mostly, though, we talk about nothing in particular in the way of well-matched, if unlikely, companions.

What makes us unlikely? She's a woman, first of all. A single woman. Dark hair cut short, blue eyes blazing out of a darkly Irish complexion. Unlike me, she comes from money, though of the unshowy, northeastern kind. A tennis-camp Connecticut youth, followed by a seemingly effortless gathering of high-powered degrees, a successful private practice in Boston, and now Columbia, where only last year she stepped down as head of the Psych Department to concentrate more on her own research. A winning résumé, no question. But not exactly the profile for a married guy's drinking buddy.

Diane has never directly complained about our friendship. In fact, it's something she's encouraged. Not that this has stopped her from being jealous of our Oyster Bar celebrations, our midweek sports bar watching of hockey games (O'Brien and I are both now provisional Rangers fans, though born to other teams, she the Bruins, I the Leafs). Diane has no choice but to accept O'Brien, as to deny our friendship would be to concede that there is something Elaine gives me that Diane cannot. That this is true and plainly known to all three of us is what can make coming home after a night out with O'Brien especially chilly.

The thought that I might cut off our friendship as a peace offering to Diane has occurred to me, as it would to any husband in a floundering marriage who still wants it to work, against all odds and good advice. And I *do* want it to work. I admit to more than my fair share of failings—the undefined pool of shade that lies at the bottom of who I am—but none are intentional, none within grasp of my control. My imperfections haven't prevented me from doing everything I could think of to be a good husband to Diane. But the thing is: I need Elaine O'Brien in my life. Not as a chronic flirtation, not as a sentimental torment of what might have been, but as my counsel, my more articulate, clear-thinking inner self.

This may sound strange—it *is* strange—but she has taken the place of the brother I lost when I was a child. While I could do nothing to prevent his death then, I cannot now let O'Brien go.

What's less clear is what she gets from our association. I've asked her, from time to time, why she wastes so many of her sparse social hours on a melancholic Miltonist like me. Her answer is always the same.

"I'm meant for you," she says.

We find stools at the long bar and order a dozen New Brunswick malpeques and a couple martinis to get us started. The place is jostling and loud as the floor of the Stock Exchange, yet O'Brien and I instantly find ourselves cocooned in our shared thoughts. I begin by relating my encounter with Will Junger, adding some sharper putdowns to the ones I actually delivered earlier that afternoon (and leaving out the raw confessions of worry about Tess). O'Brien smiles, though she detects my embellishments (and likely my omissions, too) as I knew she would.

"Did you really say all that?"

"Almost," I say. "I certainly *wish* I had said all that."

"Then let's say you did. Let the record show that the slippery snake, William Junger of Physics, is right now licking the verbal wounds inflicted by the dangerously underestimated Dave Ullman of Old Books."

"Yes. I like that." I nod, sipping my drink. "It's like a kind of superpower, when you think of it. Having a friend who accepts your version of reality."

"There's no reality but versions of reality."

"Who said that?"

"Me, as far as I know," she says, and takes a long drink herself.

The vodka, the consoling pleasure of being next to her, the confidence that, for now, nothing of any real danger could be visited on us—all of it makes me feel it would be okay to plunge forward and tell O'Brien about my meeting with the Thin Woman. I'm wiping my lips with a napkin in preparation when she begins before I do.

"I have some news," she says, slurping down a malpeque. It is the kind of introduction that suggests top-tier gossip, something startling and necessarily sexual. But then, after swallowing, she announces: "I have cancer."

If there was anything in my throat, I would have choked on it.

"That a joke?" I say. "Tell me that's a fucking joke."

"Do the oncologists at New York Presbyterian joke?"

"Elaine. My God. No. *No.*"

"They're not exactly sure where it started, but it's in the bones now. Which would explain my piss-poor squash game of late."

"I'm so sorry."

"What is the bargain-store Zen mantra these days? *It is what it is.*"

"Is it serious? I mean—of course it's *serious*—but how far along?"

"Advanced, they say. Like it's a grad course or something. Only cancers having already received their prerequisites need apply."

She's doing an astonishing job at being good humored—it's being with me that helps, I can tell, along with the bracing courage of the martini—but there's a tremble at the corner of her mouth that now I can see is a battle against tears. And then, before I know it, I'm the one who's crying. Throwing my arms around her, knocking a couple empty oyster shells off our ice tray and onto the floor.

"Easy, professor," O'Brien whispers into my ear, though she holds me just as tightly as I hold her. "People might get the wrong idea."

And what would the right idea be? An embrace such as this could never be confused with lust or congratulation. It is a hopeless refusal. A child clinging to a departing loved one at the station, fighting the inevitable to the end, instead of the adult's polite surrender.

"We'll get help," I say. "We'll find the right doctors."

"It's beyond that, David."

"You're not just going to *accept* this, are you?"

"Yes. I'm going to try. And I'd like to ask you to help me."

She pushes me back from her. Not from embarrassment, but so she can show me her eyes.

"I know you're afraid," she says.

"Of course I'm afraid. This is a pretty devastating—"

"I'm not talking about the cancer. I'm talking about you."

She takes a long breath. Whatever she is about to say requires energy she may not have. So I grip her arms to support her. Bend close to listen.

"I've never been able to figure out what you're so scared of, but there's something in you that's got you backed into a corner so tight your eyes are closed against it," she says. "You don't have to tell me what it is. I bet you don't even know yourself. But here's the thing: I probably won't be around for you when you face it down. I wish I could be, but I won't. You're going to need someone. You won't make it if you're alone. I don't know of anyone who could."

"Tess."

"That's right."

"You want me to look out for Tess?"

"I want you to remember that she's as scared as you are. That she thinks she's alone, too."

"Not sure I'm getting—"

"Your *melancholy*. Or depression. Along with nine-tenths of the afflictions I've studied, diagnosed, attempted to treat. Call them whatever you like, but they're just different names for loneliness. That's what lets the darkness in. That's what you have to fight."

Loneliness. As though O'Brien was at my lecture today, taking notes.

"I'm not alone."

"But you *think* you are. You've thought you've been all on your own your whole life—and what do I know? Maybe you have. It nearly took you down. If you didn't have your books, your work, all the shields of your mind, it *would* have. It still wants to. But you can't let it, because there's Tess now. And no matter how far away she'll drift from you, you can't give up. She's your *child*, David. She is *you*. So you have to prove your love for her every goddamn minute of every goddamn day. Anything less and you fail the Human Being Test. Anything less and you really are just alone."

Even here, in the A/C-challenged Oyster Bar, O'Brien shivers.

"Where is this coming from?" I ask her. "You've never said anything like that about Tess before. That she's . . . like me. By which you mean she has what I have."

"More than eye color and height passes through the bloodline."

"Hold on a second here. Are you speaking as Dr. O'Brien the shrink? Or my pal O'Brien, the friendly kicker of ass?"

This question, intended to return us to lighter ground, only seems to confound her. And in the moment she struggles to find an answer, her illness passes over her features. Her skin pulls close over her face, her color fades. In a transformation that would be invisible to anyone but me, she now looks as though she could be the Thin Woman's sister. A likeness that ought to have been apparent from the time I saw the woman sitting outside my office, but revealed, in a private second of horror, only now.

"It's just something I know," she answers finally.

We carry on for a while. Order another round, share a lobster as we normally do. The whole time O'Brien expertly keeps us from returning to her diagnosis, or her oddly portentous insight into my lifelong affliction. She has said all that she meant to say about it. And there is the unspoken assurance between us that even she isn't sure of its full implications.

When we're done, I walk her back up to the main terminal floor. It's quieter here now, the commuters outnumbered by the gawkers, the picture takers. I'm ready to wait with O'Brien at the entrance to her platform until her train up to Greenwich is ready to go, but she stops me at the gold clock.

"I'll be okay," she says with a weak smile.

"Of course you will. But there's no point waiting alone."

"I'm not alone." She links her hand around my wrist in a show of gratitude. "And there's someone waiting for you."

"I doubt that. These days, Tess just locks herself in her room after dinner, gets on the computer. DO NOT DISTURB in neon on her door."

"Sometimes people close a door because they're trying to figure out a way to get you to knock."

O'Brien releases my wrist and slips away into a pack of German tourists. I would follow, or try, but she doesn't want me to. So I turn and head off in the opposite direction, down the tunnel to the subway entrance, the air getting hotter the farther from the surface I go.

$\mathcal{I}$ EMERGE FROM THE 86TH STREET STOP ON THE UPPER WEST Side. This is where we live, my little family among the other little families of our neighborhood, our street often crowded with latte-holding parents pushing state-of-the-art, single-child strollers. It's magazine perfect for people like us: educated professionals with a prejudice against the suburbs and a faith that living here, in relative safety yet also a short walk to Central Park, the Museum of Natural History, and high-rated public schools, will give our only children what they need to become us one day.

I like it here, in a permanent tourist sort of way. I grew up in Toronto, a city of a more modest scale and modest temperament, relatively unmythologized. Living in New York has, for me, been a process of getting better at pretending. Pretending this is really my home and not a fabrication from novels, from movies. Pretending we will ever pay off the mortgage on our roomy three-bedroom apart-ment in a "prestige building" on 84th Street. I'm often troubled by the fact that we can't really afford the place, though Diane likes to point out that "nobody *affords* things, David. It's not 1954 anymore."

Things are bad between us, perhaps irreparably bad. But as I rattle upward in the old elevator to our floor I'm readying the news of this strange day, deciding what to lead with, what to bury. I want to tell Diane about O'Brien, my chat with Will Junger, the Thin Woman, because there is no one else to share these particular items with, each too intimate, in their own ways, to lay out before a colleague or at a dinner-party table. But there is also the hope of reaching her. Revealing something that might give her pause, arouse her interest, her sympathy. A delay of the inevitable, which is maybe all I can play for these days.

I open the door to the apartment and find Diane standing there, waiting for me, a nearly empty wine glass in her hand. What's her expression say? It says whatever story I may tell will make no difference.

"We need to talk," she says.

"The four most dreaded words in the history of marriage."

"I'm serious."

"So am I."

She leads me into the living room, where another wine glass (this one full) awaits me on the coffee table. Something to dull the blow she is about to deliver. But I don't want to be dulled. That's been her problem all along, hasn't it? That I'm rarely present in the moment. Well, whether it's the strange and terrible events of the day or a new resolution I've just now arrived at, I feel pretty damn present in this moment.

"I'm moving out," Diane says, her tone one of practiced defiance, as though this is an episode of courage for her, of daring escape.

"Where will you go?"

"My parents' place on the Cape for the summer. Or part of the summer. Until I get my own apartment in the city."

"Two Manhattan apartments. How can we pay for that? You win the lotto?"

"I'm proposing there's no 'we' anymore, David. Which means I'm talking about just one apartment. Mine."

"So I shouldn't mistake this for a trial separation."

"No, I don't think you should."

She takes the last sip from her glass. This was easier than she thought. She's almost out of here, and the idea of it is making her thirsty.

"I'm trying, Diane."

"I know you are."

"So you can see that I am?"

"It hasn't stopped you from being like someone you pass every day and say hello to but never really know. You *think* you do, but when it comes down to it, you don't."

"There's nothing I can say?"

"It's never been about saying. It's been about doing. Or *not* doing."

I can't argue with any of this. And even if I could, we've never been the arguing kind. Maybe we should have been. A few more nasty accusations, a few more passionate denials and confessions might have done the trick. But I'm not sure how that sort of thing is done.

"You going to live with him?" I ask.

"We're talking about that."

"So when I saw him today, when he 'bumped into me,' he was just rubbing my face in it."

"Will's not like that."

You're wrong, Diane, I want to say. *That's* exactly *what he's like.*

"What about Tess?" I ask.

"What about her?"

"Have you told her yet?"

"I thought I'd leave that to you," she says. "You're better with her. You always were."

"It's not a competition. We're a family."

"No, that's over now. It's over."

"She's your daughter, too."

"I can't *reach* her, David!"

At this, Diane surprises herself by bursting into loud, if brief,

31

sobs. "There's something *wrong* with her," she manages. "Nothing you could ask a doctor about, that's not what I'm saying. Nothing that would show up in a scan. Something *wrong* you can't *see*."

"What do you think it is?"

"I don't know. Being eleven years old. Almost a teenager. The moods. But that's not it. She's like you," she says, a coincidental, if angrier, echo of O'Brien's words. "The two of you holed up in your private, untouchable little club."

She's lonely. I see this now as clearly as the lipstick stain on the rim of her clenched glass. Her husband and child share some troubling darkness and, among its many side effects, it has left her on the outside. I am standing here—as I have always stood here—but she is alone.

"Tess in her room?" I ask. Diane nods.

"Go," she says, dismissing me. But I'm already gone.

EVEN ROBERT BURTON'S 1,400-PAGE *Anatomy of Melancholy* DOESN'T state whether the condition is hereditary or not. I suppose Tess and I make as strong a case for the affirmative as any. In just the last year or so she has outwardly shown signs of bluesy distraction, the whittling down of friends, the shift from broad interests to singular obsession, in her case the keeping of a journal I have never attempted to sneak a peek at, in part to respect her privacy, but also in part because I fear what I might find in it. This recent slide is what troubles Diane most. But the truth is I recognized myself in Tess at a much earlier age. A shared distance from the clamor of life that we continually attempt to bridge, only ever with partial success.

I knock on her door. At her word of medieval permission— "Enter!"—I come in to find her closing her journal and sitting up straight on the edge of her bed. Her long, Riesling-colored hair still in the braid I tied for her this morning. Hair care being a territory I claimed since Tess's toddlerhood, my patience greater than Diane's at brushing out the knots or scissoring the dried gum free. An odd task for a dad, perhaps. But the truth is we have some of our best conversations in the bathroom before eight, the air foggy from a succession of hot showers, the two of us selecting from ponytail, single braid, or "pigs."

My Tess. Looking up at me and instantly reading what has transpired in the living room.

She shifts over. Makes room for me to sit next to her.

"Is she coming back?" Tess asks, the first part of our exchange passing unspoken between us.

"I'm not sure. I don't think so. No."

"But I'm staying here? With you?"

"We haven't discussed it in detail. But yes, this is still going to be home. For both of us. Because I'm sure as hell not going anywhere without you."

Tess nods as though this—me staying here with her—is all she needs to know. It's really all I need to know, too.

"We need to do something," I say after a time.

"Like family therapy? That kind of something?"

Too late for that, I think. *Too late for the three of us together. But there's still you and me. There will always be you and me.*

"I'm talking about something fun."

"Fun?" She repeats this word as though it belongs to an ancient language, a forgotten term in Old Norse she needs help with.

"You think you could be packed for the morning? Clothes for three days? Just hop on a plane and get out of here? I'm talking first-class tickets. Four-star hotel. We'll be rock stars."

"Sure," she says. "This for reals?"

"Absolutely for reals."

"Where we going?"

"How do you like the sound of Venice?"

Tess smiles. It's been so long since I've seen my daughter spontaneously show her happiness—and at something I have done, no less—that I cough on a sob that takes me by surprise.

"Heaven's purest light," I say.

"That old man Milton again?"

"Yes. But it's also you."

33

I squeeze her nose. The little thumb-and-forefinger pinch I stopped trying a couple years ago after her irritated protests. I'm expecting another one from her now, but instead she replies the way she did as a child, when this was one of our thousand games.

"Honk!"

She laughs. And I laugh with her. For a moment, silliness has been returned to us. Of all the things I thought I'd miss when my child was no longer a child, I had no idea that the permission to act like a child yourself would be at the top of the list.

I get up and start for the door.

"Where you going?" she says.

"To tell Mom."

"Tell her in a minute. Just stay with me awhile, okay?"

So I stay awhile. Not speaking, not trying to conjure some soothing platitude, not faking it. Just staying.

THAT NIGHT, I DREAM OF THE THIN WOMAN.

She is sitting on her own in an otherwise empty lecture hall, the same one where I teach my first-year course but altered, widened, its dimensions impossible to estimate as the walls to the right and left dissolve into darkness. I stand behind the lectern, squinting at her. The only lights are the dim ones that illuminate the aisle stairs and the two blazing-red EXIT signs at the rear doors, distant as cities across a desert.

She sits in the middle of a row, halfway up. Nothing is visible of her but her face. Diseased, malnourished. A black-and-white newsreel face. The skin ready to tear open over her nose, the tops of her cheeks, the brittle jaw. It leaves her eyes to bulge out from their sockets as though fighting for escape.

Neither of us speak. Yet the silence is full with the sense that something has just been said aloud that never ought to have been. An obscenity. A curse.

I blink.

And she's standing in front of me.

34

Her mouth opens. The bared throat papery as a discarded snake-skin. A rank breath passing up from within her and licking against my lips, sealing them shut.

She exhales. And before I can awaken, she releases an endless sigh. One that forms itself into an utterance that grows in volume and force, until it billows out of her as a kind of poem.

A welcome. A heresy.

Pandemonium . . .

4

I'M THIRTY THOUSAND FEET OVER THE ATLANTIC, THE ONLY PAS-
senger with his reading light on in the first-class cabin as Tess dozes
fitfully beside me, her closed journal on her lap, when for the first
time since the Thin Woman visited my office I let my mind turn to
what could possibly await me in Venice.

Yesterday offered such a variety of curveballs it's been difficult
to decide which to field first—my best friend's terminal illness, the
once-and-for-all failure of my marriage, or why an emissary suspected
to be from an agency of the Church would offer me a pile of dough
to visit—well, visit *what*? The only aspect of my expertise she specifically cited was my knowledge of Milton's work. No, not even that. A
demonologist.

Even here, in our floating Boeing hotel, I don't feel comfortable fol-
lowing this line of thought, however absurd. So I return to my reading.
A stack of books all belonging to what, in truth, is my favorite genre.
The travel guide.

I am the sort of bookwormy fellow who has read about places more than he has visited them. And for the most part I'd *rather* read about them than visit them. It's not that I dislike the far away, but that I am always aware of my own foreignness, an alien among natives. It's how I feel, in varying degrees, no matter where I am.

Still, I'm looking forward to Venice. I've never been, and its fantastical history and storied loveliness is something I'm eager to share with Tess. My hope is that the beauty of the place will shake her out of her current state of mind. Maybe the spontaneity of this adventure and the magnificence of the destination will be enough to return the brightness to her eyes.

So I keep reading the blood-soaked back stories of the city's monuments, the wars waged for land, for trade, for religion. Along the way I note the restaurants and sites that stand the best chance of pleasing Tess. I will be the most well-informed, customized tour guide for her that I can be.

The trip has already been sort of thrilling. Tess telling Diane about our plans just this morning (she asked few questions, the calculations of how all this would give her some unexpected time with Will Junger playing across her eyes), and then the harried packing, the trip to the bank for euros (the Thin Woman's certified check cashing smoothly into my account), and the limo ride out to Kennedy, the two of us giggling in the backseat like school friends playing hooky.

Because there wasn't time to call, I texted O'Brien from the airport. I debated over how much of the trip to tell her about. Describing the Thin Woman on a cell-phone keyboard in the first-class lounge proved impossible, as did the parameters of my "consultation" on a "case," about which nothing has been revealed, other than my over-generous compensation. In the end, I wrote only:

Off to Venice (the Italian one, not the Californian one) with Tess. Back in a couple days. Explanation TK.

Her reply came almost instantly.

WTF?

I get up to stretch my legs. The jet humming and whistling, soothing as a mechanical womb. This, and the sleeping passengers on either side of me, give the odd impression that I am a transatlantic ghost, hurtling through space, the only wakeful spirit in the night.

But there's another. An elderly man standing between the washroom cubicles at the top of the aisle, looking down at his shoes in the way of the politely bored. When I approach he looks up at me and, as though in recognition of an unexpected companion, he smiles.

"I am not alone," he says in welcome. His accent charmingly Italian flavored. His face mildly lined and handsome as a commercial actor's.

"I was reading."

"Yes? I, too, am a lover of books," he says. "The *great* books. The wisdom of man."

"Just travel guides, in my case."

He laughs. "Those are important, too! You must not become lost in Venice. You must find your way."

"All the books say that becoming lost in Venice is among its greatest charms."

"To wander, yes. But to be lost? There is a difference."

I'm pondering this when the old man puts a hand on my shoulder. His grip strong.

"What takes you to Venice?" he asks.

"A job."

"Job! Ah, you are a thief."

"What makes you say that?"

"Everything in Venice is stolen. The stone, the relics, the icons, the gold crosses in every church. All of it comes from somewhere else."

"Why?"

"Because there's *nothing there*. No forest, no quarries, no farms. It is a city that is an affront to God, built solely upon man's pride. It even stands upon water! Could such an act of magic possibly please the Heavenly Father?"

Despite the devout meaning of his words, his tone somehow communicates its opposite, a kind of undercutting joke. He isn't the least concerned about the offenses of "man's pride" or the displeasure of the Heavenly Father. On the contrary, such things excite him.

He looks over my shoulder at the slumbering passengers.

"The blessed innocence of sleep," he remarks. "Alas, it no longer visits me with its comforts of forgetfulness."

Then his eyes find Tess.

"Your daughter?" he asks.

All at once, I'm struck by the certainty that I've gotten this guy wrong. He's not an elderly charmer making conversation with a fellow insomniac. He's pretending. Hiding his true wants. Along with his reason for standing here, now, with me.

I consider various replies—*None of your goddamn business* or *Don't even look at her*—but instead just turn and head directly back to my seat. As I go, I hear him enter the washroom cubicle and shut the door behind him. He's still in there when I settle in my seat.

I pretend to read, keeping my eye on the cubicle door. And though I remain awake for the next hour or so, I don't notice him come out.

Eventually I get up and knock on the door myself, but it's unlocked. When I pull it open, nobody's there.

VENICE SMELLS.

Of what? It's hard to say at first, as it is an odor of ideas more than any particular source. Not cooking or farming or industry, but the stink of empire, of overlapping histories, the unbleachable taint of corruption. In the New World, when a city has a smell, you can say what it is. The sugary rank of an iron-belt paper mill. The roast chestnuts and sewer belches of Manhattan. But in Venice, our North American nostrils are met instead with the unfamiliar reek of the grand abstractions. Beauty. Art. Death.

"Look!"

Tess points at our vaporetto as it arrives to pick us up and take us along the length of the Grand Canal to our hotel. *Look!* is about all she's said since we landed. And she's right: There is so much to see, so many details in every building's façade, there is a constant danger of missing new evidence of the astonishing. I am more than happy to follow her pointed finger, my daughter close to me, sharing the exhilaration of awakening to a different world.

We board the vaporetto and it chugs off, cutting through the chop of the other delivery boats and gondolas. Almost instantly we are out of sight of any evidence of the modern.

"It's like Disney World," Tess notes. "Except it's real."

So I point out some of the realities learned over my crash-course reading on the plane. There the gray Fondacco dei Turchi with its imposing, dead-eyed windows. And here the Pescheria, with its neo-gothic hall operating as a fish market since the fourteenth century ("Smells like some of the fish have been on sale since the fourteenth century," Tess observes). Over here, the Palazzo dei Camerlenghi, where tax evaders were once imprisoned in the cellar.

In what feels like only a handful of minutes the Grand Canal narrows, and we pass under the Rialto Bridge, its span so weighted with tourists I worry it will collapse upon us in an avalanche of digital cameras, sunglasses, and carved stone. Then the canal bends and widens once more. We pass under the less burdened Ponte dell'Accademia and the course gives way to the larger Bacino di San Marco and, beyond it, the glinting breadth of the lagoon.

The vaporetto slows and turns toward the dock of Bauers Il Palazzo, our hotel. Brass-buttoned valets secure our boat, hauling our luggage inside and offering a gloved hand to Tess. Within an hour of landing we have been transported from the anonymous anywhere of an international airport to the almost unthinkable particularity of one of the finest hotels of Venice, of all Europe.

Tess stands on the dock, taking mental snapshots of the gondolas, the lagoon, the San Marco clock tower, and a stupefied me.

"Glad we came?" I ask.

"Don't be dumb," she answers, linking her arm around mine.

THE THIN WOMAN WASN'T KIDDING AROUND.

"This place is *nice*," Tess confirms, noting the polished, brown marble floor of the Bauer's lobby, the Bevilacqua and Rubelli fabrics draping the windows. "Who's *paying* for this?"

"I'm not entirely sure," I confess.

Once checked in, we go up to our room to freshen up. Up to our *rooms*, that is: two bedrooms, two bathrooms, and an elegant living room with eleven-foot glass doors opening onto a balcony overlooking the Grand Canal.

We shower, get changed, and head up to the rooftop lounge for lunch. From our table, looking one way we can view the lagoon, looking another the whole plaza of San Marco. It is, as the tour guide boasted, the finest vantage point in Venice. And the highest.

"You know what they call this restaurant?" I say. "*Il Settimo Cielo.* Guess what it means."

"I don't speak Italian, Dad."

"Seventh Heaven."

"Because it's on the seventh floor?"

"Give the girl a kewpie doll."

"What's a kewpie doll?"

"Never mind."

Lunch arrives. Grilled trout for me, *spaghetti alla limone* for Tess. We eat ravenously, as if merely looking about us the last couple hours has earned us fierce appetites.

"What's that place?" Tess asks, pointing across the canal at the white dome and elegant columns of the Chiesa della Salute.

"A cathedral," I say. "One of the plague churches they built in the seventeenth century, as a matter of fact."

"Plague church?"

"They built it to protect themselves when a terrible disease—the Black Death—came to Venice. Took out almost half the population. They didn't have the medicine to fight it at the time, so all they felt they could do was build a church and hope God would save them."

"And did he?"

"The plague eventually lifted. As it would have whether anyone built a church or not."

Tess twirls a new bundle of noodles around her fork.

"I think it was God. Even if you don't," she says decisively. Takes a cheek-bulging mouthful. Chews and grins at the same time.

THAT EVENING, TIRED BUT EXCITED, WE GO FOR A SHORT STROLL along the twisting *calles* surrounding the hotel before bed. I have a better-than-average sense of direction (it comes with the travel-guide map study) and can see our course in my head: three jagged sides of a square and then back again. Yet shortly after setting out, the turns become unexpected, the lane breaking off into two smaller canalside *fondamenta*, forcing a decision—left? right?—I didn't think I'd have to make. Still, I figure I'm holding to the idea of going around the square and returning to the Grand Canal, even if it takes us a little longer.

After half an hour, we're lost.

But it's okay. Tess is here. Holding my hand, oblivious to my internal calculations, my attempts to guess north from south. The old man on the plane was wrong. Being lost in Venice is as charming as the guide books say it is. It all depends on who walks next to you. With Tess, I could be lost forever. Then it occurs to me, with the sharp pinch of emotion, that so long as I am with her, I could never be truly lost.

Just as I am about to abandon my masculinity altogether and ask someone for directions, we come upon the doors to Harry's Bar. *Hemingway had his own table here for the winter of 1950.* The guidebook returns this fact to me, along with the more useful recollection of the map of the area. We aren't too far off. We probably never were. The Bauer is just around the corner.

"We're home," I tell Tess.

"We were lost back there, weren't we?"

"Maybe a little."

"I could tell from your face. It does this thing sometimes"—she hardens her brow—"when you're thinking."

"Your face does the same thing."

"Of course it does. I'm like you, and you're like me."

The simple truth of her observation stops me, but Tess walks ahead. My guide, leading me to the hotel doors.

THE NEXT DAY MY PLAN IS TO DO A LITTLE SIGHTSEEING, VISIT the address the Thin Woman provided me in the afternoon, then wipe my hands of my official business and enjoy the evening and tomorrow with Tess unencumbered. Yet as we start out in a private gondola, Tess marveling at the long boat's smooth progress through the chop, I begin to suspect my timing is a mistake. I should have gotten my work (whatever it is) over with first thing, because my speculation over what I have been asked to observe here has, even over breakfast, graduated to niggling worry. The strangeness of my assignment was sort of thrilling over the last twenty-four hours, a distraction from unwelcome realities. I could see the episode playing out as something to be retold in the lecture hall, a winning, screwball anecdote at conference wine-and-cheeses. Now, though, in the gold haze of Venetian light, the butterflies in my stomach have turned to warring wasps, churning and stinging.

What had the Thin Woman called it? A case. A *phenomenon*. Not the analysis of a discovered text or interpretation of verse (the only sort of fieldwork I might be expected to lend my expertise to). She came to me for my knowledge of the Adversary, one of the Bible's many names for the Devil. *Apocryphal documentation of demonic activity in the ancient world.*

None of this, of course, can be discussed with Tess. So I play cheerful tour guide as best I can. All the while struggling to tell myself that this day is merely a little out of the ordinary, that I shouldn't fear the unusual simply because it takes me out of my habitat of library, study, and seminar room. Indeed, maybe more days like this would have made me more present, as Diane had wished I'd been. Excitement makes you more alive.

But the fact is, as the morning sun rises to beat shadowlessly down on the old city, it feels less like excitement and more like fear.

◆　◆　◆

WE START AT THE DOGE'S PALACE. IT'S A SHORT WALK FROM THE
hotel to San Marco, and once we step out onto the broad plaza, we
take in the structure's immensity from a distance. It's true what one
of the guidebooks said: the long arcade of columns on the building's
lower level lend the walled floors atop them the illusion of floating.
I hadn't expected the sheer size of it, the tons of stone, no matter
how gracefully assembled, suggesting long-buried narratives of labor,
injury, lost lives.

Among these lost lives, I tell Tess, were the condemned men
brought here to be given a final chance at salvation.

"Why were they condemned?" she asks.

"They'd done bad things. And then they had to be punished."

"But they were brought here first?"

"So the story goes."

"How *does* the story go?"

I tell her about the column. The book said it was on the exposed
side facing St. Mark's Basin, opposite the island of San Giorgio.
Count three columns in and there it is: worn around its marble base
from all the prisoners and, over the centuries since, curious tourists
attempting the impossible. The challenge is to put your hands behind your back (as the prisoners' hands would have been bound) and,
facing outward, step around the entire column. For the condemned,
it was a cruel offering of potential freedom, as the myth holds that
the task has never been achieved.

Tess thinks I should go first. I slip my fingers into my belt and get
up onto the base's edge. A single sliding step and I'm off.

"Can't do it," I say.

"My turn!"

Tess reverse-hugs the marble, faces me, grinning. Then she starts.
Little shuffles on her heels, inching around. And keeps going. I stand
there with my iPhone video camera ready to capture her fall, but instead she disappears as she circles the column. A moment later she
emerges again, still shuffling around. Except now the grin is gone. In

45

its place is a blank look I take to be severe concentration. I return the iPhone to my pocket.

When she's made it all the way around to the starting point she stands there, looking out over the water, as though listening to whispered instructions from the lapping waves.

"Tess!" A shout meant to awaken her from wherever she's gone as much as to celebrate her accomplishment. "You did it!"

She steps down. And with her recollection of who I am and where she is, her smile returns.

"What do I win?" she asks.

"Your place in history. Apparently nobody's ever done that before."

"And salvation. Do I win that, too?"

"That, too. C'mon," I say, taking her hand. "Let's get out of this sun."

WE WALK ACROSS THE ALREADY-CROWDED PLAZA TO THE BASILICA. The sun, aloof but scorching, makes even this short journey fatiguing. Or maybe the early rising after a long flight has me weaker than I figured. In any case, by the time we enter the cool of the cathedral, I'm feeling tilted, as though standing on the deck of a sailboat.

It's partly an excuse to regain my balance when I stop to point up at the mosaic decorating the dome above us. The images tell the story of Creation: God's invention of light, Adam in the garden, the serpent and his temptation of Eve, the Fall. There is an astonishing simplicity to the images, especially in the context of the building's overwhelming, Byzantine architecture. It's as though the builders intended to distract one from the real materials of faith, rather than depict them. Yet here, in this overhead pocket, is the familiar narrative of Genesis, laid out in an almost children's book illustration, and the impact of it takes my breath away.

At first, I assume this is an aesthetic response: a man in awe of towering artistic achievement. But it isn't the beautiful that transfixes me. It is the sublime. The unsettling presence of the serpent and its implications not only upon the iconic "Eve," but the two real people pictured in the mosaic, a man and woman touched not by a symbol, but by a physically embodied evil. The green-scaled length. The forked tongue.

And then, in the hushed tomb of the church, the sound of a whisper next to my ear. The serpent's eyes focused not on a girl holding out her hand for an apple, but upon me.

"Dad?"

Tess has her hands against my lower back.

"What's wrong?"

"Me?" she says. "What's wrong with *you*? I'm holding you up."

"Sorry. Got a bit dizzy for a second there."

She squints. Knows I'm not giving her all the details and determining whether she needs to hear them now or not.

"Let's go back to the hotel," she suggests. "We can have a rest before your meeting."

She's your child, the imagined O'Brien qualifies in my head as Tess leads me out into the piazza's bustle. *She knows more than you could ever hide.*

I'M FEELING MUCH STRONGER AFTER LUNCH. THE BABYSITTER THE
concierge has arranged for arrives at our room to look after Tess for
the couple hours I will be away. Stout, matronly, "fully registered,"
as the hotel assured me. I trust her at once. As does Tess. The two of
them engaged in Italian lessons before I'm out the door.

"Be back soon," I call to Tess, who rushes to deliver a farewell kiss.

"*Arrivederci*, Dad!"

She closes the door behind me. And I'm alone. It's only once I'm
down among others in the ordered comings and goings of the lobby
that I feel able to pull out the address the Thin Woman gave me.

Santa Croce 3627.

A typically Venetian designation. No street name, no apartment
number, no postal code. Even the most extensive online map zoom-
ing could provide only a couple-hundred-square-meter area where it
might be. To find the doorway I'm to knock on, I'll have to be on the
ground, looking for signs.

I board a vaporetto at the hotel's dock and head back along the

Grand Canal to the Rialto stop. The bridge is as busy today as when we passed under it yesterday, and as I work my way across it to enter the Santa Croce *sestiere* on the other side, my hesitations about whatever awaits me at 3627 lift away, and I am merely a visitor among visitors, passing the vendors' stalls and asking "How much?" in the languages of the world.

Then I'm following the relatively easy route highlighted in the printout I unfold from my pocket. There are people here, too, other map readers like me, though as I proceed their numbers diminish. Before long there are only locals returning to their homes with grocery bags. Kids kicking soccer balls against ancient walls.

I should be close. But how can I know? Only some of the doors have numbers next to them. And they aren't in anything approaching order. 3688 is followed by 3720. So I turn back, thinking the numbers will get smaller, only to find 3732 comes after 3720. Much of the time, I'm just trying to remember landmarks to which I can stick a mental pin: these drooping window-box flowers on the second floor, those stern-faced old men drinking espresso outside a café. Yet when I cut back and follow what I'm sure is the same path, the café is gone, the flower box replaced by an undershirt left out to dry.

It is only at the moment I start to head back in the direction (or what I believe to be the direction) of the Rialto that I find it.

Stenciled in chipped, gold paint on a wooden door smaller than any other is 3627. It must be an original, maintained since the time when it was built for shorter, seventeenth-century Venetians. Its size, along with the tiny script of the numbers, gives the impression of an address that has long done its best to avoid notice altogether.

A doorbell button flickers like a nightlight even now at midday. I press it twice. It's impossible to know whether it makes a sound within or not.

In a moment, the door is pulled open. From out of the interior shadows, a middle-aged man emerges wearing a gray flannel suit far too hot for the temperature of the day. His eyes blink at me through the smudged lenses of his wire-frame glasses, the only evidence of dishevelment in his otherwise excessively formal appearance.

"Professor Ullman," he says. It is not a question.

"If you know my name, I must be at the right place," I answer, a smile meant to invite him to participate in some humor at the strangeness of our meeting, but there is nothing in his expression that registers anything other than my presence at his door.

"You are late," he says in accented but perfectly articulated English. He opens the door wider and makes an impatient, sweeping motion with his hand, ushering me inside.

"There was no designated time for my arrival that I was aware of."

"It is late," he repeats, a hint of weariness in his voice, suggesting he is referring to something other than the time.

I step into what appears to be a waiting room of some kind. Wooden chairs with their backs against the walls. A coffee table with Italian news magazines that, judging by the acts of terror and block-buster movies featured on their covers, are more than a few years old. If it *is* a waiting room, no one else waits here. And there is nothing— no signage, reception desk, explanatory posters—to indicate what service might be provided.

"I am a physician," the man in the suit says.

"Is this your office?"

"No, no." He shakes his head. "I have been commissioned. From elsewhere."

"Where?"

He waves his hand. A refusal, or perhaps an incapacity, to answer.

"Are we the only ones here?" I ask.

"At the moment."

"There are others? At other times?"

"Yes."

"So shall we wait for them to arrive?"

"It is not necessary."

He starts toward one of three closed doors. Turns the knob.

"Wait," I say.

He opens the door, pretending not to hear. It reveals a narrow set of stairs leading up to the floor above.

"*Wait!*"

The physician turns. His anxiety undisguised on his face. It's clear he has a job to do—lead me up these stairs—and has a distinctly personal investment in getting it done in the quickest manner possible.

"Yes?"

"What's up there?"

"I don't understand."

"You are about to show me something, right? Tell me what it is."

The various answers he might give can almost be read in his eyes. It is a process that seems to bring him pain.

"It is for you," he says finally.

Before I can ask him anything else he starts up the stairs. His polished leather Oxfords pounding on the wooden steps with uncalled-for force, either to prevent hearing any further comments from me, or to signal someone else of my arrival.

I follow him up.

The stairwell is warm and dark, the rising heat thicker with each step higher, the plaster walls slippery with condensation. It's like entering a throat. And with the arrival of this impression, a sound: the subdued breathing of something other than myself or the physician. Or, more accurately, two breaths, overlapping and in time. One high and weak, a deathbed struggle. The other a bass tremor that is felt rather than heard.

It's pitch dark when I reach the second floor. Even looking back the way I've come reveals nothing but the palest reach of light from the waiting room.

"Doctor?"

My voice seems to reanimate the physician, who switches on a powerful flashlight, blinding me.

"*Le mie scuse,*" he says, lowering the beam to the floor.

"Are the lights not working?"

"The power. It has been turned off for the building."

"Why?"

"I have not asked. I believe it is to be"—he works to find the phrase—"off the grid."

I study the man's face for the first time. His features are underlit by the downcast light, so that his near-panic is caricatured.

"Why are you doing this?" I ask. The question alone provokes a clench of discomfort.

"I cannot say."

"Is someone forcing you to do this?"

"There is no action without choice," he says, the words spoken in a slightly modulated accent, as though quoting someone else's answer to the same question.

"Are we safe here?"

The plaintive urgency of my question surprises me, though not the physician, who briefly shuts his eyes against some recollection of irreparable regret.

Then, with a sudden motion, he reaches for something on a table behind him, and the flashlight swings about in his other hand, showing we are on a landing with access to at least three closed doors. The space free of any art or decoration. Only the slight glitter of humidity on the white walls.

The physician shines the light on me again, focuses the beam on my chest. And what I see is him offering what looks to be a brand-new digital video camera.

"For you," he says.

"I don't want it."

"For *you*."

He drops the camera into my hand.

"What am I supposed to do with this?"

"I was not told what you are to do. Only to give it to you."

"This wasn't part of the deal."

"There is no *deal*," he says, flinching as though in prevention of rude laughter. "What you do with it is for you to determine, Professor."

The physician starts to move. At first, I assume he is going to accompany me inside one of the doors he will open, or perhaps guide me to a higher floor altogether. But then he steps by me—a whiff of sour body odor as he passes—and I see he is about to start back down the stairs.

"Where are you going?"

He pauses. Casts the light on the farthest door.

"*Per favore*," he says.

"You will wait for me? Downstairs? You'll be here if I need you, yes?"

"*Per favore*," he repeats. He has the yellowish look of someone doing his best to hold on before he can make it to the closest toilet so he can be sick.

One minute.

This is all I'm thinking as I take a step toward the door.

One minute to make my observations, report them to this man or whoever awaits me downstairs, then leave. Take the free holiday and the money and run. Honor my promise.

The truth? I open the door and step inside not for the Thin Woman's payment or to fulfill my end of the agreement I made with her. It's simpler than that.

I want to see.

A MAN SITTING IN A CHAIR.

He appears to be asleep. His head slumped forward, chin touching his chest. While I can't see his face, his position allows a good view of his thinning salt-and-pepper curls and the small pink patch of crown that is the badge of male middle age. He wears dress pants, a pinstripe business shirt, and leather loafers. A wedding band. His otherwise trim frame betrayed by the slightly rounded stomach of someone used to fine food, but still vain enough to fight its effects through obligatory exercise. Everything about him, in a first appraisal, suggests a man of good if unadventurous taste, a professional, a father. A man like myself.

But then, with a single step closer, other details reveal themselves, invisible a second earlier.

He is soaked through with sweat. His shirt clinging to his back, dark moons under his arms.

His breathing. A hoarse rattle so deep it seems to be drawing air to somewhere other than his lungs.

And then the chair: each leg screwed to the wooden floor with industrial bolts. Rough leather straps of the kind used to bridle horses wrapped around the man's chest, holding him in place.

A kidnapping. They have taken this man and are keeping him for ransom.

Then why have they brought me here? No demand has been made of me other than my presence.

You are about to be imprisoned here, too. Or worse. They have given you the camera to record something terrible. Torture. Murder. Something they will do to the man.

But why bring a witness, if that's what I am, all the way from New York?

They're going to take you, too.

For what purpose? Not money. I don't have enough of that to make it worthwhile. And if they want to imprison me, why wait as long as they have?

Hitchcock's North by Northwest. *They've got the wrong guy.*

But the Thin Woman knew exactly who I was. As did the ticket agent at the airport and the clerk at the Bauer, all of whom studied my passport. She wanted David Ullman here. And now I am.

This internal debate, I realize, has been conducted with an imaginary O'Brien. There is a pain in my chest as I wish she were with me now. She would have answers that the O'Brien of my making doesn't.

I turn on the camera.

I don't try to run, don't try to call the *polizia*. For some reason I am certain that I'm not in any immediate physical danger, that I haven't been brought here to be strapped to a chair.

The man before me is why I am here. He is the "case." The phenomenon.

I press REC and look through the camera's viewfinder, square it on the man in the chair. In the corner of the frame, the digital clock starts to tick away as the footage rolls in. The autofocus briefly blurs him before it adjusts to render him clearly on the screen. Still asleep.

I test the zoom button. Push in closer to exclude the floor, the walls.

1:24

Then closer still, so that only his upper body and head fill the frame.

1:32

Suddenly, his head jumps up straight, throwing wet tendrils of hair off his forehead. Eyes wide open, at once alert and glossed with exhaustion. For however long he rested his chin on his chest, they never closed. He was never asleep at all.

He stares directly into the camera's lens. And I hold it on him. Recording his expression as it shifts from a blank apprehension to recognition. Not of the room, but of me. A smile spreads over his face as though at the arrival of an old friend.

But the smile grows *too* wide, his mouth stretching open until the corners tear open old scabs there from when he last performed this trick. It bares all of his teeth.

He snarls.

Fights against the restraints that hold him in place. Thrashing his torso to one side, then the other, testing the chair's fix on the floor. The screws remain secure, but the force of his struggle sends creaks through the room's entire structure, the light fixture swinging over my head. In case it falls, I take a step forward. A step closer to him.

A slight pause before he lunges his head at me. Stretching his neck and shoulders as far as the restraints allow. And even farther. His body elasticized, extending forward whole inches past what I would have guessed the natural length of his spine would allow.

I step back again to a safe distance. Record what feels like minute after minute of his seizure. Barks. Spits of white froth. Voices emanating from within him, growling and hissing.

He is insane. A violent madman in the middle of an extended fit.

Or this is what I try to convince myself it is. It doesn't work.

Everything he does is too intentional to be a sickness of the mind. It *appears* to be the random, pointless sufferings of some advanced neurological corrosion, but isn't. What is being shown is the revelation of an identity, however alien. It has the patterns, the crescendos, the dramatic pauses, that come from some internal consciousness. One meant for the camera to record. For me.

More unsettling than his most explicit shocks—the feminine cackle, the agonized whinnies, the eyes rolling back in his head to reveal whites so bloodshot they appear as tiny maps of pain—are the moments when he suddenly sits still and looks at me. No words, no contortions. His persona is "normal," or what I take to be what remains of his formerly sane self: a man of roughly my own age, unsure of his whereabouts and trying to calculate who I am, how he might alter his situation, find the way home. A man of intelligence.

And then, each time, his expression changes. He remembers who he is, the nature of his plague, and a cascade of sensations—images? emotions? memories?—returns to him in a rush.

That's when he screams.

A voice wholly his own. The note rising in his throat, then shattering into a kind of sob. His terror so instant and crystalline it dehumanizes him in a way that even his most grotesque displays cannot equal.

He looks at me and reaches out his hand.

It reminds me of Tess at two years old, learning to swim on a summer holiday on Long Island. She would take a step from the shallows and feel the sandy bottom slip deeper beneath her, at the same time as a wave washed over her. Each time she spat out a mouthful of sea her hand would shoot up for me to save her. She could repeat this near-death experience a dozen times in a single afternoon. And although she was lifted into my arms within a quarter-second each time, her desperation was the same.

The difference between Tess and this man is that while Tess knew what frightened her—the water, the deep—he doesn't have any idea. It isn't a disease. It is a presence. A will a thousand times stronger than his own. There is no fighting it. There is only the recognition that he is damned, coming to him anew each time.

Finally, he stops. Slumps into a sleep that is not a sleep.

4:43

Only now do my hands start to shake. For the preceding moments the camera might as well have stood on a tripod, it was held so firmly in place. Now, as the impact of all I've just seen hits me, the frame wobbles with nauseating jerks and corrections, as though with the man's stillness the camera itself has come to life.

5:24

A voice.

The sound of it stills my hands. Frames the man in the chair squarely once more. Yet he doesn't move. The voice comes from him—it *must* come from him—but there is nothing in his form to confirm that it has.

Professor Ullman.

It takes a moment to recognize that the voice has directly addressed me. And that its language isn't English, but Latin.

Lorem sumus.

We have been waiting.

The voice is male, but only in its register, not in its character. In fact, though it commands in the way of a human utterance, it is strangely non-gendered. An unoccupied medium, in the way even the most sophisticated computer-generated voice is detectable as a surrogate for a real human presence.

I wait for the voice to go on. But there is only the terrible breathing, louder now.

6:12

"Who are you?"

My voice. Sounding tinny and scratched as an old 78 record.

His head lifts again. This time his expression belongs to neither the snarling madman nor his terrified "normal" self, but something new. Becalmed. His face bearing the insinuating smile of the priest, the door-to-door salesman. Yet with a fury beneath the surface. A hate contained by the skin but not by the eyes.

"We do not have names."

I need to challenge what it says. Because what happens next will decide everything. Somehow I know this. It's essential to not let it see that I think it might be anything other than a symptom of mental disease. *This isn't real*. The reassurance offered to a child reading a story of witches or giants. *There's no such thing*. The impossible mustn't be allowed to gain purchase in the possible. You resist fear by denying it.

"'We,'" I start, doing my best to smooth the trembling from my words. "Don't you mean your name is Legion, for you are many?"

"We *are* many. Though you will only meet one."

"Aren't we meeting now?"

"Not with the intimacy of the one you will come to know."

"The Devil?"

"Not the master. One who sits with him."

"I look forward to it."

It says nothing to this. The silence highlighting the vacancy of my lie.

"So you can foretell my future?" I go on. "This is as common a delusion as one believing one is possessed by spirits."

It takes a breath. A long pull that, for a moment, empties the room of all its oxygen. It leaves me in a vacuum. Weightless and suffocating.

"Your attempts at doubt are unconvincing, Professor," it says.

"My doubt is real," I say, though the tone betrays the words. *You are winning*, it says instead. *You've already won.*

"You must prepare for an education in what frightens you."

"Why not begin now?"

It smiles.

"Soon you will be among us," it says.

At this, part of me floats up and away from my body. Looks down on myself to see my mouth ask a question it has already asked.

"Who are you?"

"Man has given us names, though we have none."

"No. You won't tell me who you are because there is power in knowing the name of one's enemy."

"We are not enemies."

"Then what are we?"

"Conspirators."

"Conspirators? What is our cause?"

It laughs. A low, satisfied rumble that seems to come up from the foundations of the house, from the ground beneath it.

"New York 1259537. Tokyo 996314. Toronto 1389257. Frankfurt 540553. London 590643."

When it stops, the man's eyes roll back in his head to show the bloodshot whites. It takes an impossibly long breath. Holds it. Lets it out in words that carry the acrid sting of charred flesh.

"On the twenty-seventh day of April . . . the world will be marked by our numbers."

The head falls forward. The man's body still again. Only the low breathing that keeps him this side of death.

8:22

Three minutes. That's how long I was in conversation with it. With *them*. Three minutes that already feel like a whole chapter of my life, a stretch like Adolescence or Fatherhood in which the terms of selfhood are fundamentally redefined. The time between 5:24 and 8:22 will be *When I Spoke to the Man in Venice*. And it will be a period marked by regret. A loss I can't guess the shape of yet.

Time to go.

If I was brought here to witness the symptoms of this diseased man's mind, then I've seen enough. Indeed, the wish that I'd never entered this room at all is so strong I find that I'm shuffling backward toward the door, putting inch after inch of distance between myself and the sleeping man, trying to pretend that I might rewind the last quarter hour and erase it from my memory as easily as I could erase it from the camera that records my retreat.

But there will be no forgetting. The camera will hold the man's words with the same vividness that I will.

And then he does something that will be even more impossible to erase.

He wakens and raises his head. Slowly this time.

It is the man's face, though altered in a way perhaps I alone could detect. A number of fluid, minute adjustments to his features that, collectively, shift his identity from whoever he once was to someone else, someone I know. The eyes slightly closer together, the nose longer, the lips thinned. My father's face.

I try to scream. Nothing comes out. The only sound is the voice the man speaks with, my father coming out from within. His seething accusation, his bitterness. The voice of a man who has been dead for over thirty years.

"It should have been you," it says.

I STUMBLE FROM THE ROOM AND DOWN THE STAIRS. FIND MY FEET, lurch through the empty waiting room—no sign of the physician— and out to the narrow street. I run from 3627 without looking back, though part of me wants to, a part that knows if I look the man will be standing at the second-floor window, released from his restraints, grinning down at me.

It's only after the fire in my chest forces me to rest against a wall protected from the sun that I realize I am still holding the camera. And that it's still recording.

11:53

My thumb presses STOP. The screen blackens.

All at once I'm doubled over, retching onto the bricks. An ache in my bones, angry and unforeseen. It bears a similarity to every other flu I've ever had, though there's something distinct about it in addition to its suddenness. The nearest I can come to describing it is that it's not physiological, not an illness at all, but a *thought*. The infection of a virulent idea.

I wipe my lips on the shoulder of my jacket and carry on.

Tess.

I've got to get back to her. Make sure she's okay, then get on the next flight to New York—to anywhere—whether I've got malaria or worse. *We have to go.*

First, though, I've got to find my way to the Grand Canal. Any vaporetto stop will do. It shouldn't be too hard. Not that I have any idea where I am. So long as I keep moving, I'll eventually come out at the water.

It doesn't work.

I'm lost even worse than I was with Tess in our stroll around the hotel last night. And instead of charm, what I feel now is a crushing panic so great I'm grinding my teeth on tears. There is the need to return to Tess, the anxiety of not knowing where I am, the fever that twists the *calle* before me into an undulating tunnel. And there is also the certainty that I am being pursued. Something hulking and close, just behind me.

I break into a run again. Turn a corner. As I do, before I see what's there, I smell it. The same barnyard smell that clung to the Thin Woman.

But it isn't she standing in the lane in front of me. It's a herd of pigs.

A dozen of them or more. All turned my way, nostrils flaring. Impossible, yet undeniably *there*. Too detailed in their appearance to be a side effect of whatever is making me feel poisoned. Too aware of who I am.

The animals come at me. Squealing as though scalded. Their hooves clattering over the stone.

I back up and swing around the corner I just turned. Wait for their teeth to find my skin, to break it open and eat.

But they don't come. I look around the corner. The *ramo* is empty.

Don't stop to understand. You may never *understand any of this.*

My internal O'Brien again.

Just keep going.

So I keep going.

64

And at the end of the next *calle* I turn onto—one whose length I'm sure I have already run down at least once if not three times—there is the Grand Canal. Appearing out of nowhere as though at the turning of a page.

Don't stop.

Something is happening.

But she's safe.

There's no such thing anymore.

How do you know?

Because it knows who she is.

I SIT AT THE BACK OF THE BOAT, BITING AT AIR. TRY TO THINK only of Tess, of returning to Tess, of escaping with Tess. Relieving the babysitter, calling the airlines, arranging a water taxi. Putting this sinking city behind us.

Yet other thoughts muscle through. My professor's brain providing footnotes, interpretations. The text at hand is the last hour of my life. And the reading—nonsensical, unstoppable—is that my experience reflects what has been written of previous encounters between man and demon.

I try to bring Tess's face to my mind. Instead the man in the chair appears. His skin pulling away to reveal the true face of the thing inside him.

It swings my thoughts away to something else.

The Gerasene demon. Twice noted in the gospels by Luke and Mark. In the telling, Jesus came upon a naked, homeless man living in the tombs, a man "which had devils a long time." Upon seeing Christ, the demon begged not to be tormented. Jesus asked its name, and it answered "Legion," for it was not a single demon but many that possessed the man. And the savior cast them out, transferring them into a nearby herd of pigs.

Then went the devils out of the man, and entered into the swine: and the herd ran violently down a steep place into the lake, and were drowned.

The man strapped to the chair at Santa Croce 3627, bound as the possessed man at Gerasene had been repeatedly and unsuccessfully bound, also claimed to be without a name, though composed of many. And then the herd of pigs stampeding toward me in the maze of lanes. Either I hallucinated it, or it is a coincidence well beyond the random.

Stop this! the O'Brien in my head tells me.

But it can't be stopped.

Another ancient text, this one apocryphal. The *Compendium Maleficarum,* written by Brother Francesco Maria Guazzo in 1608, has been taken by the Vatican and other theological bodies as a primary guide in the matters of demonic possession and exorcism. Guazzo offers fifty ways to tell if possession is real, and includes the sensation of ants under the skin, along with accurate foretellings of future events and voices in your head saying things beyond your own understanding, but which are nevertheless true.

These three signs come to me in particular, as my flu-like symptoms include a maddening whole-body itchiness that has me considering jumping out of the vaporetto to be cooled by the waters of the Grand Canal. And what is to be made of the list of cities the presence within the man uttered, along with the numbers? Is it a code? Addresses? Phone numbers? Whatever they are, they came attached to a date a few days from now. April 27th. When "the world will be marked by our numbers."

And then my father's voice. Telling me it should have been me.

I told you not to think, O'Brien says.

All the landmarks I'd learned from the guidebooks slide past as the vaporetto approaches the hotel, but I can't recall their names now, let alone the tidbits I'd learned about their histories. They are merely old, pretty buildings. Free of the reverence I'd brought to them yesterday, the façades suggesting only falsehood today, elaborate decoration meant to disguise their original owners' lusts and greed. How can I see this? It seems that with my flu-that-isn't-a-flu has come a kind of X-ray vision, one capable of looking into structures—into the people who made them—and seeing their base motivations. A perspective that brings with it a terrible despair. The claustrophobia of being human.

It's a feeling that precedes the return of a memory. Something I have expertly ignored through scholarship, family life, the thousand little tricks of avoidance the mind can be trained to perform every day. But now it comes back with such vividness I am powerless to dim its images.

My brother, drowning.

His arms thrashing at the water of the river behind our family's cabin, his head under and not coming up. Then his arms stop, too. He drifts downstream. Slower than the current, as though his feet dragged along the river bottom in resistance even in death.

I was six years old.

"Mister Ullman?"

Someone is standing over me. A man in a black suit, reaching down.

"Yes?"

"Welcome back to the Bauer. You have enjoyed your afternoon?"

I RUSH UPSTAIRS TO OUR SUITE. IT ONLY TAKES A MINUTE OR TWO, but feels torturously longer. What draws it out are the new horrific images of what I will find in the room once I open the door.

Tess hurt.

Tess snarling and thrashing like the man in the room, the babysitter helpless to restrain her.

Tess gone.

I've failed her. I was tricked, sent to the house in Santa Croce as a diversion. The goal was not to record a phenomenon, but to separate me from my daughter in a foreign city so that she might be taken away.

Yet when I kick the door to our suite open, she is there. The sitting room's glass doors open wide, the Grand Canal sparkling outside them. Tess writing in her journal on the sofa, the babysitter watching a muted soap on the TV.

"Dad!"

Tess rushes over to me. Rewards me with an embrace that is almost enough to make my illness lift away from me.

"You're all hot," she says, touching my hands, the sides of my face.

"I'll be okay."

"Your eyes."

"What about them?"

"They're all, like, *seriously* bloodshot."

"Just a touch of flu. Don't worry, sweetheart."

The babysitter stands behind Tess, trying to maintain her smile. But she too finds my appearance distressing. A glance at the front hall's mirror and I see why.

"Thank you. *Grazie.*"

I hand her a wad of euros roughly double the negotiated fee, yet she takes the bills with some reluctance, as though whatever ails me might transfer from the paper to her.

When she's gone, I tell Tess we have to go.

"Because you're sick?"

"No, baby. Because . . . I don't like it here."

"*I* like it here."

"It's not the *place*. What I mean—" I start, then try to think of a palatable fiction. Decide on the truth instead. "I mean I'm not sure we're safe."

I don't intend to frighten her. And she *isn't* frightened. Her face shows something else I can't quite read. Something like resolve. The grimace that shows a willingness to take on a fight.

Whatever it is, it's my fault. What the hell was I *thinking*, saying that?

The answer is it wasn't me who said it. It's the thing that's followed me here. A being other than Tess or me in the room with us.

"Pack your things," I say. "I've got a couple calls to make."

MAYBE IT IS THE FOCUS REQUIRED IN THUMBING MY iPHONE, CALL-ing the airlines, finding a flight that leaves that night (getting lucky with Alitalia to London, then British Airways to New York). Or maybe it's just a matter of bringing some distance between myself and the man at 3627. Either way, I feel almost instantly better. The breeze through the open doors cools the sweat on my neck, my stomach calmed. Even more welcome, the dark thoughts that plagued my return journey on the vaporetto have retreated, leaving me more buoyant than I can remember feeling for the last few weeks. Has the day been weird? Sure. A conspiracy cooked up in the underworld? Not too damn likely.

So what to do about the video camera? When I'm done on the phone I spot it on the coffee table. The eye of its lens staring at me. Inside the machine is the man in the room. His gnashings and flail-ings. But also the cities and numbers. The lifeless voice. My father.

I consider leaving it there but quickly pack it instead, burying it under my socks as though concealing it might render its contents impotent. I'm too addled at the moment to say how I know this, but the documentation it contains may be important. Not that I will ever view its contents again. But the academic in me—the archivist, the enlightened opposer to the destruction of historical record—doesn't like the idea of it disappearing. In the manner of any text, it may have something crucial to say that isn't evident on the first reading.

I zip up my suitcase. Comb fingers through damp hair.

Good-bye, gloriously expensive hotel suite. Good-bye, magnifi-cent Chiesa della Salute, postcard-framed by the window. Good-bye, Venice. I won't be coming back. And when the next plague comes, go ahead and build another church. Whether they cure the sick or not, they're certainly beautiful.

"Tess? Time to go, honey."

I roll the suitcase to the living room, expecting to find Tess there. She isn't, though her bag is. The handle extended but the case lying on its back on the floor, as though abandoned.

"Tess?"

Check her room. Both bathrooms. Open the suite's door and go outside to stand in the empty hallway.

"Tess!"

The living room window. Doors open wide, the curtains coaxing in the hot breeze.

I run to the balcony, look over the side. Below, the arrivals and departures of the hotel's dock. But no commotion. No Tess.

Call the front desk. That's what I should do. Have hotel staff look everywhere at the same time. The police, too. If she left the hotel it would take no time at all to become lost in the city's maze.

Don't just run around. *Think.* I have to put the next steps in the right order. What I do now will decide everything—

She's on the roof.

O'Brien's voice interrupts again. Except this time it's not my imagined O'Brien, but somehow the real thing. My friend here with me.

Il Settimo Cielo. Go, David. Go now.

Even as I'm running out the door and taking the stairs up to the seventh floor, I'm wondering if this voice, among all the others of this day, can be believed. It could be a lie. Maybe everything I heard in the room at 3627 was a lie.

But this one is true.

I run out onto the patio restaurant atop the hotel, and there she is. My daughter standing on the edge of the roof. Meeting my eyes alone through the crowd of panicking patrons and waiters.

"Tess!"

There is something authoritative about my shout—I know her *name*—that parts the crowd, quieting the calls for the police, for someone to *do something*. It allows me to approach in what I hope to be a calming pace, my steps as sure as I can make them.

All the while Tess's eyes stay on me. But as I get closer I see that I'm wrong. They are her eyes, blue as mine. Yet it is not Tess who sees

72

with them. It's not my daughter who stands on the edge, her arms out at her sides, fingers splayed apart to feel the wind pass through them. There is a rigidity in her stance that betrays an unfamiliarity, the testing of balance and strength. Her posture is that of someone contained within a prison of bones and skin. Her body, but not her.

When I'm almost close enough to reach her, she rears back. Extends her leg out behind her so that she is balanced on one foot, the other wavering in the air.

It's meant to stop my approach. It works.

Hello, David.

An entirely different voice this time. Male, measured, the fine pronunciation that marks the affect of sophistication. A voice not unlike the ones I hear at university conferences or from the country-club parents of students who donate money in order to put their names on campus buildings.

"You're the one I was told I would meet," I say.

We're going to be so close. Not friends, perhaps. No, certainly not friends. But unquestionably close.

It lowers Tess's leg so that she stands on both feet once more. Yet to show this isn't a gesture of concession, both feet shuffle backward an inch. It leaves her heels hanging off the edge.

"Let her go."

It replies in what sounds like Tess's voice, though it's not. The same phrase, the same intonation she used when I said I wanted to leave Venice less than an hour ago. A brilliant mimicry, though emptied of life.

I like it here.

"Please. I'll do whatever you ask."

It's not about my asking you to do anything, it says, speaking in its own voice again. *This is for you, David. A journey of your own making. A wandering.*

That word again. *Wander.*

The old man on the plane had used it, too. And the Thin Woman had said that about herself, hadn't she? That she was not a traveler, but a wanderer. Even at the time I'd noted this term bears particular meaning for Milton. Satan and his underlings wander about the earth and in hell, self-directed but without destination. It is widely inter-preted as connoting the homeless nature of demonic existence, the drifting movement within purgatory. Ungrounded, loveless.

And then, as though reading my mind, the voice cites *Paradise Lost* itself.

Wandering this darksome desert, as my way
Lies through your spacious empire up to light
Alone, and without guide, half lost, I seek . . .

"Then tell me," I say, my voice breaking. "What are you seeking? I promise I will help you find it."

I have already found what I seek. I have found you.

Tess's feet scratch back another inch. All of her weight gripped to the edge by her toes like a highboard diver.

There is much to discover, David. Though little time.

"How much?"

When you see the numbers, you have only until the moon.

"Why? What happens then?"

The child will be mine.

I lunge forward. Grab Tess's hand.

Even though I pull as hard as I can—even though she is an eleven-year-old girl less than half my weight—it's all I can do to just hold her there. Her strength is not her own but the voice's. And what it shows me at the touch of Tess's hand is of his design, too. A collage of pain, colliding and burning.

My brother inhaling the river's water.

Tess screaming, alone, in a dark forest.

My father's face.

A severed thumb, spouting blood.

Tess's lips part. Say something I hear but can't immediately make sense of. Because she's going and I'm trying to hold her. There is nothing but the effort to not let go. Her fingers drawing closed. Slipping through mine.

"TESS!"

And she's gone.

Her freed hands held out wide like wings. She doesn't push away from the edge but merely falls back, slowed by the buffeting air. Her face stricken in terror—*her* face again, *her* eyes—but her body still and composed, her braided hair pointed straight up above her head like a noose.

I rush to the edge and watch her tumble, once, before crashing into the canal.

And with the impact comes the words she whispered to me before the fall. Whispered not in secrecy but because it took all of her strength to push aside the other being within her. A gap when she was in command of her own tongue long enough to utter a plea.

A girl, mine. Calling for me to bring her home.

Find me.

THE BURNING LAKE

8

$\mathcal{B}$RIEF HAS A COLOR.

It has other characteristics, I know now, collectively forming a personality of sorts. An antagonizing figure that arrives in your life and refuses to leave or sit anywhere but next to you or stop whispering the name of the departed in your ear. But for me, more than this, grief expresses itself primarily as a shade of paint. The same disheartening turquoise on the kitchen walls of the cabin where we spent our summers and, after we had to sell our house in town, where we lived until Dad walked out into the woods one Sunday in July carrying only a photo of my brother and a shotgun and never came back.

It is the color of my mother crying while standing at the sink, her back to me. The color of my father sitting alone at the kitchen table through the night, rousing only to pick up the unringing phone and ask "Hello?" of the dead line. The color of the river my brother drowned in.

And now all of New York is washed in turquoise. I see it everywhere. The smallest splashes of it leaping out and demanding my attention, a guerilla ad campaign promoting nothing. A bleeding turquoise that touches everything, like a watercolor that spreads out from where the brush meets the paper. I see the city through an aquamarine gel, the Chrysler Building, the storming cabs, and the canyons that crosshatch Midtown all brushed by an underwater glaze. Even my closed eyelids are backlit by sadness. It is the color of seniors' home interiors and bus station bathrooms. The color of the Grand Canal.

It has been two days since I returned from Venice, five since Tess fell from the top floor of the Bauer Hotel into the water below. I would have returned sooner, but the police in Venice were searching for her remains all that time and I couldn't leave until they stopped looking. They never found her. It was, apparently, not unusual for those who drowned in the canals to disappear, drawn out of the city by tricky, stronger-than-you'd-guess currents, through the lagoon, past the outer islands and into the Adriatic Sea. And there were all the underwater buttresses, tunnels, and waste passages of the city itself, a network of invisible pockets where a body might become lodged. They had scuba divers working the case (ours was briefly a news story meriting mention and a photo of frogmen jumping into the canal with a striped-shirted gondolier in the background) but they found nothing, which seemed not to surprise them.

Nobody ever suggested she might still be alive. I didn't think it possible myself. But it had to be asked, and I asked. Every time I did it provoked the same look. The kind of look you give someone who has suffered a brain injury that has stolen coherence from their faculties and therefore there is no reply to offer aside from a compassionate stare.

The point is Tess was never returned to me, and when they called off the search (promising to remain diligent and in frequent communication) they encouraged me to go home, as there was nothing more for me to do in Venice. I have never felt more disloyal as when I boarded the plane and left my daughter's body somewhere in the waters below.

Diane and I have spoken, of course, both on the phone from Italy and in person, a couple times, here in New York. And O'Brien has left multiple messages, offering to move into the apartment for as long as I need the company. I declined via text. Instead of accepting offers of comfort, I have spent my time clogging up the Venice police's answering machine with queries to every department that may be of relevance to searching for victims of drownings. That, and wandering around the turquoise city. Remembering Tess.

Wandering.

Maybe this is what the voice meant when it said what awaited me. To move about aimlessly like this is to come as close to the dead as the living can get. Trekking from Wall Street to Harlem and down again, detouring at random. Unnoticed and absent as a phantom.

And as I go, some backstreet of my mind is making impossible connections.

This is the beginning of madness. Guilt so unbearable it twists the mind. To think these thoughts is to let go of the world and, if they are to be even partway believed, never return.

Knowing this doesn't stop me from thinking them.

Maybe the voice that came out of Tess's mouth was an independent presence, a spirit that took control of her for the last twenty minutes of her life. Maybe it was what pulled her hand from mine. Maybe it wasn't suicide that claimed my daughter (as the coroner and authorities unavoidably concluded, once suspicion directed my way was erased by witness accounts) but a murder committed from within. Maybe the voice belonged to the demon promised to visit me by the man in the chair.

Certainly not friends. But unquestionably close.

Maybe this presence piggy-backed on me from the room with the man in the chair back to the hotel, and from there transferred to Tess. It would explain some things. Why I felt so suddenly ill after I escaped from Santa Croce 3627—and then suddenly better again once back in our room at the Bauer. Why I saw the screeching pigs in the street. Why Tess went up to the roof. Why the last words she spoke asked me to find her. Why her body hasn't been found.

This is how far I've fallen.

No. Not true. I've gone even further than that.

What if the personality trait Tess and I share, the mostly disguisable birthmark of melancholy, was never just a temperament but an indication of our being chosen from the very start? If this were a lecture hall and the question I've just asked myself came from a student, I'd know the precedent I'd recite from heart: Mark 9. Another instance of Jesus casting a demon out of an afflicted soul. A boy this time. His father begging the savior to relieve his son of a foul spirit that had often thrown him "into the fire, and into the waters, to destroy him."

The waters.

Suicide. Demonically provoked.

Christ asked the father how long the boy had suffered in this way.

And he said, From childhood.

HERE'S ANOTHER DEFINITION OF WANDERING: EMOTIONS SO GREAT they require superstition to explain them. This is the core observation of my field of study, after all. Fear—of death, of loss, of being left behind—is the genesis of belief in the supernatural. For someone like me to suddenly find himself entertaining the myths of primitives can only be seen as symptomatic of a psychotic break of some kind. I know this to be as verifiable as the street numbers I walk past, as the time on my watch. *I am proposing that a demon took my daughter from me.* Just stop and say that out loud a few times. Just *hear* it. It is the sort of theory that rightly justifies locking someone in Bellevue for long-term observation.

So I move on. Surrounded by blue-green people on blue-green blocks.

And feel almost nothing.

That is, I miss Tess, I mourn for her, I am heartbroken. But to "miss," to "mourn," to acknowledge a "broken heart"—these are words so inadequate they border on the offensive. It's not about finding a way to *go on.* It's not about being angry at God. It's about dying. About wishing to be dead.

The only things that register are children. It's always been that way. There probably isn't a parent alive who can watch strangers' children play and not think of their own child. The laughter, the invitations to give chase, the anguish at the scraped knee or pilfered toy. All of it leads back to how our own did these same things, the quirks that marked them as both like and unlike every other child in the world.

There: A girl playing hide-and-seek with her mother amid the boulders and trees near the Turtle Pond in Central Park. It reminds me of playing the same game with Tess. Every time she hid—even if it was within our own apartment—there was always a half-second of real terror as I looked for her in the usual places and didn't find her. *What if, this time, she was really gone? What if she was hidden so well that looking behind trees or under beds or in laundry hampers wouldn't be enough?*

And then, just as the fizz of panic started up from the bottom of my throat, she was there. Jumping out at the first surrendering call of "Okay, I give up!" from me.

This time, Tess is hidden and never coming back.

Yet she begged me not to give up.

Find me.

I stop by an iron gate and watch the mother pause to look about her. Pretending to be stumped by her daughter's location. But when she tiptoes over to a maple and pokes her head around—*Gotcha!*—the girl isn't there. And instantly, the worry comes. The thought that this time the game is not a game.

"Momma!"

The girl rushes out from the quack grass that surrounds the edge of the pond and the mother picks her up, the girl's legs flying out behind her. Then the mother spots me. A man standing alone by the gate. It's the first time anyone's fully registered me since my return to New York.

I turn from them, shamed by my inadvertent invasion of their privacy. But the mother is already bundling the girl into her arms and starting away. Protecting her from the man who's clearly missing some essential part. Someone not entirely there but all the more dangerous for that.

A wanderer.

◆ ◆ ◆

THE TURQUOISE DAY TURNS TO TURQUOISE NIGHT. I RETURN TO THE apartment and make toast. Butter the slices and cut it into fingers the way Tess used to like it. Sprinkle them with cinnamon sugar. Throw them out without tasting them.

I pour myself a vodka on ice. Walk around the apartment and notice the light on in Tess's room. The *Lion King* poster over the bed (we'd taken her three times to the Broadway show, requests from two birthdays and a Christmas). A map of North Dakota on the wall (part of a school project, an in-depth study of one of the fifty states). The crayon drawings I'd honestly praised and had framed. The stuffed animals on the floor next to the chest of drawers, toys now long ignored, though still loved enough to avoid removal to the closet. The room of a girl in transition from childhood to the murky confusions of whatever follows.

I'm about to leave when I spot Tess's journal on her bedside table (I'd placed it there after bringing it home from Venice, returning it to where it often rested after her jottings). I'd never thought to read it when she was alive, my fear of her discovering my betrayal far greater than any curiosities I may have had about her secret thoughts. Now, though, the need to hear her, to bring her back, outweighs discretion.

A movie ticket stub marks the entry dated the day we left for Venice. Which means she must have written it on the plane.

Dad doesn't know that I can see how hard he's trying. The "funny" smiles, the hype about all the stuff we're going to see. Maybe he is kind of excited. But he still wears the Black Crown.

I can see it more today than ever. It's even like it's moving. Like there's something alive in it, making a nest. Worming around.

The trouble with Mom is part of it. But not all. There's something waiting for us he doesn't have a clue about. The Black Crown is coming with us. He's wearing it but doesn't know it's there (how can he NOT know it's there??).

Maybe the thing that waits on the other side wants to meet Dad, too.

All I'm sure about is that it wants to meet me.

This is followed by a page or so about the flight over, the vaporetto ride to the hotel. And then the journal's final entry. Dated the day she fell. Written in our room at the Bauer during the time I visited the address in Santa Croce.

It's here.

Dad knows it now, too. I can feel it. How scared he is.

How he's talking to it RIGHT NOW.

It won't let him go. It likes that we're here. It's almost happy.

Maybe we were wrong to come. But staying away wasn't a choice. It would find us. Here or there. Sooner or later.

Better that it's happening now. Because we're together, maybe there's something we can do. If not, it's better if it takes us at the same time. I wouldn't want to be the one left behind. And if we have to go THERE, I don't want to go ALONE.

He's coming now.

They're coming.

The journal drops from my hands with a whisper of pages.

She went to Venice to face it.

I turn off the light and close the door. Rush to the bathroom to kneel retching over the toilet.

She went to wear the Crown so I wouldn't have to anymore.

When I'm able, I head back toward the kitchen to freshen my drink and notice Tess's door is open. The light on.

It's an old apartment, but there's never been a draft that could open a door. And we've never had electrical problems. So I *hadn't* closed the door and turned off the light.

I turn off the light. Click the door shut. Start away.

And stop.

Only steps from Tess's room and there is the clear *snick* of the door-knob being turned. The squeak of the hinge.

I swing around in time to see the light go on. Not *already* on. The room going from dark to yellow as I blink it into focus.

"Tess?"

Her name passes my lips before the puzzlement settles in my mind. Somehow I know this isn't a hallucination, isn't a waking dream. It's Tess. In her room. Maybe the only place she could be strong enough to reach out to me. Tell me she's still here.

I rush in. Stand in the middle of her room with arms outstretched, fingers grasping.

"Tess!"

There is nothing to feel but the room's air-conditioned emptiness. Though the light remains on, she is no longer here.

I am, as crime reporters say of their sources, a "highly credible witness." I hold a Cornell PhD, a handful of distinguished teaching awards, publication credits in the most respected critical journals in my field, a medical history free of mental disturbance. More, I am an insistently rational sort, a spoilsport by nature when it comes to the fantastical. I've made an entire career out of doubt.

Yet here I am. Seeing the unseeable.

IN THE MORNING I AWAKEN TO FOUR MESSAGES ON MY PHONE. One from Diane, asking, in the tone and script of bill collector, to call her back as soon as possible "to resolve an outstanding issue." One from the detective in Venice I've been primarily corresponding with, informing me of the news that there is no news. And two from O'Brien, demanding to see me, the second of which advising me that I'll "go batshit crazy up there all alone if you don't talk to someone, and by 'someone,' I mean me."

Because she's Tess's mother, and because I can only manage one human-to-human conversation this morning, I prop myself against the headboard and call Diane back. It's only as her phone is ringing that I realize I've slept in Tess's room.

"Hello?"

"It's David."

"David."

She says my name, her husband of thirteen years, as though it is an obscure spice she's trying to remember if she's ever tasted before.

"This a bad time?"

"Stupid question."

"Yes, it was. Sorry."

She takes a breath. Not the hesitation of someone reluctant to cause pain to another, but merely, again, the pause of the bill collector, pulling out the right dialogue sheet for a particular subcategory of delinquent.

"I wanted to make it official," she says. "My moving out. Beginning the process."

"Process?"

"Divorce."

"Right."

"You can use Liam if you'd like," she says, referring to the lawyer in Brooklyn Heights who did our wills. "I've already spoken to someone else."

"Some Upper East Side tiger to take on Liam the tabby cat."

"You can choose the counsel you wish."

"I didn't mean to accuse. I was just being . . . myself."

She makes a sound that could be a small laugh, but isn't.

"I just don't understand the urgency," I say.

"This has been going on for a long time, David."

"I know that. I'm not fighting it. I will be the most helpful, acquiescent cuckold in the history of New York State matrimonial law. I'm just asking, why this morning? Less than a week after Tess went missing."

"Tess isn't missing."

"They're still looking."

"No, they're not. They're waiting."

"*I'm* still looking."

A silence. Then: "Looking for what?"

You can go as balls-out insane as you want to. My inner O'Brien, coming to my rescue. *But do you have to let her know you've lost it?*

"Nothing," I say. "I'm not making sense."

"So you'll speak to Liam? Or whomever? Expedite the application?"

"I'll expedite. You've never seen such expediting."

"Fine. Good."

She is in pain, too. Not that she's shown me any of it. I can only assume Will Junger is offering the comfort and bearing the brunt, though he doesn't strike me as much of a brunt bearer, not for long. In any case, Diane is Tess's mother and now her daughter is gone and it can only be tearing her into tiny, useless pieces as it is me.

Yet here's the thing: I can't stop wondering if I might be wrong about that. There is loss in her voice, and resolution. But there's an awful satisfaction in there, too. Not about Tess never coming home, nothing so monstrous as that. But satisfaction that I was the one who was there—that it was my failure—when it happened.

"I don't care if you blame me. If you hate me. I don't care if we never speak again," I say. "But you have to know that I tried to save her. That I didn't let go. That I didn't just *stand by*. I *fought* for her."

"I acknowledge what you're trying to—"

"Every parent says—or at least thinks—they'd lay down their lives for their child. I don't know, when the test comes, if that's true for everyone. But it's true for me."

"But you *didn't!*"

This shout comes so bright and hot down the line that I have to pull the phone from my ear. "You *didn't* lay down your life for her," she says. "Because you're still here. And she's not."

You're wrong about one thing, I want to say. *I'm not here.*

Instead, as I'm readying some farewell, an acknowledgment of our time together and the one thing we did right, the one thing we'd never regret, she hangs up.

WHO SITS IN A CHURCH IN THE MIDDLE OF A WEEKDAY AFTERNOON? Drunks, runaways, addicts in all their varieties. The lost who have only themselves to blame. I know because I sit among them. Praying for the first time in my adult life.

Or trying to pray. The iconography, the forced quiet, the stained glass, all of it feels overcooked. Yes, it's a church: it's *supposed* to be churchy. But I feel no closer to holiness here than I did outside on 43rd Street moments ago.

"You get disconnected?"

I turn to find a slightly grizzled man in his midfifties. Rumpled suit, hair in need of all manner of attention. A businessman—or former businessman—belonging to the drunken class, would be my guess.

"Sorry?"

"Your prayer line. To the Big Guy. He put you on hold? Does it to me all the time. Then damned if you don't get disconnected."

"I never even dialed the number."

"You're better off. If you'd gotten through, it would have been press '1' for miracles, press '2' for picking the winning horse in the eighth at Belmont, press '3' for 'I'm sorry for what I did . . . but not *so* sorry I wouldn't do it again.'"

"Might as well just go to my shrink."

"Yeah? She good at picking horses?"

She. Are most therapists women? Or could I possibly know this guy? A guy who knows both me and O'Brien?

"She doesn't gamble," I say.

"No? Well, you know what they say. Can't win if you don't play."

He leans his arms across the back of the pew. It brings a whiff of recently applied deodorant. A crude perfume meant to cover the earthy scent beneath it.

"I don't mean to pry, but you look a little lost, my friend," he says.

He offers a look of real concern. And then it comes to me: He's one of those street missionaries. A recruiter for the church in civilian clothes, prowling the pews.

"Do you work here?"

"Here?" He looks around, as though noticing where we sit for the first time. "They got *jobs* in here?"

"I'm just not up for a sales pitch for salvation. If that's what you do."

He shakes his head. "What do the T-shirts say? 'You've mistaken me for someone who gives a shit.' I just saw a kindred spirit sitting here and thought I'd say hello."

"I'm not trying to be unfriendly. I'd just prefer to be left alone."

"Alone. Sounds nice. Hard to find a moment's peace where I live. Pandemonium. A man can't *think*. And believe me, friend, I'm a thinker."

That word again. The same one O'Brien used to describe Grand Central. Milton's hell.

Pandemonium.

"I'm David," I say, and offer my hand. And after a pause, the man takes it.

"Good to meet you, David."

I wait for him to share his name, but he just releases my hand.

"Think I'll be moving on," I say, standing. "I just came in here to get out of the sun for a minute."

"Can't say I blame you. Personally, I'm an indoors cat."

I make my way to the aisle and, with a parting nod, start toward the open doors. The day blazing beyond.

As I go, the man recites part of a poem in the pious murmur of a prayer.

> *O sun, to tell thee how I hate thy beams*
> *That bring to my remembrance from what state*
> *I fell*

Milton. Writing Satan's words.

I turn. Slide along the pew to where he sits, his head now lowered, hands reverently clasped. Grab his shoulder and give him a rough push.

"Look at me!"

He jerks away in a defensive reflex. Winces up at me in anticipation of a blow. Not the man who was sitting here a moment ago. A priest. Young and clean-shaven, his skin blushed in alarm.

"I'm so sorry," I start, already backing away. "I thought you were someone else."

As I make for the aisle again, the young priest's expression changes. His surprise turning to a smile.

"I'm ready to hear your confession," he says.

His laugh follows me all the way out onto the street.

IT WAS THE VOICE AGAIN. I'M SURE OF THIS AS I LURCH AWAY FROM St. Agnes' to Lexington and lean against the doorway to an Irish bar, catching my breath. It was the same presence that passed from me to Tess, that spoke to me on the rooftop of the Bauer. Quoted from *Paradise Lost* just as the man in the church just did. And the Thin Woman, too, though I'm less sure she was an incarnation of the voice herself—the being I have started to think of as the Unnamed—rather than an on-the-ground, human representative. For some reason, I had to travel to Venice, to Santa Croce 3627, for the Unnamed to be introduced into my life, and it was the Thin Woman's job to see to it that I accepted the invitation to do just that. Which would suggest she didn't work for the Church or one of its agencies as I suspected.

O sun, to tell thee how I hate thy beams

In Milton's poem, this is Satan speaking. Cursing the light of day as a painful reminder of his fallen state, of all he'd lost in his self-imposed exile in the darkness. Is that who the Unnamed is? The Adversary? The man in the chair—or the plurality of voices speaking through him—said it was not the "master" whom I would soon meet, but "one who sits with him." In *Paradise Lost*, this would mean the fallen angels who formed the Stygian Council of ruling demons in hell, with Satan sitting as Chair. They were thirteen in number, each given distinctive personalities and skills by the poet. It would seem that the Unnamed is one of them. An originating demon, cast out of heaven. A being capable of the most convincing shapeshifting and mimicry, assuming human form—the old man on the plane, the drunk in the church.

Then again, perhaps these are borrowed shades of those who have already lived and died. Perhaps the Unnamed is limited to inhabiting the skins of those in hell.

It's clear now. I have lost my mind.

Instead of grieving Tess head on, I'm creating gothic distractions, Miltonic puzzles, demon dialogues—anything but facing the unfaceable. I'm using my mind to protect my heart, and it's a cheat, a dishonor to Tess's memory. She deserves a father to mourn her, not construct an elaborate web of paranoid nonsense. I'm sure the shrinks have a term for this. Cowardice will do.

By the time I get back to the apartment and check my phone, more messages have been left for me, a couple notes of sympathy from colleagues at the university, and two grave warnings from O'Brien that if I don't call her back soon, she'll be forced to take matters into her own hands.

Why *don't* I call O'Brien back? I honestly can't say. Every time my finger hovers over the button to speed-dial her it loses the will to press it. I *want* to speak to her, to see her. But what I want has been negated by another purpose, an influence I can feel in my veins as an alien weight, heavy and cold. A tingly sickness that, above all, doesn't want O'Brien anywhere near me.

And besides, I'm busy.

Opening the medicine chest and pulling out the bottle of Zolpidem that Diane left behind. I fill a glass of water and go to Tess's room. Sit on the edge of her bed and, one by one, swallow the pills.

Suicide? And with sleeping pills? Chickenshit and cliché.

O'Brien is here with me, but at a great distance. Easy enough to ignore.

Will I see you, Tess, when it is done?

Yes. She is waiting, says a voice, neither my own nor O'Brien's. *Go on, Professor. Sip. Swallow. Swallow. Sip.*

I don't believe what it says. Yet it's impossible to resist.

Sip. Swallow.

SMASH.

A framed photo falls to the floor. Shards of glass now winking

92

over the rug, lodged in the cracks between the boards. The nail still firm in the wall, the wire the frame hung on still intact and secure.

I know what photo it is, but I go to it anyway. Bend and turn it over.

Me and Tess. The two of us laughing at the beach near Southampton a couple summers ago. Below us, out of view, our sand castle being dissolved by the incoming tide. What's funny are our hopeless efforts to save it, to buttress the walls with fresh sand, bail out the courtyard with our hands. The picture shows the pleasure in our being together in the sunshine, on vacation. But it also shows the joy in taking on a task with someone you love, even if that task is too great to be achieved.

"Tess?"

She is here. Not just in the memory the photo evokes. She was the one who pulled it off the wall.

I crawl to the bathroom. Stick a forefinger down my throat. Empty my stomach of tap water pinkened by tranquilizers. When I flush it away, the heavy thing in my blood goes with it.

For a while I lean against the tiled wall, my legs out before me. If I don't move, it's easy to pretend this isn't my body. There is no order I could give that would make any part of me move.

Find me.

I'm being the old David again, the man of inaction Diane was probably right to leave. Because there is still something to be done. An impossible task, admittedly: find and retrieve the dead—or half-dead—from darkest limbo.

And then there is the matter of not having any idea how to begin.

I stand under the shower fully clothed. Feel the bookish references and snippets of poetry slide off me like oil. Soon there is nothing left.

Except for the feeling I'm not alone.

My eyes open against the spray of hot water. Steam fills not only the glass-walled shower stall but the whole bathroom, so that the room is alive with billowing fog.

Nothing there. But I stare into it just the same.

And watch Tess come out.

Shaking with hunger, with fear. Her skin bruised by cold. Reaching out to me but stopped by the glass. Her palms as darkly lined as ancient maps.

"Tess!"

She opens her mouth to speak just as a pair of arms slips around her and pulls her back into the fog.

Arms too long, too grotesquely muscled to be a man's. Blackened by hair thick as fur. Their claws soil-stained as a beast's.

ONCE I'VE CHANGED INTO CLEAN CLOTHES AND AT LEAST PARTLY cleared my head, I get the digital camera the physician gave me in Venice and download the footage I recorded of the man in the chair onto my laptop. The reason I do this occurs to me only after I'm done.

This is important.

I don't know why yet. But it was the one thing the physician insisted on. *For you.* So whoever was giving him his instructions wanted me to have it. To train the lens on the man in the chair and record what he said, what he did. Why else give me the camera at all?

So what *did* the man do and say?

I watch the recording on my laptop's screen. Its reality pulses out at me in the way that even the most vivid news clip or documentary has never done before. A physical blow to my chest that forces me back on the sofa. And it's not just the disturbing sounds and images that do it. There is something about the effect the recording has that is distinct from its content. How to put it? An aura of the pain from which it originates. A subliminal glimpse of chaos. A Black Crown.

There are the voices, the words, the tortured writhings of the body. But the only thing I write down in my notebook is the list of cities and numbers the voice said would be of relevance on April 27th. The day after tomorrow.

New York 1259537
Tokyo 996314
Toronto 1389257
Frankfurt 540553
London 590643

The presence offered this as a piece of what is to come. A snapshot of the imperceptible future that, if correct, would prove its skills, its power. Its reality.

As the recording continues, I close my eyes when the man's face changes into my father's. It doesn't prevent me from hearing the old man's voice.

It should have been you.

As awful as it is to interpret his words, I can't help feeling he means something even worse than his wishing I'd drowned instead of my brother.

Rewind. Again. Eyes open this time.

I watch his image on the screen and know, inarguably, that it is my father speaking to me from wherever he went after we buried him. And he is revealing a secret that I can't fully understand yet. An invitation to seek him out, nearly as irresistible as Tess's.

When the recording is finished replaying, I close the laptop and return it to its leather travel bag. Then I wrap the camera in an old jewelry bag of Diane's and put them both inside a briefcase. I think of simply placing it on the top shelf of my bedroom closet, but something tells me it requires more care than that. There is no hiding place in the apartment good enough.

I start out with the briefcase, with the absurd idea of going to a pawnshop and getting a pair of handcuffs so that I might attach the handle to my wrist. As I walk, however, I come up with some better ideas. What I need to do is stash it where even I won't be able to access it until after the 27th, when the prediction it contains can be proven true or false without any question of my tampering with it.

Do they have safe deposit boxes big enough for a briefcase? Here's the thing about banks I learn over the next three hours: They have safe deposit boxes big enough for a sedan if you're ready to pay.

And they'll do more or less anything else for money, too. For instance, whether you have an account or not (I choose a Midtown main branch I've never entered before), they will place your belongings in a box in a vault that can only be opened by way of a numerical code of your own devising. They will bring in a silver-haired senior partner at a prominent law firm to prepare a document ensuring no bank employee or manager will allow anyone—including myself—to access the box until after April 27th, then have the manager sign it and register copies with the bank, the law firm, and an envelope for my pocket. They will provide a written guarantee that the box will not be opened for at least ninety-nine years unless either myself or someone with my signed permission and the numerical code shows up. They even offer you a cup of reasonably decent coffee while you wait for it all to be done.

On the way home, I put in a call to a guy I know in the IT department at Columbia. After some roundabout, isn't-this-heat-a-bitch chat, I ask him some questions. In particular, I want to know if it would be possible to alter the time a video download is registered to have occurred on a hard drive after it's happened or, alternatively, to make any record of the download having happened go away.

He pauses, and I imagine the internal dialogue in his mind:

Q: Why would a professor of literature want to know that?
A: Porn.

Eventually, he answers no. It would be "pretty damn difficult" to erase a download entirely or make one saved on the 25th look like it happened on the 28th. "Stuff like that always leaves fingerprints," he says with a verbal wink, a warning for the next time I want to grab something nasty off the Internet without the wife finding out.

What I don't tell him is the wife is gone. And that I don't want to erase my download. What I want is to ensure that the time I transferred it from the camera to my laptop says the same thing as the date and time recorded on the footage itself: that the document reflects events—and spoken cities and numbers—that occurred *before* April 27th.

Like a magician ensuring nothing is up his sleeve, I feel like I've done everything I can to establish the conditions for a real trick. If I'm able to figure out what the cities and numbers mean on the 27th, and if they correspond to verifiable reality, the magic of the recording is real.

And as the *Compendium Maleficarum*'s Brother Guazzo would note, if miracles are one way the savior proves his identity, magic is the way demons prove theirs.

LATER, ANOTHER CHURCH. THIS ONE OURS, IF ONLY NOMINALLY, AS our attendance has been limited to three Christmas Eves of the last five and an annual donation from Diane's personal account. Church of St. Paul and St. Andrew, uptown on West 86th Street. Chosen by Diane for its progressive congregation and fuzzily inoffensive denomination (United Methodist). A community we chose but didn't, in practice, belong to.

Though today it's serving a purpose. Tess's memorial service. Hastily arranged by Diane and announced to me only yesterday in an e-mail buckshot with "healing" and "process" and "closure." I've come for her sake, to present a united parental front. It's what you do on occasions such as these. You show up.

But now that I'm here, standing across the street from the building's octagonal tower I'd barely noticed before but which today looks ominously Venetian, watching the dark-suited colleagues and peripheral friends and members of Diane's extended family all hauling wreaths and their hesitant selves up the steps, I know I *can't* go in. To enter would be the same as admitting that Tess is dead. If she isn't, it might pull her away from me. And if she is, I don't need the help of near-strangers to remember who she was.

I watch the last of them return their phones to their pockets and slip inside. But before I start away, Diane steps out into the sunshine. She must have been welcoming the guests at the door, letting them pat the back of her hand and replying with the appropriate phrases she'd be good at credibly repeating. Now, with the organ starting its prelude, she's come to take a last look around. A last look for me.

I wait until she finds me. There is nothing on her face. A more honest expression than any she'd offered those within. It's her feeling of vacancy, I see now, that is intolerable for her, and today's service is part of an effort to start filling up the space. With activity, with words, with starting out *here* and heading off to *there*.

She raises her palm, as though to show me the lines drawn on it and invite a reading of their meaning. It's a half wave, perhaps, or merely a twitch. Something unintended or abandoned. Then, once she's returned her arm to her side, she backs into the darkness and the doors are pushed shut from inside.

THERE'S SOMEONE WAITING FOR ME ON THE STREET OUTSIDE MY apartment.

That is to say, there's a man in his midthirties standing with his hands in his pockets near the entrance to my building, casually glancing into traffic from time to time as though waiting for a cab, yet when one comes along, he turns his back on it like he's changed his mind. There is no indication, when I spot him the moment I turn the corner off Columbus Avenue, that he is waiting for me. I've never seen him before in my life. And he is, at this distance at least, a near-perfect composite of the nondescript: white cotton shirt rolled up his forearms, weekend jeans, dark hair cropped short. Not tall but solid, a frame used to delivering and absorbing blows. He could be ex-military. And he could hold one of the vaguely rough-and-ready jobs so many former servicemen hold in New York. Limo driver, personal security, doorman, bartender.

So what is it that sets him apart? His lack of distinction. Every posture, the way he's tucked in his shirt, the calculated curl of his lower lip. He is someone who has been trained not to stand out. And given the visitations over the last week of my life, when a man like that stands by my door, he stands there for me.

Yet, as I approach, he doesn't seem to notice me at all. I'm almost past him when he addresses my back.

"David Ullman?"

"Who are you?"

"My name is George Barone."

"Doesn't ring a bell."

"It wouldn't."

I stare at him a moment.

"*Es vos vir aut anima?*" I ask him in Latin. *Are you man or spirit?*

He doesn't appear to understand the question. Nor does he seem surprised that I've just addressed him in an ancient language.

"Can I buy you a coffee?" he says. "Perhaps the street isn't the best place for conversation."

"Who says we're having a conversation?"

"I'm sure this neighborhood isn't lacking for cafés. I would be pleased if you would guide me to your favorite," he says, ignoring my question, coming up alongside me so that his shoulder sidles against mine. From twenty yards away, we would look like old friends paused in deciding whether to head east or west to grab a drink.

"Why should I talk to you?" I ask.

"It's in your best interests."

"You're here to help me?"

"I wouldn't go that far."

Normally, I would walk away from an exchange with a stranger like this. But now I have to open every door, accept every invitation. Even if it doesn't feel like it could lead to much good.

To get closer to Tess, I will have to say yes to everything.

A journey of your own making.
"Sure," I say. "There's a good place this way."

WE WALK WEST TO AMSTERDAM, AND AROUND THE CORNER TO the The Coffee Bean, where we find a table at the window. The man who calls himself George Barone buys me a cappuccino, but nothing for himself.

"Ulcer," he explains as he delivers my coffee and sits across from me. Relaxed and friendly, but only *seeming* relaxed and friendly. I'm no expert in this area, but something about this man suggests a capacity for violence, the carrying out of unthinkable assignments. What gives him away is how he pays attention only to me. No pretty girl—or handsome boy—who comes near our table attracts even the briefest glance from him. When a barista drops a tray of mugs and they explode on the tiled floor, he doesn't blink. His focus like a bird of prey.

"Stress," I say. "Always is with ulcers."

"My doctor says otherwise."

"Oh yeah? What's he say?"

"Coffee. Cigarettes. Booze. He recommends the avoidance of pleasure."

"Sorry to hear that."

"Don't be sorry. Keeps me sharp."

"What do you do, Mr. Barone? What do you keep so sharp for?"

"I'm a freelancer."

"You write?"

"No."

"Your business is more practical, then?"

"I pursue. Let's put it that way."

"A professional pursuer. And your current quarry is me?"

"Only indirectly."

He waits, as though I am the one expected to report something to him. I sip my coffee. Stir it. Add sugar. Sip it again.

"Are you an assassin?" I ask finally.

"Are you still alive?"

"As far as I can tell."

"Then let's not worry about it."

"What *should* we worry about?"

"Nothing. If you help me, right now, nothing at all."

He touches a fingertip to the table, picks up a crystal of sugar. Stares at it as though determining the quality of a cut diamond.

"The man you saw in Venice," he says. "Do you know who he was?"

"What do you know about that?"

"Quite a lot, in some respects. Though I am informed of only the facts that will assist me in my task. I'm sure you have questions I can't answer."

"Who do you work for?"

"Like that, for instance."

"Is it the Church? Do you know who sent that woman to my office?"

"I'm not aware of any woman. I'm only aware of us. Here. Right now."

And it's true. He *is* only aware of us. His calm concentration negating the world with a hypnotist's gaze.

"That's very Buddhist," I say.

"Is it? I wouldn't know. I'm just an altar boy from Astoria with a job to do."

"So you're some kind of Vatican thug? That it?"

"I hope you're not being rude."

"Who else would you be working for? Does the Devil hire meatheads like you—sorry, *pursuers*? Either way, they flew me first class, you know. Whatever they're paying you to harass me, you've got to ask for a raise."

"Let me ask you again," he says, ignoring my attack. "Do you know who the man at Santa Croce 3627 was?"

"Was? What happened to him?"

"Suicide. That's what the authorities have ruled it, anyway. History of depression, strange and uncharacteristic behavior of late, then went AWOL altogether. It's a pretty easy file to close."

102

"How did he die?"

"Painfully."

"Tell me."

"Toxin ingestion. Battery acid, to be precise. A difficult thing to swallow a liter of, even if your goal is to end your life. Trust me. That shit *burns*."

"Maybe somebody helped him."

"There you go. *Now* you're picking up steam, Professor."

"You think he was murdered."

"Not in the conventional sense."

"What's the unconventional sense?"

"Foul play," he says, and smiles at the phrase. "There was most likely some very fucking foul play."

"You did it."

"No, not me. Something worse."

I feel my knees click together under the table, and it takes a second to set them apart again.

"You haven't answered my question," the Pursuer continues.

"I'd forgotten you'd asked one."

"Do you know who he was?"

"No."

"Then let me tell you. He was you."

"How's that?"

"Dr. Marco Ianno."

"I've heard the name."

"I figured you might have. A fellow academic. A professor of Christian studies at Sapienza for some years now. Father of two, married. Quite well regarded in his home country for his defenses of the Church, though, interestingly, not personally a member of the Church himself. His writings concerned the necessary relationship between human imagination and faith."

"Sounds like one of my lectures."

"There you go again. They don't just hand out those PhDs for nothing."

"Why are you telling me this? You came here to deliver a warning?"

"I'm not a courier."

"So what do you want from me?"

He presses the sugar crystal on his finger onto the table with a tiny, audible crunch.

"I believe you have a document," he says.

"I got plenty. You should see my office."

"It may be written, or a photograph. Though my bet is it's a video. Am I correct?"

I don't answer. And he shrugs slightly, as though he is well used to this kind of initial resistance.

"Whatever it is," he goes on, "you have something that you took from that room in Venice that I'd like you to give me."

"Don't tell me. You're going to write an astronomical sum on this napkin in return for it."

"No. It's a matter of accounting. Paper trails. There can be no residue to the transaction."

"I'm just supposed to hand this thing—this *document*—over. That it?"

"Yes."

"What's my motivation?"

"The possible avoidance of following in Professor Ianno's footsteps. And me, of course. There's avoiding me."

"Go to hell."

Something passes over his face. So quick I might have only imagined it. A twitch at the top of his cheek. A switched gear.

"You don't want to play it like that, David."

"There was a time, not long ago at all, when a fellow like you, saying the things you're saying, would frighten me. But not anymore."

"I suggest you reconsider that."

"Why?"

"Because I *should* frighten you. And if not me, there are other things. Really quite remarkable things."

"The things that killed Marco Ianno."

"Yes."

"You're in control of these things?"

"No. Nobody is. But they seem to have an interest in you."

I raise my cup, but the sight of the sludgy coffee, the floating island of milk, almost makes me gag.

"The man in that room was mentally ill," I say. "He was vulnerable to becoming convinced of impossibilities."

"We all are." The Pursuer almost smiles. "Maybe none more so than you."

"He killed himself."

"Just the same as they're saying your kid did. Like they might end up saying about you."

"You're threatening me?"

"Yes. I most certainly am."

I get up. My knees knocking against the side of the table and overturning my cup. The still-hot cappuccino spills over the table, splashing onto the man's legs. It must scald him. But he doesn't flinch. Grabs my wrist as I move to go.

"Give me the document."

"I don't know what you're talking about."

I feel the turned heads of the other customers behind me. But he doesn't notice.

"You misunderstand me," he says, slowly and patiently. "I'm not a nuisance you can just walk away from."

He lets go of my wrist. Expecting me to walk. But instead I bend low so that I'm inches from his face.

"I don't care what you do. I'm not giving you a goddamn thing," I say. "You lose what I've lost, and you hold on to whatever you've got left. In my position, there's no protecting yourself, because I don't *have* a self to protect anymore. So go ahead. Pursue away. And tell your employers they can go fuck themselves. Okay?"

Now I walk.

Up Amsterdam a block and a half, take a right onto my street. I don't look back. But even after I turn at the corner, he's watching me.

I know this as certainly as I know who Dr. Marco Ianno was.

I DIDN'T RECOGNIZE HIM AS THE MAN IN THE CHAIR AT THE TIME. But as soon as I heard Marco Ianno's name moments ago he was returned to me. A colleague who witnessed the most unprofessional moment of my career.

It was at an unusually glitzy conference held at Yale seven or eight years ago. Rome was rumored to be quietly picking up the tab. "Future/Faith" was the title of the proceedings, as if belief were a tired product in need of some snappy rebranding, which I suppose it is. Top scholars and philosophers and op-ed pundits from around the world were assembled to discuss "the issues Christianity faces in the new millennium." My job was to deliver a punched-up, PowerPoint version of my standard lecture about how Milton's Satan is an early advocate for the dissolution of patriarchy. "The Devil has father issues," was my laugh-getting opening zinger.

After my talk, the house lights were raised for a brief Q&A. The first to stand was a theologian whose work I was aware of, a priest (fully collared and frocked for the occasion) who was known to be a policy advisor to the Vatican, devising defenses that might hold the line against creeping modernizations in Church doctrine. He was polite, his question a softball about some citation or other he failed to make note of. Yet something about the man instantly set me against him. I became uncharacteristically aggressive in my replies to his follow-up questions, until, within minutes, I'd worked myself up to spitting insults from the lectern ("Maybe that thing around your throat is choking off the circulation to your *brain*, father!"). The room seemed to enlarge and contract, breathing like the bellows of an awakening giant. There was no stopping, no control. It was as though I was involuntarily playing a part, someone wholly other than myself. I remember the coppery film in my mouth when I bit the inside of my cheek and drew blood.

Then it got truly strange.

The priest stared at me, puzzled, seeing something he'd just noticed. He took a step back and bumped into the legs of the person sitting behind him. His hands searching the air for balance.

"What is your name?" he asked.

And I couldn't answer. I couldn't, because I no longer knew.

"Professor Ullman?"

A new voice, coming from the rear of the hall. Kindly and sympathetic. An accented voice belonging to a man who was advancing with sure purpose and a familiar smile so that, when he finally stood next to me and took me by the elbow, I seemed to have known him all my life.

"I believe our allotted time has expired," Dr. Marco Ianno said, offering *I'll handle this* nods to those seated in the rows and leading me toward the doors. "Perhaps you would like to join me for a refreshment, David?"

Once we were outside in the bracing air of the quad, I felt like myself again. Close enough to myself, in any case, to thank Ianno and assure him I was fine, that I needed only to return to my hotel for some rest. It was the end of an embarrassing performance, later requiring letters of apology and the fictional excuse of a fever that had taken sudden hold of me. An unsettling incident, to be sure, but over now.

Yet Ianno, a man I knew only through his written work and never saw again until the room in Santa Croce, called after me as I left him standing in the New Haven cold. A message I dismissed as mistranslated Italian at the time, and remembered only when the Pursuer mentioned his name moments ago.

"What happened in there—it has happened to me, too," he said. "I believe we may have been wrong in thinking they were just words on a page, Professor!"

I DON'T GO STRAIGHT HOME. IT'S NOT WORRY THAT THE PURSUER will follow me there or break down the door once I'm inside. There'd be no point: He knows what he seeks won't be in the apartment. He's most likely *already* been through the apartment. He's looked in all the obvious places, but now requires me to tell him what he needs to know. He asked politely today. Next time he will employ harder persuasions.

Why not just give the "document" to George Barone? It would be easy enough. And I believe if I did, I would be left alone. He was concerned about residue: killing a Columbia prof would leave even more stains than a cash payoff. It would be the easiest thing in the world to accompany my Pursuer to the Chase Bank at 48th and Sixth in a couple of days (when the legal instructions will permit me reentry to the box) and hand him the laptop and camera, the only evidence of my dialogue with the late Dr. Ianno.

But I can't do that. Because if the Pursuer wants it—or if whoever is paying his freelance fee needs to get it as badly as they seem to— then it has value. Without it, I might not be worth any more visits, might not be receptive to any more signs. Even if holding on to what the Pursuer called the document endangers me, I have no choice but to keep it mine and remain a target. Only as a wanted man will I retain my part in the story. And while I have no real idea *why* I'm wanted, I've got to stay in the show if I'm to find a way to Tess.

One thing is clearer now that the Pursuer has introduced himself: there is less time than I had guessed.

I call O'Brien, and she picks up halfway through the first ring.

"David," she says with relief. "Where *are* you?"

"Here. In New York."

"So why are you avoiding me? I'm your *friend*, you jerk."

"I'm sorry."

"What's going on?"

"I'm not sure I could give it a name."

"Don't diagnose yourself. Just tell me what you've been up to. Because I know there's something happening. Surprise trip to Venice, what happened with Tess. And no calls from you even once you got home. That's not you, David."

"I am well and truly messed up."

"Of course you are. You've lost so much. It's unimaginable."

"It's not just Tess. There are . . . aspects to her disappearance I can't explain."

"Disappearance? It was suicide, David."

"I'm not sure that's true."

She absorbs this. "You're speaking as to how it happened?"

"As to *why*."

"Okay. What else?"

"I've had . . . visits."

I can hear O'Brien measuring this. Giving me an opportunity to share everything. But suddenly, on the street, on the phone, I worry what we're saying might not be private. Phone hacking. *They can do that pretty easily now, right?* And the last thing I want to do is imperil my friend. She's got enough to manage on her own without me sending a Pursuer to knock on her door.

"You are sounding genuinely weird," she says.

"You're right. This is just unprocessed emotional stuff morphing into twisted, paranoid stuff. Stuff, stuff, *stuff*."

O'Brien pauses. She seems to understand my aversion to saying anything more isn't a dismissal of the topic, but a concern about privacy. In any case, when she speaks next, it's in a code known only to us.

"Well, I just wish we could get together," she says. "But I'm up to my neck in a dissertation evaluation right now. And then there's a whack of late freshmen papers to grade. Total pandemonium."

That word. The demons' palace. Our meeting place.

"Sorry to hear that. Would've been good to get together."

"Definitely. Another time. Soon, okay? Be well, David."

"Thanks. You, too."

She hangs up.

And I'm hailing a cab.

"Grand Central Station," I tell the driver, and we swerve out into the currents of traffic heading downtown.

AT LEAST WE'RE *supposed* TO BE HEADING DOWNTOWN. THE DRIVER must be new. Or stoned. Or both. He heads south on Columbus before taking an aggressive, spontaneous right that throws me against the door. Then he's going around the block and, even when he has the chance to correct himself, keeps heading all the way to Central Park West.

"I asked for Grand Central. As in the *railway station*," I call up to him through the cash receptacle of the plexiglas shield. "You know something I don't know?"

He doesn't answer. Pulls over to the curb somewhere in the mid-seventies.

"Why are you stopping?"

I knock on the plastic. He doesn't turn.

"I need to keep going *that* way," I say, pointing straight ahead.

"You're here," the driver says. The voice barely audible but distinctly wet-sounding, as though he's just had dental surgery that's left his mouth drooling and numb.

"I'm going *downtown*."

"This is where . . . you have to go."

He doesn't move. In the rearview mirror only part of his face is visible. And half of that is obscured by aviator sunglasses, as well as a black, chest-length, Middle Eastern beard. In short, he looks like a cab driver.

Except for the tongue. Sliding out past his lips, glistening and obscene. The tip twitching. Tasting the air.

As soon as I'm out I slam the door shut and he's skidding away. I try to get his car number as he goes but he's blocked by traffic in an instant. A battered yellow sedan among others.

Now I'm here. Half a block north of 72nd Street. Where the grand old Dakota Apartments building overlooks the park. Not the more famous south end, where John Lennon was shot (a drop-off point for an inexhaustible number of ghoulish tourists) but the north corner, famous for nothing. If the driver intended for me to see one of New York's best-loved bloodstains, he got even *that* wrong.

I decide there is something to this.

It's an act of will on my part as much as deduction. There are no accidents anymore, only meanings and prophecies. I'm an overnight fundamentalist interpreter, seeing confirmation of some Great Plan in the Virgin's face appearing in the outline of a cloud or what's spelled out in my alphabet soup.

He dropped me off at the north corner of the building. North of the Dakota.

North Dakota.

The map on Tess's wall. The state she'd selected for her school project. Or, now that I think of it, the state she'd been assigned.

"Why North Dakota?" I remember asking her the day she'd brought the map home and started rummaging around for the scotch tape so she could put it up.

"I don't know. It was chosen for me."

"By the teacher?"

"No," she'd said, pretending to be engrossed by digging through a kitchen drawer.

"Then who, honey?"

She didn't answer. But had her shoulders stiffened as the answer paused in her mind, before pulling the tape from the drawer and running off to her room? It's certainly how I remember the moment now, though it meant little at the time, other than a preteen's impatience with her father's nagging.

It means considerably more now.

If the point of my wandering is to look for signs, maybe this is one of them. Whether he was one of the good guys or the bad, the driver brought me here for a reason. I was meant, like the apostles, to see significance in coincidence. I have to, for Tess's sake.

Blind faith. Though in my case, a faith not in heaven but those at war with it.

I DON'T CALL ANYONE. WHO WOULD I CALL? DIANE DOESN'T NEED to know. And though Tess is gone, maybe *she* already does.

Then there's O'Brien. Who I've now stood up. I would text her to say I'm not coming, but I'm underground, taking a subway uptown to my campus office. There, I quickly gather the only things I can think of being of use other than the credit cards in my wallet. Books. A hastily assembled personal library of demonology pulled down from my shelves and stuffed into a leather satchel. *Paradise Lost. The Anatomy of Melancholy.* The King James Bible. Along with the unrelated but just as necessary *Road Atlas of the United States.*

I walk off campus into Harlem and buy a car. Renting would certainly be cheaper, but I worry my whereabouts will be easier to trace if I'm beholden to Budget or Avis to return their property at some point. And there's a used car lot up on 142nd I've passed on my way to a good Mexican place (that is, a good margarita place) O'Brien and I have been to a few times. It turns out they take credit cards for full payment and don't ask for ID when I give my name as John Milton for the registration forms.

The better decision would probably be to go generic, some reliable Japanese four-door in a gray or beige. Instead, I buy a custom black Mustang. Not a vintage model but a chunky newer one—two years old, just eight thousand miles on it, if the odometer is to be believed—with chrome hubcaps and leopard-fluff seat covers. Subtle, as drug dealer rides go, yet still something of a standout on the muted highways and byways of today's America. I've never driven a car like this—never really been into cars at all—and now, walking through the small lot of repossessed Mercs and fat-assed SUVs, the contradiction of a wire-rim bespectacled, comfort-fit Levi's me (the permanent undergrad look, as Diane called it) emerging from an inner-city hot rod appeals to me. It's funny. If Tess were here, she'd find it funny, too. She'd also be jumping to get into the passenger seat, settle into the spotted fake fur, and tell me to gun it. So I give it a go in her honor. A polite tire squeal out of the lot and then south to the apartment, where I throw some clothes in a bag. Along with Tess's journal.

Then north again, into the merging lanes that lead onto the George Washington Bridge that takes me off the island. From there, westward on I-80, entering the grid of interstates that, with its GOOD FOOD! diners and KIDS STAY FREE! motels is an exclamation- marked world unto itself. A paved gateway to widening spaces and progressively fewer people. Leaving the fixed certainties of New York behind and rolling toward the wilder possibilities of the less scrutinized cities and towns, the forgotten plains. North Dakota. The Overlooked State.

Not that I'm going to get anywhere near there today. A collected fatigue hits me as I roll over the Pennsylvania state line, and I start looking for a rest stop. Also to call O'Brien. She didn't deserve my rudeness earlier today, and she's likely worried after I didn't show up. But it felt like I had to get out of the city right away, an urgency fueled by the notion of the Pursuer as well as the timely puzzle piece of the Dakota.

This one looks nice. Weed-free picnic area, only a few balls of hamburger paper rolling around the overflowing bins. I park in the far corner of the lot and speed-dial.

"You okay?" O'Brien asks when she picks up. The worry in her voice triples my guilt.

"Fine. Listen, I'm sorry I didn't make it this afternoon."

"So you understood my code."

"Oh yeah. That was good, by the way."

"I'm blushing."

"I was on my way downtown when . . . I had to change my mind."

"What happened?"

How to answer that? "I got a sign," I say.

"A sign. From the heavens sort of sign?"

"Not heaven, no."

"David, could you please tell me what the hell is going on with you?"

How to answer *that*? How about the truth? The impossible truth I'm halfway to believing but haven't allowed myself to say aloud or even think to myself until now.

"I think Tess might be alive," I say.

"Have you heard something? The Italian police—they've found her? There's been a sighting?"

"Not a sighting, no."

"Oh my God! David! Has she *contacted* you?" At the next thought, O'Brien darkens. "Is it a kidnapping? Does somebody have her?"

Yes, somebody has her.

"Nobody has called me," I say instead. "The police haven't found anything. In fact, they've more or less given up looking. All they're waiting for are her remains to show up. They think she's dead."

"And you don't?"

"Part of me knows she must be. But there's another part that's starting to think otherwise."

"Where is she, then?"

"Not in Italy. Not here either."

"Okay. Pretend I'm holding a map. Where should I look?"

"Good question."

"You don't know?"

"No. But I'm feeling something. That she's alive, but not alive. Waiting for me to find her."

O'Brien breathes. It's something like a sigh of relief. Or perhaps it is the breath that signals the summoning of the energy she requires to carry on a session with a friend who is now, with these last words, confirmed to be certifiable.

Yet it turns out to be something else. She is adjusting the direction of her mind so that she can travel along my line of thinking. Not that she's accepting what I'm saying. She's just gone into diagnosis mode.

"Are you talking about her spirit?" she starts. "Like a ghost?"

"I don't think so, no. That would imply she's already fully gone."

"Purgatory, then."

"Something like that."

"She told you this?"

"I tried to take my life yesterday," I say, and it comes out simply, matter-of-factly, like I've just confessed to having my teeth cleaned.

"Oh, David."

"It's okay. Tess stopped me."

"The memory of her, you mean? You thought of her and couldn't do it."

"No. *Tess stopped me*. She threw a photo off the wall to let me know she was there. That I had a job to do."

"And what job is that?"

"Following signs."

"How does that work, precisely?"

"There's nothing precise about it."

"How does it *imprecisely* work?"

"I think it's about opening my mind. Using what I know of the world, of myself. All that I've studied and taught, all that I've read. Thinking and feeling at the same time. Screwing the lid off my imagination so I can see what I've trained myself—what we've all trained ourselves—not to see."

"Darkness visible," she says.

"Maybe. Maybe it's hell I'm being lured into. But if it is, maybe Tess is there, too."

O'Brien sighs again. Except this time I know what it is. A shiver.

"You're scaring me," she says.

"Which part? The me believing Tess wants me to search for her in the underworld part? Or the me as runaway mental patient part?"

"Can I say both?"

She laughs a little at this. Not because it's funny, but because she's just heard some things any sane person would have to laugh at.

"Where are you now?" she asks.

"Pennsylvania. I'm on the road."

"You think Tess might be there?"

"I'm just driving. Looking for signs that'll take me closer."

"And you're going to find them in Pennsylvania?"

"North Dakota, I'm hoping."

"What?"

"It's complicated. I'd feel like a bit of an idiot if I told you."

"David? The truth? You already sound like a bit of an idiot."

"I appreciate that."

"Seriously. I don't know what to make of all this."

"I'm crazy."

"Maybe not entirely crazy. But I have to tell you, you've got me worried. Do you hear what you're saying?"

"Yes. It's got me pretty goddamn worried, too."

A pause now. It's O'Brien readying to go where she has to go.

"David?"

"Yeah."

"What really happened in Venice?"

"Tess fell," I say, deciding I've said far too much already. "I lost her."

"I'm not talking about that. I'm talking about what took you there in the first place. Why Tess did what she did. Because you *know*, don't you? You don't believe it was suicide."

"No, I don't."

"So tell me."

I want to. But the story of the Thin Woman and the man in the chair and the voice of the Unnamed is all too much to share. It would risk alienating the fragile link I still have to O'Brien, and I need her to be on my side. And then there's the matter of her safety. The more she knows, the greater danger I am putting her in.

"I can't," I say.

"Why not?"

"I just can't. Not yet."

"Fine. But answer me this."

"Okay."

O'Brien takes a breath. Slow and rattling. She doesn't want to ask what's coming next, but she can't stand with me if she doesn't.

"Did you have any part in what happened to Tess?"

"Any part? I don't understand."

"Did you *hurt* her, David?"

As stunning as this question is, I immediately see where it's coming from. My talk about signs and spirits and purgatory may be the result of guilt. O'Brien's doubtlessly seen it before in her practice. An unbearable conscience that seeks relief through fantasy.

"No. I didn't hurt her."

As soon as this is out I'm struck by its not-quite-truthful aspects. Wasn't I the one who brought the Unnamed back to the hotel from Santa Croce 3627? Wouldn't Tess be here today if it weren't for my accepting the Thin Woman's money? I didn't harm my daughter. But there's still guilt.

"Forgive me," O'Brien says. "But I had to ask, you know? To clear the deck."

"No apology necessary."

"This is just a lot to digest."

"I get that. But O'Brien?"

"Yes?"

"Don't call the guys in white coats to bring me in. Please. I know how I must sound. But don't try to stop me."

This isn't an easy one for her. I can tell by how long it takes her to calculate the risks of making such a promise, the responsibility she now carries if something bad were to happen to me. Or, it occurs to me now, if I were to do something bad to someone else.

"Okay," she says finally. "But you have to call me. Got it?"

"I will."

She wants to know more, but she doesn't ask. It gives me a chance to ask about how she's feeling, what the doctors are saying, if she's in any discomfort. Other than "a little stiffness in the mornings," she reports she's feeling fine.

"And who gives a shit about the doctors?" she says. "They've given me enough opiate scripts to entertain a dozen rehab patients for a month. The doctors are done with me. And I'm done with them."

With O'Brien, I know she's serious. She will manage her illness and, when the time comes, her death, with defiance and dignity. Yet when speaking about the cancer, buried just beneath the surface of her words, there is a serrated edge of anger, too. Just like me. We've both decided to get pissed off at the invisible thieves that have sneaked into our lives.

"I'm going to get back on the road," I say when I can tell she doesn't want to linger on the topic any longer.

"I hope you find what you're looking for."

"Even if you think it's a mirage."

"Sometimes mirages turn out to be real. Sometimes there's water in the desert."

"I love you, O'Brien."

"Tell me something I don't know," she says, and hangs up.

I TRAVEL ON INTO THE IRON BELT OF PENNSYLVANIA, THE INTER-state cozying up to the outskirts of pulp mill and foundry towns, the faded billboards promising them as A GREAT PLACE TO LIVE! and suggesting I STOP ON BY . . . YOU'LL BE GLAD YOU DID! But I don't stop. Keep rolling on into early evening, the sun drowsing behind the smokestacks and tree lines.

At one point, a ladybug lands on top of the dash. The windows are closed, and I hadn't noticed it before. And yet there it is, staring back at me.

It makes me think—as nearly all things do now—of Tess. A memory that surprises me in its possibilities for rereading. What it says about her. About us. The things she might have been able to see from almost the very beginning, even as I was perfecting my blindness to them.

Once, soon after she'd turned five, Tess asked me to leave the bedside lamp on when I was putting her to bed. Until then, she'd never displayed any fear of the dark. When I asked her about it, she shook her head in you're-not-getting-it-Dad frustration.

"It's not the dark I'm afraid of," she corrected me. "It's what's *in* the dark."

"Okay. What's in the dark that's got you scared?"

"Tonight?" She pondered this. Closed her eyes, as though summoning a vision to her mind. Opened them again once she got it. "Tonight, it's a ladybug."

Not ghosts. Not the Thing That Lives Under The Bed. Not even spiders or worms. *A ladybug.* I tried to stifle it, but she caught me laughing anyway.

"What's so funny?"

"Nothing, honey. It's just . . . ladybugs? They're so small. They don't sting. They have those cute little spots."

Tess looked at me with an intensity that pulled the smile off my face.

"It's not how a thing *looks* that makes it bad," she said.

I promised her that, good or bad, there were definitely no ladybugs in the apartment. (It was the middle of winter. Not to mention I'd never seen one the whole time we'd lived there, or anywhere else in Manhattan for that matter.)

"You're wrong, Daddy."

"Yeah? How are you so sure of that?"

She pulled the bedsheet up to her chin and turned her eyes to the bedside table. When I followed her line of sight, it led to a single ladybug on its surface. Not there a moment ago.

Thinking it a toy or the dried husk of some long-dead creepy crawler discovered under a rug—and placed there by way of clever sleight of hand on Tess's part—I leaned closer in to inspect it. With my nose only a couple inches away, it scuttled around to face me. Opened its shell to test its black wings.

"Sometimes, monsters are real," Tess said, rolling over, leaving me alone with the ladybug staring up at me. "Even if they don't look like monsters."

WHEN THE MUSTANG STARTS TO BUCK AND I GASP AWAKE TO FIND I've drifted onto the gravel shoulder, I figure it's time to look for a place to spend the night. The next town coming up? Milton. Pop. 6650. Another sign. Or empty coincidence. I'm too tired to decide.

There's a Hampton Inn just off the highway ("FREE CNT. BKFST! CBL TV!") and I check in, buy a six-pack and a burger and eat in my room, the curtains drawn. Outside, the interstate hums and yawns. Television advertising alive within the walls.

When she was younger, one of the games Tess and I used to play together was Warmer/Colder. She would choose some item in the apartment and whisper it to Diane—her princess hand puppet, the kitchen juicer—and I would have to search for it with only her calls of "Warmer!" and "Colder!" as a guide. Sometimes, the secret item would be herself. And I would shuffle closer to her, hands out, feeling the air like a blind man. *War-mer! Waaaaar-mer! Hotter! RED HOT!* My reward was a giggling hug as I mercilessly tickled my prey.

Now here I am, in Milton, Pennsylvania. Searching in the dark.

"Am I getting warmer?" I ask the room.

The silence brings on a new wave of worry. And a gnawing in my gut unquieted by the double bacon-and-cheese. Missing someone feels like hunger. An insatiable emptiness right at the core of yourself. If I linger here, thinking about her, it will swallow me up.

And I can't disappear yet.

I grab Tess's journal from the car. Start from the beginning this time. Much of what she records is what you'd expect. The normalcy of her observations—the "dippy" boys in her class, the loss of her best friend who moved to Colorado, the at-the-blackboard humiliations of her "onion smelly" math teacher—are a relief to me. The longer her entries remain on this ground, the longer I can entertain the possibility that she was as she appeared. A smart, bookishly aloof girl, defender of fellow nerds, happy in all the ways that matter.

Yet even the recollection of happiness can have a countereffect. Knowing a moment is not only past but never to be spoken of again brings a whole new kind of pain.

I'm probably the only kid in school who likes going to the doctor and the dentist and the guy who checks your eyes. Not because I like dentists or doctors or eye guys. It's because most of the time when Dad signs me out to do this stuff, we're actually skipping school.

It started maybe a year or two ago. Dad had to take me to the dentist, and when we were done instead of dropping me back at school we took the rest of the day off and visited the Statue of Liberty. I remember the wind was so strong on the ferry going over that his Mets ball cap with the sweatstain around the edge that drives Mom INSANE blew off his head and dropped into the river. Dad pretended he was about to jump in after it and this lady thought he was really going to do it and screamed her head off! After Dad calmed her down he told me only an idiot would jump into the Hudson to get a Mets cap back. "If it was the Rangers? Then maybe . . ."

After that, we started skipping school on purpose.

Here's how the scam works:

Dad signs me out—showing up out of nowhere, so I never know when I'm gonna get sprung—and we decide what to do only after we hit the street. Most of the time we just walk and walk around the city, looking at stuff, talking and talking. Dad calls it "Playing tourists in your backyard." I call it Wandering Around New York. Doesn't matter. It's the BEST.

So far this year, we've ended up on this street in Chelsea with these weird art galleries (there was this one sculpture of a man with flowers growing out of his bum!), went for not one, not two, but THREE carriage rides around

Central Park, and had a Vietnamese noodle picnic halfway across the Brooklyn Bridge.

This week we joined a line without knowing what the line was for. Turned out to be the Empire State Building. I hadn't been up there before. Neither had Dad.

"I've seen the photos," he said.

"Photos are never the same as the real thing," I said.

After about an hour we went up the elevator and out to where you can see the whole of Manhattan. The park, the two rivers, what looked like little TVs in Times Square.

It was weird how quiet the city is from up there. What's noise on the street is like a hum. Something tuning up. You can't tell if it's getting ready to howl like an animal or sing like an angel.

I read on. Not sure what I'm looking for. More, I suppose. More of her. More of what I knew, as well as what I didn't.

And I find it.

There's a boy who's coming to visit a lot lately. Not in this world, but the Other Place. A boy who is no longer a boy.

His name is TOBY.

He's so sad it's almost too hard to be with him. But he says he is meant for us. Because something Very Bad where he comes from has a message for Dad. And TOBY is going to deliver it.

TOBY says he's sorry. That he wishes he could just hang out, show me he's still just a kid, like me. Once, he said he'd like to kiss me. But I know, if the thing asked him to, he would pull my tongue out with his teeth if we ever did.

I don't know a Toby. And as much as I don't *want* to know this one, I believe I soon will.

She is you, O'Brien said. But Tess acknowledged her demons—our demons—in a way I never could.

Until now.

On the next page there's a drawing. Like me, Tess was more a writer and talker than a drawer, and the image she has sketched here is rudimentary. At the same time, the image is all the more striking for its simplicity. The few details that distinguish it, that make it more than just "A Man Outside a House," indicate the intent behind them. In a glance I can see that Tess has witnessed this scene before. Or had it shown to her.

A flat horizon. So broad it travels from one page over to the next, though no part of the picture appears on the second page other than this straight line of land and towering sky. It works to isolate the subject matter even more.

On the first page, a square house with a single tree in the yard, a straight gravel lane leading up. A fat wasps' nest under the topmost point of the gabled roof. A rake leaning against the tree. And me. Approaching the front door with a mouth drawn straight-lined to show grimness, or perhaps pain.

Only two words on the page. Darkly etched beneath the ground I stand on like a system of roots.

Poor DADDY

I close the journal with shaking hands.

TV. I get it now. It's the crushing loneliness of motel rooms that makes everyone turn on the TV immediately upon entering.

I flip the channels until I hit CNN. And there it all is: the great American pageant of distraction. I crack open a can of Old Milwaukee and let my vision blur at the split-screens and ticker tapes of information. Body counts, celebrity rehab ins-and-outs, box-office takes. The talking heads wearing so much foundation they look like ingeniously animated figures from Madame Tussaud's.

I'm not really watching. Not really listening. But something draws me closer to the screen.

It takes a while to stir myself to full attention and figure out it's not a passing news item or spoken name that struck me, but numbers. A series of digits skittering across the bottom of the screen. Each of them preceded by a city. The world's closing stock market indexes for April 27th.

. . . NYSE 12595.37 . . . TSE 9963.14 . . . TSX 13892.57 . . . DAX 5405.53 . . . LSE 5906.43 . . .

New York. Tokyo. Toronto. Frankfurt. London.

The world will be marked by our numbers.

And it has been.

But what does it mean? Proof. That's what the man in the chair had promised. At the time, the voice that wished to be known as a collective of demons didn't answer *what* the numbers would prove. It would be clear when the time came. Which it is, now. The correctly foretold stock market closings prove the voice was right, that it predicted a series of events beyond any reasonable chance of coincidence or opportunity for trickery, something a man in a Venetian attic, sane or otherwise, could never do. The passing of one of Brother Guazzo's tests. One that establishes the voice as inhuman.

That it is *real*.

I'm up. Tossing the beer can in the garbage, where it attempts a leaping escape with spits of foam. Pacing back and forth, from washing hands at the bathroom sink to squinting out the peephole at the highwayside night.

The Unnamed had made a promise of his own.

When you see the numbers, you have only until the moon.

The moon itself isn't a time. But it belongs to a rhythm, a way of *measuring* time. The beginning of the cycle being the new moon, when its surface is darkest. As close to the total absence of sunlight as the world comes. It's why it plays such a large part in witchcraft lore, a tool for biblical diviners and Egyptian magicians alike. Demons, too. It's a way to foretell a person's death, among other things. I recall a particular method from my readings where the Moravian Jews would fix the new moon between the forks of a tree branch. In time, the face of a loved one would appear. If the leaves of the branch fell, they were destined to perish.

So the next moon is to be the darkest hour for me, too. The moment when Tess will be out of reach once and for all.

The child will be mine.

I grab my phone, look up a site that shows a detailed worldwide lunar calendar. Find when the next new moon arrives. Read the result twice. Then again, slowly. The date—the exact hour, minute, and second—all inscribed to memory.

If I cannot find her first, my daughter dies at 6:51:48 on the evening of May 3rd.

Six days from now.

12

𝔍 HAD A PROFESSOR ONCE WHO, IN ONE OF HIS WILDLY OFF-TOPIC, possibly alcohol-fueled rants, argued that if you were to ask the average American why we bothered to fight the last war in Europe, and if that average American were to be perfectly honest, his answer could be distilled to something like "A Twenty-four-Hour Denny's in every town." It got a big laugh. In part because it was likely true.

So here's to a Mac 'n' Cheese Big Daddy Patty Melt (from the special "Let's Get Cheesy!" menu) with a side of onion rings at 11:24 PM at the Denny's in Rothschild, Wisconsin. Here's to wide-beamed waitresses with coffee pots glued to their palms. Here's to the comforts of a clean, well-lighted place, a deep-fried oasis along the open four-lane. Here's to freedom.

I'm not myself.

Having driven all day, bidding hellos and farewells from behind the Mustang's windshield to passing Ohio, Illinois, and Indiana vistas, spinning the AM radio dial between raving evangelicals and Lady

Gaga, then switching it off to drift in long, haunted silences, I am ravenous and lonely. And Denny's provides a salve for both conditions.

"More coffee?" the waitress asks, the coffee pot already half-tipped in the direction of my cup. I need more caffeine like I need a Louisville Slugger to the head, but I accept. It would seem rude, if not unpatriotic, to do otherwise.

My phone vibrates in my pocket. A mouse awakened from its lint-nested slumbers.

"I've been thinking," O'Brien says when I answer.

"So have I. Not always a good thing to do. Believe me."

"I want to suggest something."

"The Maple Bacon Sundae?"

"What are you talking about?"

"Ignore me."

"David, I think you're creating your own mythology."

I sip the coffee. The taste of liquefied rust. "Okay."

"It's a delusion, of course. I'm sure a very real-seeming experience for you, but a delusion nonetheless."

"So you've decided I'm nuts."

"I've decided you're grieving. And your grief has taken your mind in a particular direction, led it to a place where its pain might be rendered in a comprehensible way."

"Uh-huh."

"You're a professor of myth, right? You teach this stuff, live it, and breathe it: the history of man's efforts to make sense of pain, of loss, of mystery. So that's where you are, what you're actively creating. A fiction that works in a tradition of previous fictions."

"You know what, O'Brien? I'm tired. Can you give me the summer school version?"

O'Brien sighs. I wait for her, gazing out the window next to my booth. The parking lot is floodlit as though in anticipation of a sporting event, a game of football to be played among the reversing pickups and minivans. Yet there are still dark corners where the light doesn't reach. In the farthest one, a parked, unmarked police car. The dark

outline of its driver's head just visible over the seat. A trooper catching forty winks.

"Remember Cicero?" O'Brien starts.

"Not personally. A couple millennia before my time."

"He was a father, too."

"Tullia."

"That's right. Tullia. His beloved daughter. And when she died, he
was crushed. Couldn't work, couldn't think. Even Caesar and Brutus
sent letters of condolence. Nothing helped. So he read everything
he could get his hands on about overcoming grief, conquering the
cold fact of death. Philosophy, theology, probably some black magic
thrown in, too. In the end, though—"

"'My sorrow defeats all consolation.'"

"A bonus point for the correct quotation, Professor. All of Cicero's
reading and research didn't help. There was no spell he could cast to
bring Tullia back. End of story."

"Except it *wasn't* the end of the story."

"No. Because that's where myths are born. At the point where the
facts end and the imagination carries on, masquerading as fact."

"The burning lamp."

"Exactly. Somebody in Rome digs up Tullia's tomb in the fifteenth
century and finds . . . a lamp! Still lit after all these centuries!"

"Cicero's undying love."

"Impossible, right? A *literal* fire could never burn that long. But a
figurative fire could. The symbol is powerful enough—useful enough
for all those who have ever lost a loved one, which is *everyone*—for the
myth to be sustained. Perhaps even believed."

"You're saying I'm Cicero. Except in my case, instead of lighting
eternal flames, I'm inventing evil spirits sending me on a wild goose
chase."

"That's not the point. The point is you're a *father*. What you're
experiencing, these feelings, they're normal. Even the secret signs and
omens are to be understood as normal."

"Even if they're not real."

"And they're not. They're almost certainly not."

131

"Almost. You said *almost* certainly not."

"I have to."

"Why?"

"Because it's you."

Out in the parking lot, the dozing cop awakens. His head rising, a hand adjusting the rearview mirror, to wipe the sleep from his eyes. But he doesn't yet turn the keys in the ignition. Doesn't step out of the car.

"There's a problem with your analogy," I say.

"Yes?"

"I'm not claiming I've found a lamp burning for hundreds of years. Everything I've seen, I've seen with my own eyes. And none of it, strictly speaking, is scientifically impossible."

"Maybe not. I wouldn't know. You haven't *told* me what you've seen. But look where it's led you. Driving across the country following clues left behind by—who? Tess? The Church? Devils? Angels? And to what purpose? To reclaim your daughter from the hands of death."

"I didn't say that."

"But it's what you're thinking, isn't it?"

"Something like that."

"And I'm not saying it's wrong. I'm saying it's *okay*. You've lectured about Orpheus and Eurydice, what, a dozen times? Two dozen? It makes sense that, in this time of distress, your brain would summon that old story and refashion it into your own."

"I'm on a journey to the underworld. That it?"

"*I'm* not saying that. *You* are. To find the one closest to your heart. The age-old human yearning to step beyond the bounds of mortality."

"Orpheus had a lyre that charmed Hades. What have I got? A head full of essays."

"You've got knowledge. You know the territory. Even if that territory is completely made-up."

"You're smart, O'Brien."

"Then you'll come back to New York?"

"I said you were smart. Didn't say you were right."

As I watch, the light inside the state trooper's car goes on. It reveals enough of the interior details to show that I'm wrong. Though it is one of those big Crown Victorias the police use, it's not one of theirs. And it's not a trooper behind the wheel. It's Barone. The Pursuer. Grinning at me in the rearview mirror.

"I'm gonna call you back," I say, getting to my feet and dropping a fifty on the table as I go.

"David? What's going on?"

"Orpheus has got to run."

I hang up and head out the door to my car. But before I do, the waitress calls after me. An intended pleasantry that, in the Midwestern manner, comes out as a stern command.

"Have a good one, now!"

BUT THIS ISN'T A GOOD ONE.

Driving dog-tired through the night, taking exits at random, parking on farmhouse lanes with the lights off to confirm I'm no longer being followed.

It seems to work. By the time the first colorings of dawn push up against the horizon, there's no longer any sign of the Pursuer. It allows me to consult the map and plot out my advance on North Dakota. I decide to stick to the secondary roads and avoid the interstates. Forgo sleep and just keep driving. Use the jittery energy of all-nighters and see how far it will take me.

Trouble is, this kind of thing has its side effects. Pasty sweats. Indigestion. Along with seeing things.

Like the person up ahead, for instance. A girl with her thumb out in the universal beckoning of the hitchhiker. Except the girl is Tess.

I come down heavier on the gas just to put the vision behind me. As I pass, I make a point of keeping my eyes off her, as I know it *can't* be her, and if it *isn't* her, then it's more likely to be something nasty. A nightmare mask donned by the Unnamed for the hell of it. For the pain it causes.

Yet when I risk a glance in the rearview after I fly by, she's still

133

there. Not Tess at all, but a few years older than her. Looking more scared than I am.

I pull the Mustang over and she runs along the shoulder, a soiled Dora the Explorer knapsack bumping against her hip. There is the urge to drive on. Even if she is not involved in what O'Brien believes is my deluded mythmaking, there is little good that can come from picking up human strays on Iowa country roads. I am breaking the New Yorker's rule of not getting involved.

Yet even as she comes into more particular view in the mirror, her run now slowed to a walk, I can see she has the blank-faced look of those who've been on their own for too long. Attempting escape. She looks less and less like Tess with each approaching step she takes. But she has more in common with me.

She opens the door and plops into the passenger seat before she looks at me. And when she does, it's not at my face, but my hands. Gauging to see if they are capable of harm.

"Where you going?" I ask.

She peers ahead. "Straight."

"That's not a place."

"Guess I'm not sure where I'm going."

"Are you in trouble?"

She looks me in the face for the first time. "Don't take me to the police."

"I won't. Not if you don't want me to. I just need to know if you've been hurt."

She smiles to show a surprising mouthful of yellow teeth. "Not the hospital kind of hurt, no."

She turns to look out the rear window, as though she's being followed, too. I roll back onto the road and put a mile behind us before looking at her again.

"You look like a dad," she says.

"Is it the gray hair?"

"No. You just *do*." And then: "You look like my dad."

"Funny, because you look a little like my daughter. But she's younger. How old are you?"

134

"Eighteen," she says. And now, in the Mustang's close quarters, she doesn't look like Tess at all, which makes my saying she did a lie, too.

"You still live with your family?" I ask.

But she's not listening. She's picked up my iPhone from where I'd stuck it in the car's cup holder, touching its screen, her fingers jumping back from the actions they cause as though she's never seen such a thing.

"It's a phone," I say. "You want to talk to somebody?"

She ponders this a moment. "Yes."

"Go ahead. You know the number?"

"They don't have a number."

"The phone lines don't reach them where they live?"

She makes a sucking sound through her teeth that may be a smothered show of mirth. Continues to play with the screen, moving through apps with greater speed as though she is learning the device's capacities as she goes. It gives me a chance to steal glances at her without being noticed. Reddish hair in a ponytail, fat freckles, a filthy summer dress patterned with pink polka-dots. A doll. An oversized Raggedy Anne come to life. She is, it occurs to me with a flush of shame, a talking, breathing fetish. The Freckled Farmgirl. The Dirty Ragdoll. Something missing in her that has been filled by vaguely sexualized, stock details.

She closes a window on the phone and swings her head around to catch me looking at her. For the first time, her eyes assume a brightness when they meet mine. It makes me feel like she's caught me in the middle of some lewd act, the indulgence of a private perversion. And her eyes say it's okay. My secret is safe with her.

"Do you believe in God?" she asks.

A Born Againer. Maybe that's all this girl is. Just a harmless Bible thumper, thumbing a ride to some revival barbecue up the road. It would explain the flatness of her voice, the eyes at once observing and dim. Her odd, doll-like aspect has been taught. A by-product of faith.

"I don't know if there's a God or not," I answer. "I've never seen him if there is."

She stares. Not off-put by my answer. Just waiting to hear the rest of it.

"But I've seen the Devil. And I promise you, he is most definitely real."

This takes a moment to reach her. Like she's at the end of a bad long-distance connection, waiting for the meaning to arrive. When it does, she makes the teeth-sucking sound again.

I return my eyes to the road. Correct the leftward drift that has taken the Mustang into the oncoming lane.

"What's he look like?" she asks.

Like nobody. Like you, I almost say.

At first, when I feel the warmth in my lap, I think I've pissed my pants. Over-tired, too much coffee. An unstoppable flow of heat down my legs.

Yet when I look down expecting to find my jeans darkened, I find the girl's hand there instead. My fly down. Her hand inside.

"You believe here," she says, pushing the index finger of her free hand against my temple. Except the voice is no longer the girl's. It is the voice that came out of Tess's mouth on the rooftop of the Bauer. At once alive and lifeless.

"Now you must believe *here*," the Unnamed says.

With that, she squeezes.

I pull her hand out in one yank of her wrist, but it costs a fish-tailing turn of the steering wheel, so that the car dodges onto the shoulder before veering hard the other way, waggling across both lanes. To hit the brakes would start a spin, and at this speed—the needle poking against 60 mph—it would likely send us flying off into a passing field. The best thing is to get the car back in line and then slow it down. And I'm managing it, too, letting the girl go so I can return both hands to the wheel, compensating for what the back end of the car wants to do by cutting the other way with the front tires.

We're just straightening out and I'm putting my foot on the

brakes when the girl clenches her fingernails into the sides of my face. That's what starts the skid.

Sky.

Asphalt.

Daytime moon.

A spinning, flashing show.

We stop in the middle of the road. If anything comes over the rise ahead it will take us out before it has the chance to slow down.

But the girl is scratching now, screeching and chattering like a rabid animal, like the man in the chair in Venice. I push her against the passenger door and her head cracks against the frame. Not that she feels it. She just lunges at me again. Goes for my eyes.

I swing my fist again and again—half-connecting with her jaw, her ribs, a square shot to her ear. Then, when she appears to be waning, I lean over her legs and open the door.

I'm pulling myself straight when she bites.

A snarling sinking of teeth into the back of my neck. I can't tell if the scream that follows comes from her or me. The bright shock of pain lends me a seizure of new strength. It's enough to push the girl out the door, where her ass meets the road with a fleshy slap.

I get back behind the wheel. Slam it into drive.

But the girl comes with me.

In the two seconds it took me to start rolling she must have scrambled up and gripped her hands around the door's open window. The girl is now being dragged along next to the car. The door swinging out so that she scrapes along the shoulder's gravel. Then, as it swings closed again, she slams against the side.

The Mustang flies over the rise.

The girl howls.

I let my foot sink the pedal to the floor.

"Please!"

A new voice. Not the false one that belonged to Raggedy Anne, not the Unnamed's. The girl's real voice. The one that was hers when she was alive. I'm certain of this. This one word has found its way over the wall of death to ask me for help I cannot give.

It's an impression confirmed when I turn to look. The girl now being slashed along the side of the car, still holding onto the swinging door. But I don't slow down. Because she's already gone. Already his.

"Help me?"

She knows I can't. A girl who has swum all the way up to the surface only to find a stranger drowning just like she is.

But I reach for her all the same.

And she reaches, too. Releases her left hand from the door handle and throws it over the passenger seat so that it briefly grazes mine. The skin cold as meat taken from the back of the fridge.

Even still, we reach for each other again.

It forces her weight back and the door swings wide. Her legs stream blood as they drag over the asphalt, wildly bouncing like a string of soup cans tied to a JUST MARRIED! bumper. She looks at me and, even before she lets go of the door, I see the dimness returning to her eyes. Whoever she was in life slips back underwater. Now there is only this animated puppet, this freckle-cheeked shell.

Then it's gone.

The nails of one hand scratch against the side of the car, scrabbling to find a hold. A sickening thud as the Mustang's back wheel rides over her.

I stop.

Jump out of the car and scramble around to the back. Fall to my knees to check under the chassis, peer along the ditches on either side of the road. The girl is nowhere to be seen.

I wipe my hand against the back of my neck and it returns smeared with blood. And the iPhone. Still working. Still holding on to the previous minutes since she'd found the dictaphone app and pressed RECORD.

I rewind. Press PLAY.

Do you believe in God?

Whoever she was, she was here. Not a part of my mythmaking. Not a delusion. The entire conversation recorded.

. . . And I promise you, he is most definitely real.

138

I turn the recording off to avoid hearing the real girl's call for help, a sound more frightening than even the Unnamed's hollow tone.

The idea that I should erase the file crosses my mind. It's what I want to do more than anything else.

Instead I enter a name. Call the file ANNE. Save it.

𝔍 PULL OVER TO SLEEP IN TWENTY-MINUTE BREAKS. DRIVE. SLEEP. Drive. By afternoon I cross the North Dakota state line without anyone noticing. I barely notice it myself.

In Hankinson, after a gummy ham-and-cheese and an entire jug of coffee, I feel pointlessly refreshed. I'm in North Dakota. Now what? Wait for a telegram? Go door to door, flashing open my wallet to the five-year-old photo of Tess within and ask if anyone's seen my daughter? I can imagine how that would go:

SWEET OLD LADY
Oh dear. How awful. She go missing 'round here?

MAN
No, not here. Venice, actually.
And nobody believes she might be alive except me.

SWEET OLD LADY
I see. And what do you think happened to her?

MAN
Me? I think a demon has her.

SWEET OLD LADY
Henry! Call 911!

SLAM!
The screen door whacks against the MAN's nose.
He rubs it and walks on as SIRENS approach in the distance.

I decide, having come all this way, to take in Hankinson's sights. It doesn't take long. Hot Cakes Café. The Golden Pheasant Bar & Lounge. The Lincoln State Bank. A few white clapboard churches standing well back from the curb. The town's biggest boast, judging from the paint-chipped signage, is "OKTOBERFEST . . . IN SEPTEMBER!" Otherwise no sign of Tess or the Unnamed. No sign of a sign.

When I reach the Hankinson Public Library—a provisional-looking structure of cinderblock and poky windows—I walk in with the idea of taking things into my own hands. I'm a professional re-searcher, after all. I should be able to find a buried reference, a wink hidden in the text. But what *is* the text? The only book I'm working from is the real world around me. Material I've never been particularly good at interpreting.

I acquire a library card for a buck fifty and sign out one of the computer terminals. Figure I might as well begin where all my lazy undergrads embark upon their research papers these days. Google.

"North Dakota" brings up the standard wiki entries about popula-tion (672,591, which ranks it forty-seventh among states in density), capital city (Bismarck), sitting senators (one Democrat, one GOP), the highest elevation (at White Butte, which prompts a mental cata-loguing of possible puns).

But there is, farther down in the entry, a list of the state's newspapers. The *Beulah Beacon*. *Farmers Press*. *McLean County Journal*. And one that jumps out: *Devils Lake Daily Journal*. Is this where I'm supposed to go next? The name fits, though the clue strikes me as rather on-the-nose for the Unnamed, whose character (if it can be understood as *having* character) is emerging as rather more subtle, pleased with its cleverness. So no, I'm not hitting the road to Devils Lake. I'm not hitting the road to anywhere until I discover why I'm here in the first place.

Which may be the point. Perhaps I'm not expected to move, to wander any farther, but to *arrive*.

Which starts me wondering if I have come to North Dakota not to encounter another riddle to solve, but a story. Like Jesus coming upon the man in Gerasene possessed by a legion of demons, like me flying to see the fellow scholar strapped to a chair in Santa Croce, maybe I am here to witness another "phenomenon." More evidence of demonic incursions in our world. Perhaps my role—and my road to reaching Tess—is not as academic or interpreter, but as chronicler. A gatherer of anti-gospels. Of proof.

It was the disciples' job. Though they only earned their positions after professing their unquestioned faith in the messiah. Me? I'm not following the Son of God, but a defiling agent for the other team.

And for Tess, I'll do it. For her, I'll see whatever we were never meant to see.

One problem. If I'm here to look for a new "case," it's certainly not leaping out at me from the sunny, too-wide streets of Hankinson. Then again, indications of demonic presence aren't likely to be out in the open, but rather veiled as something else, masked in a different form just as the Unnamed was when he visited as the girl in the car, the man in the church, the old gent on the plane. It will be an event that *could* be rationally explained, but with something wrong about it. The kind of story picked up on the wires and reported along with the other oddball bits and pieces on Internet home pages. The passing weirdness to be found in the back sections of small-town newspapers. Something North Dakota apparently has a fair number of.

A new search. "North Dakota devils." Which takes me directly to porn.

Try again.

"North Dakota unexplained."

"North Dakota mystery."

"North Dakota missing."

"North Dakota phenomenon."

After a time, one story pops up more than any other. A short piece that presents itself as little more than a depressingly common end-of-the-line for neglected souls, more sad than unsettling.

The story first appeared on April 26th in the *Emmons County Record* based out of Linton. Just three days ago.

STRASBURG WOMAN, 77, A SUSPECT IN MISSING TWIN CASE

Delia Reyes maintains her sister, Paula Reyes, followed "voices"

By Elgin Galt

LINTON—

Delia Reyes, a 77-year-old who has spent her life working a small farm in the Strasburg area with her twin sister, Paula Reyes, has been called a "person of interest" by the sheriff investigating the latter's disappearance.

Delia Reyes contacted police six days ago, on April 20, to report her sister as a missing person. Police questioning of the woman, however, revealed a version of events that left authorities puzzled.

"According to Delia, Paula had been hearing voices coming from the cellar for some time," Sheriff Todd Gaines revealed to the *Record*. "Voices that were calling for her to come down and join them."

Delia told police that she herself couldn't hear these voices, and was concerned for her sister's mental state. Fearing she might harm herself, she made Paula promise to not go down there on her own.

Then, according to Delia, one evening Paula could resist no

longer. Her statement indicates she witnessed Paula open the door to the cellar and go down the cellar stairs. By the time Delia—who has certain physical limitations—was able to make it down herself, Paula was gone.

"It was the last she or anyone has seen of Paula Reyes," Sheriff Gaines said.

With Ms. Reyes' permission, investigators have thoroughly searched the interior and exterior of the sisters' property, but have so far discovered no sign of the senior.

When asked if there were indications of foul play, Sheriff Gaines replied in the negative. "It's a missing persons case with an aspect we view as somewhat out of the ordinary, that's all," he said.

Despite repeated attempts at contact, Ms. Reyes has declined to comment on the ongoing investigation.

Dementia in the elderly is no sure sign of demons. Nevertheless, voices inviting you to join them in an old Dakotan root cellar has something about it that may be useful. It is, this week at least, the closest thing the forty-seventh most densely populated state of the union has to offer in the way of traces left behind by the Adversary.

I debate calling the reporter, Elgin Galt, directly, but decide against it. The *Emmons County Record* doesn't need to know a New York professor has come to call on the surviving Reyes sister. Better if nobody knows at all. No advance phone calls, no request for a few minutes of Miss Delia's time.

I don't want information anyway. That's not what the Unnamed expects of me. He expects me to bear witness. To document. To assemble a dark account of his actions.

The Book of Ullman.

14

THE JOURNEY FROM HANKINSON TO LINTON IS SO WHOLLY VOID of landmarks or points of interest it is a version of hell in itself. Not the fiery, soul-crowded caverns of Giotto's paintings, but a place of torment where boredom is the primary punishment.

Yet there is, as I turn south on Highway 83 for the drive into Linton, a growing sense that I was right to come here. That is, I am *wrong* to come.

An unease that the benign landscape of early-season grain fields and long-laned farmsteads cannot wholly camouflage. A kind of sound. A high-frequency note that never entirely goes away.

At first I take it to be the buzz of cicadas, but even when I roll up all the windows, it's still audible. I'd think it was some form of tinnitus if I didn't sometimes hear something in it. Words. An indiscernible monologue or recitation delivered at a pitch just out of the range of hearing. A hissed voice addressing the world. And now, as I roll closer to the Reyes farm, I am developing the unwanted skill of learning its message.

◆　　◆　　◆

BY THE TIME I MAKE LINTON THERE'S A GRAY POWDERING OF DUSK over town. A sparse light that seems to accentuate the forsaken flags outside half the businesses, the oversized SUPPORT OUR TROOPS ribbons lashed to elm trunks and porch steps. It's too late to go looking for the Reyes place right now. So, first, a take-out Hawaiian from Hot Spot Pizza. A room at the farthest end of Don's Motel. A scorching shower. A channel surf of famine victims and talent contests. Bed.

I fall asleep only to be immediately awakened. This is what it feels like, though the clock radio on the nightstand reads 3:12 AM. The only light a pale slopover from the parking lot, spilling down the wall from under the closed curtains. And no sound. No reason to have been lifted out of sleep at all.

At the same instant I have this thought, I hear it. The creak of a metallic spring. The slap of skin on rubber. A backyard, childhood sound.

Someone jumping on a trampoline, over and over. A joyless play, without laughter or shout.

I get up and peek through the front window, knowing I will see nothing there. The sound is coming from behind the motel's outbuilding.

. . . *Reek-TICK. Reek-TICK. Reek-TICK* . . .

The jumper keeps jumping. Even louder here in the bathroom. The trampoline close by outside the open ventilation window. The nylon curtains repeatedly blown out and sucked in, as though the jumping is the sound of the night breathing, the rusty catch of its ins and outs.

I part the ventilation window's curtains. The breeze now direct upon my face. The window's frame is too small to allow much view without getting closer. To see anything aside from the patch of back lawn and marshlands beyond I have to press my nose against the screen.

. . . *Reek-TICK. Reek-TICK* . . .

Look right. Nothing there.

Press harder until the screen pops out of its frame. My head stuck out. My neck laid upon the sill.

... *Reek-TICK* ...

Look left. And she's there.

Tess's arms unnaturally rigid at her sides. Her legs bending only at the knees with each meeting with the elastic tarp that sends her up to the exact same height each time. The bare feet flat as sawed-off two-by-fours.

Her body, though it is not under her own control. Her face. From the chin up it is my daughter staring back at me in confusion, in panic. Unsure why she's here, how to make it stop. She keeps her eyes on me because it is all she knows.

Her mouth opens. Nothing comes out. I can hear it anyway.

Daddy ...

I try to push myself out through the window but the space is too small for my shoulders to pass through. So I uncork my head and run to the door. Bare feet spanking over the parking lot, then slipping on the dew-slicked grass as I round the corner.

Even when I see she's not there I keep running. Lay my hands on the trampoline's surface, feeling for a trace of her warmth.

I circle the building to see if I can catch sight of her. Launch into the marsh and sink down to my waist in sulfur-belching muck.

Of course she's not here.

Of course I keep looking.

Another hour or so of pacing the perimeter of the motel's lot. Shouting for her every few minutes even after a guest opens the door to advise me he's prepared to make me shut up if I don't do it myself. At some point, her name turns to tears in my throat. A mud-soaked madman walking about the night, howling at the half moon.

IT WASN'T WHAT YOU'D CALL A GOOD NIGHT'S SLEEP.

In the morning, I head into town for breakfast at the Harvest Restaurant & Grill, parking on the street outside. On the way to the door, a tail-wagging mutt comes up for a scratch. I wish him good morning and he responds with a lick of my wrist.

"Keep an eye on my car, would you?" I ask, and he seems to understand, lowering his rump to the sidewalk and watching me go, his ears raised teepees atop his head.

Inside, I take a booth near the kitchen, my back to the door. It's why, a minute later, I don't see the man approach who sits opposite me, tossing yesterday's *New York Times* across the table.

"Thought I'd bring you a little taste of home," the Pursuer says.

I spin around. None of the other diners seem to find anything strange about his sudden appearance. Why would they? Two strangers, traveling together, joining each other for breakfast. Come to think of it, that assessment would be more or less true.

"You found me," I say.

"Never really lost you."

"Bullshit."

"Okay. Took a few calls to catch up for a while there."

"Calls to whom?"

He bridges an index finger over his lips. "Trade secret."

The waitress arrives to pour coffee for both of us. Asks us if we're ready to order. I point to Special #4, the Farmer's Feast.

"Toast," the Pursuer says, handing back the menu without moving his eyes from mine.

The thought occurs to me that, now that he's found me again, this man intends to kill me. Not here in this diner, not at the moment. But certainly here, in Linton. It's a strange thing, but even more than my imminent murder it's the notion of dying in North Dakota that comes as a shock. I always assumed my elbow-patched life would see me expire in my bed at home, sedated and painless, quoting the poets on my way out. Taking a bullet in Hicksville belonged to another man's story. But of course, I'm living another man's story now.

"Hey, Dave," he says. "Over here. Look at me."

Should I run? Just get up and bolt out of here and hope I can make it to the Mustang faster than the Pursuer can make it to his Crown Victoria?

I'd lose. I can elude this man for stretches of time—I *have* eluded him, or I wouldn't be here—but he will find me in the end. And he will do what he will do.

"I'm not giving it to you," I say.

"That's all right. My client has altered my instructions."

I can't keep looking at the print of a hunter shooting a duck nailed to the wall over the pie fridge. So I look at him. See that he appears almost friendly.

"How so?"

"You've become interesting," he says.

"You should see me after a couple of drinks."

"My client would like to know where you're headed."

"Nowhere in particular."

He sips his coffee. Swallows. The taste of it apparently reminds him of his ulcer, as he bangs the cup down in the saucer as though he's spotted a spider drowning in it.

"Your instructions," I say. "You said they've changed."

"Temporarily. Of course, our primary interest remains in obtaining the document."

"Which you haven't even mentioned yet."

"We know it's not traveling with you. We know you are aware of its location, and that you will eventually disclose it to me. That moment has been suspended for the time being, however."

"How long do I have?"

"Not long, would be my guess."

"Your client is impatient."

"We share that."

The Farmer's Feast arrives. A nest of scrambled eggs, along with the full oeuvre of breakfast meat: sausage wrapped in bacon on a bed of ham. The Pursuer eyes it with undisguised envy.

"Want some?" I offer.

"That's crazy glue for your arteries."

"We're all gonna go one day."

"Yeah. But where are you gonna go the day *after*, Professor?"

He takes a bite of his toast. A shower of crumbs on the formica.

"What are you doing here, anyway?" I say. "If you're just following me, follow me."

"I'm here to impress upon you the severity of the situation. Because I'm not sure you're quite getting it yet."

"I get it."

"Really? Then tell me. What are you after out here?"

"It doesn't concern you."

"It's personal. I understand. My client has seen people in similar situations. People who have had a door opened for them. The kind of door you should close. Or run away from. Mostly, they do. But sometimes, people think they can walk right through, take a look around, grab a souvenir from the gift shop on the way out. Never turns out well."

"Hold on," I say, gauging whether I could reach his shirt collar from where I sit. "Do you *know* who has her?"

"See? That's my *point*. You're chasing something you shouldn't be chasing."

"That your client's advice?"

"No, that's mine. My client is interested only in having what you have and, if possible, knowing what you know."

"So this concern you're showing for me—this is coming from you alone?"

"I'll do what I'm paid to do, Professor. I'll do goddamn *anything*. But like I said before, I'm just an altar boy from Astoria at heart."

He picks up another slice of toast but, this time, doesn't have the stomach for it.

"So let's try this again, David," he says. "What brings you to Linton?"

"Hunting season."

"Hunting your kid. Tess."

"You know where she is?"

"Wouldn't *want* to know that, to tell the truth."

"So what do you know?"

"That she's gone. That you think you can fix that. Not an unheard-of sort of thing, from my client's point of view. Though, admittedly, you are regarded as a slightly special case."

"Because of the document."

"Because whatever you think has your daughter now has an interest in *you*. It's why you have the document in the first place."

"You're saying I'm *meant* to have it?"

"You think it's just because you're so smart?"

The waitress stops by to top off our coffees. It takes her a few seconds longer than it should. Taking a good look. Not at the mercenary across the table, but at a suddenly sweaty, fork-shaking me.

"You and I might have different goals," the Pursuer starts again once she's gone. "Still, if you break it down, if you forgive some of the means, we're both on the side of good ends, David."

"But you can't bring my daughter back."

"You think he can?"

"He?"

"He. Her. It. Them. I've always thought of the Devil in masculine terms, myself. Haven't you?"

"What's the Devil got to do with it?"

"Everything. He's why you're out here driving around on the plains. Why you're holding on to the thing I want. Why Tess isn't with you anymore."

It hits me all at once. A dizziness so severe I grip the table edges just to stay seated on the bench. I am saying too much. I am listening to someone else too much. And the Unnamed doesn't like it.

"He . . ."

"Speak up, Professor."

"He has my daughter."

"Maybe." He shrugs. "If he does, you're never getting her back."

"I need to speak to him."

"He's a *liar*, David. The Devil *lies*. He wants something from you. And right now, whatever it is you're doing, you're halfway to giving it to him."

"*You* want something from me."

"Yes. But maybe I can help you."

"Can you bring my daughter back?"

"No."

"Then you can't help me."

I rise from the table. And with every new inch that comes between myself and the Pursuer, my balance is returned to me. What's he going to do? Stop me here in the middle of the morning rush at the Harvest Restaurant & Grill?

That's exactly what he does.

His hand gripped to my shoulder as I push open the door. It turns me half around. So close his lips almost graze against my ear.

"I've been a gentleman this morning," he says, and digs his fingers under the muscle of my shoulder. Wrenches it up. "But when the call comes, it won't mean a thing to me. Understand?"

He releases me an instant before a shriek of pain can escape. Pushes me aside to be first out.

I MAKE MY WAY TO THE MUSTANG WITH MY HEAD DOWN AND ONLY notice the dog when I've got the keys out, opening the driver's-side door. Its body laid on the hood. A thick sheet of blood inching down over the headlights. Eyes open, ears still standing to attention.

I'll do goddamn anything.

Slipping my hands under the body and lifting it down to the street leaves me soaked through to the skin. The blood warm as bathwater.

I consider lifting it into the trunk and heading to a hardware store, buying a shovel, and digging a hole for it somewhere, but in the end I leave it where it is. Snuggled against the curb, blankly staring at the prairie sun.

How long do I have?

Not long, would be my guess.

As I get behind the wheel I venture a glance up at the sun myself. It burns.

I DRIVE BACK TO THE MOTEL AND SIT ON THE EDGE OF THE BED, wondering what the hell I'm doing here. That's not quite right: I know what I'm doing here, just not *how* I should do it. In the un-likely chance that I'm right to be chasing a real-life demon across the

American landscape, by what means do I think I might take it on? I'm not in possession of holy water or a crucifix, no gold daggers bearing seals of approval from Rome. I'm a teacher with a lapsed gym membership. Not exactly the Archangel Michael roaring down from on high.

And yet the Pursuer was right. The demon I'm after seems to have taken an interest in me. It has gone to the trouble of assuming human form to have a few words with me, most recently as the crotch-crushing girl in my car. Milton's poem offered a warning about this very thing.

> *For spirits when they please*
> *Can either sex assume, or both.*

And what was Raggedy Anne's message? That I still had more believing to do. Not just in my head, but in my body.

And the Word was made flesh, and dwelt among us . . .

The Word of the gospels tells the story of God and the Holy Son. But it also tells the story of temptation, sin, obstructions, demons. What if all of it isn't merely allusion but literal history, an account of actors performing verifiable actions, both long ago and reaching into the present? Surely now, after what I've seen, I would be forced to accept that it's possible. Imagine all the words and stories I've studied as being material, dwelling in the world. As *not* being stories.

Now you must believe here.

Destiny. The factor that determines where a character ends up in the ancient works I teach, though one presumed to leave the modern self untouched. But what if the modern presumption is wrong? What if this demon hunt has been my destiny ever since the scholarships lifted me out of the turquoise world I came from and allowed me the freedom to pursue a life of the mind?

It's certainly true that when I went to university, even more than the moneyed cliques and beautiful debutantes, it was the abundance of choices that astonished me. My devotion was to literature, I knew. But which of its many tunnels would I descend into? There were brief flirtations with Dickens, with James, the Romantics. Then, to my atheistic surprise, the Bible took up an immovable place in my study carrel. And Milton soon after. His blank verse that seemed to defend the indefensible. The poem that, upon my first reading, made me weep with self-recognition when the villain tried to set aside his past and find a way out of the darkness, to use his mind alone to talk himself out of his suffering.

> *What though the field be lost?*
> *All is not lost*

I remember nights as a graduate student in the old Uris Library at Cornell, reading these lines and deciding *This is it*. A rallying cry that spoke directly to me, a fellow outsider seeking triumph not through optimism but denial. I decided I would dedicate myself to making the case for this character, this Satan, as I would make a case for myself, also fallen, also alone.

Though I never admitted it to anyone, I sometimes saw another in the stacks with me on those evenings. A presence that seemed to nudge me deeper in my commitment to my chosen course of study. At least, that's how I interpreted the glimpses of my drowned brother. Lawrence. Dripping water onto the floor as he sat swinging his legs on a chair at the end of my table, or slipping away around the corner of a shelf, leaving a circle of greenish river water behind. Yet perhaps what I took to be encouragement was in fact a warning. Maybe Lawrence appeared to me to demonstrate how the dead—both those known in life and imagined in books—are never quite as dead as we've willed ourselves to believe.

So if this journey I've embarked on is my fate, what is my role in it? I had always seen myself as standing outside of things, a harmless expert of cultural history, an interpreter of a forgotten language. But perhaps the Thin Woman was closer to naming my real vocation. *Demonologist*. Getting to Tess will require that I apply my life's study in a practical way I'd never considered before. Start taking the mythology of evil seriously.

The first step in such a game is to determine which version of demonology we're dealing with. Old Testament or New? The Jewish *shedim* of the Talmud or Platonic demons (intermediary spirits, neither god nor mortal but something in between)? Plato, now that I think of it, defined *daimon* as "knowledge." Demonic power proceeds not from evil, but from knowing things.

In the Old Testament, satans (for their appearances are almost always pluralized) are wardens over the earth, carrying out tests of man's faith in their capacity as devoted servants of God. Even in the New Testament, Satan himself is one of God's creations, an angel who went astray. How? The abuse of knowledge. Darkness isn't the matter from which the Antichrist was formed, but intelligence. Foreknowledge.

Like knowing the world's stock market results a week in advance.

Clearly my demon wished to demonstrate his power in this way. To prove its intellect as much as its ability to possess, to steal.

It.

He. She.

The Unnamed.

All along, in every encounter, from the Thin Woman to Anne, the presence has refused to provide a name. It's another way of mocking me. But it's also one of its vulnerabilities. According to the Catholic Church's official rite of exorcism, using the demon's name against itself is a primary means of denying its authority.

I need to figure out the demon's identity. From there, I might find out what it wants. Find Tess.

If I approach the question using the whole library of possibilities, throwing every demonic figure from every faith and folkloric tradition into the mix, it would be impossible to finger a suspect. But my demon has chosen me. A Miltonist. Its repeated citations from *Paradise Lost* can't be seen as accidental. It is the version of the demonic universe through which it wishes to be viewed.

Which would lead us to Pandemonium. The council chambers where Milton described Satan assembling his disciples for their debate over the best ways to undermine God's rule.

We know their names.

Moloch.
Chemos.
Baalim.
Ashtaroth.
Thammuz.
Astoreth.
Dagon.
Rimmon.
Osiris.
Isis.
Orus.
Belial.

My Unnamed is among these. And I have only three days to figure out which one.

Satan himself can be eliminated, if the voice that spoke through Marco Ianno is to be taken at its word. Indeed, the fact that the Unnamed arranged for a preintroduction, a kind of fanfare prior to its appearance, says something of its character. Pride. Conceit. Showmanship. And the reliance on Milton provides more than just clues. It shows how the presence sees itself as a scholar, too. A kinship—as well as a competition—with me.

I will have to discover the name of the Unnamed through a reading of its personality. Milton ascribed characteristics to the members of the Stygian Council, a way of distinguishing them, "humanizing" them.

So that's what I will be. A demon profiler.

FINDING THE REYES PLACE TURNS OUT TO BE AS EASY AS OPEN-ing the phone book in my motel room and mapping the address on my iPhone. Not far. Only 6.2 miles from where I sit, apparently. If I start now I'll be there well before lunch.

There is the problem of the Pursuer, of course. If I drive out to the Reyes farm with him on my tail it might not only alert him to the twin sisters' little mystery, it may be enough provocation for his client to give him the order to take me down. I need to find out if I'm right or wrong about coming to Linton. Without him.

This has me stumped until I look out the front window and see the Pursuer's Crown Victoria parked just twenty feet from the Mustang. It appears he's a guest here now, too. And he doesn't mind my knowing it.

Aware that he's likely watching my every move, I walk out to the motel's office and ask to borrow a screwdriver and an ice bucket. Fill the latter with water. Walk back toward my room (looking like a man ready to plop some cubes into his soda) and stop by the side of the

Pursuer's car. Use the screwdriver to wrench the locked gas tank flap open, then screw off the cap. Pour the ice bucket's water into the tank.

Then I'm running.

I'm behind the wheel of the Mustang and reversing by the time the Pursuer comes out of his room—unhurried at first, then, when he sees the gas cap on the ground, a focused alarm—so that I'm able to take in the full fury of his glare.

It's all different now, he's telling me. No more dead dog threats, no more warnings. When the order comes, he'll not only carry it out, he'll take his time.

But I can't linger on this, not least because he's now running himself. At me. His hands held out before him like he's prepared to claw his way through the windshield.

My foot comes down on the gas and I shoot past him, purposely taking the wrong turn and then going around the block and heading south out of town unseen. It won't take him long to get new wheels.

But mine are already rolling. Already gone.

IT'S A SHORT DRIVE SOUTH OUT OF LINTON TO THE CROSSROADS hamlet of Strasburg, then west a couple miles to the Reyes farm. Not that there's much growing on the land at the moment. The fields on either side of the property's gravel lane have been tilled but unseeded, so that only stray weeds poke up from the earth. It leaves the Reyes' farmhouse to stand out even more than it otherwise would. A white clapboard toy sticking out on the endless horizon.

The same house—the same horizon—as the one Tess drew in her journal.

Out front, the lone tree with a rake leaning against it, the handle split from long exposure to the sun. Under the highest eave, a gray wasps' nest glued to the wood, a black hole at the bottom seething with furious comings and goings. On the ground, weeds grown thick and thorned as rolls of barbed wire along the front path. It's as though the entire farm and the work once done on it stopped some years ago, and now it is halfway to becoming something else, a return to undisciplined scrub.

And me. Now making my way up to the porch, my face stiffened in apprehension.

Tess had seen all of this. Had known I would come.

Poor DADDY.

The front door is ajar. The police? A neighbor dropping off a basket of eggs? For some reason, I didn't expect competition for Delia Reyes' time. As I knock on the frame of the screen door I start editing my planned niceties in my head. The longer I take getting in, the greater the odds someone else might show up to haul me out.

I'm about to knock again when the inside door is pulled open to reveal a sinewy woman dressed in what appears to be layers of old sweaters and an ankle-length denim skirt. Her long hair held back in an elastic that leaves the ends bunched and brittle as the head of a broom. Brown eyes wide and alive, flickering with humor.

"Mrs. Reyes?"

"Yes?"

"My name is David Ullman. I'm not with the police. I don't work for one of the papers."

"Glad to hear it."

"I just came here to speak with you."

"Seems you're already doing that."

"I'll come to it, then. I understand that something unusual has happened to you, in this house, over the last few days."

"I should say so."

"A similar thing has happened to me. I was wondering if I might ask some questions to see if you could provide me with some answers."

"You've had someone go missing, too?"

"Yes."

"Someone close."

"My daughter."

"Lord."

"It's why I've come all this way to show up uninvited at your door like this."

She pulls the screen door wide.

"Consider yourself invited," she says.

The kitchen is large and cool, with a butcher-block table in the middle used, apparently, for both the preparation and consumption of meals. An ancient Frigidaire huffing and sighing in the corner. Side-by-side enamel sinks. A spider plant doing its best to block out the light from the window. All of it adding up to a clean, museum-quality old Dakotan farm kitchen. A heartening place if not for the turquoise walls. The color of melancholy. Of grief.

As I stand next to the table the old woman shuffles past to take the seat she was occupying when I knocked. This is what I assume anyway, given the lone coffee cup by her hands. Yet, glancing into it, it appears not only empty but clean, as though pulled off the shelf as a plaything or prop.

"Paula Reyes," she says, offering her hand. It's only when I take it that the significance of the name strikes me.

"Paula? I thought you were lost."

"I was. But I'm found *now*, aren't I?"

"What happened to you?"

She traces the rim of the coffee cup with a finger.

"I don't properly know. Isn't that something?" she says, and answers herself with a short blast of laughter. "Must have hit my head or something. Some old-lady blunder! All I remember is walking in that screen door this morning and Delia sitting right in that seat there, the one you're leaning on, drinking coffee from this very cup, and the two of us hugging and Delia making me eggs like not a thing had passed between us."

"That's Delia's cup?"

"Um-hm."

"It's empty."

"She finished it."

"But it looks untouched."

She looks into the cup's bottom, then back at me. "So it does," she says.

"Are you all right?"

162

She doesn't appear to hear the question.

"Do you have a sister, Mr. Ullman?" she asks.

"No. I had a brother, though. When I was young."

"Well, then you'd know the place kin like that keep in your heart. There's no scrubbing out that kind of stain, is there?" She shakes her head. "Blood runs deep."

At the mention of blood I notice, for the first time, the spots on the woman's most exterior sweater, a cardigan with the pockets hanging off. A fine spatter around her middle. Along with crumbs of earth, field dirt. Smudges here and there on her clothes and under her nails.

"What's that?"

She looks down. Wipes at the blood and soil with the back of her hand.

"Don't know how that got there, to tell the perfect truth," she says, though with what could be a tremble of uncertainty now. "But when you work a farm, you stop wondering how the dirt and such gets on you."

"Doesn't seem there's been much work around here for a while."

Her eyes look up at me, instantly drained of warmth. "You calling my sister and me lazy?"

"It came out awkwardly. Forgive me."

"I'm not in the forgiving business, Mr. Ullman," she says, suddenly smiling again. "You want *that*? Get on your knees."

I can't tell if she means this literally or not. Something hard behind her smile suggests this last remark wasn't a joke, but a command. There's no choice but to pretend I hadn't noticed.

"The voices you heard," I say. "The ones that called you down to the cellar."

"Yes?"

"What did they say?"

She ponders this. A brow-scrunched search of what seems a distant past, as though I've asked her the name of the boy who sat next to her in kindergarten.

"It's a funny thing," she answers finally. "But though I know it

163

was words, I can't recall them as words. More like a *feeling*, y'know? A sound that put a *feeling* inside you."

My tinnitus on the drive to Linton. *A sound that put a feeling inside me.*

"Could you describe it?" I ask.

"An *awful* thing. You'd rather be doubled over sick. You'd rather drive a nail through the back of your own hand."

"Because it was painful."

"Because it opened you up from the inside out. Made things so clear they were cast in pure darkness instead of light. A darkness you could see *better* than any light."

No light, but rather darkness visible
Serv'd only to discover sights of woe

"This may seem a strange question," I say. "But have you ever read John Milton? *Paradise Lost?*"

"Not much of a reader, sorry to say. Other than the Good Book, of course. Too busy with the day-to-day."

"Of course. Can I go back to that feeling you mentioned? What did you see in that visible darkness?"

"What real freedom could be. No rules, no shame, no love to hold you back. Freedom like a cold wind across the fields. Like being dead. Like being nothing." She nods. "Yes, I believe that captures it. The liberty of being nothing at all."

I know something about that. It's the feeling I carried with me from Santa Croce 3627 to the Bauer Hotel. The disease that infected Tess. Made her fall. *Like being dead.* But worse. An unnatural death because it was more final than death. *Like being nothing.*

"Where's Delia now, Paula?"

"She went down to the cellar just before you came."

"The cellar?"

"Said she had to straighten something out. Now that I'd come home and all."

"Do you mind if I go down and have a word with her?"

"Be my guest. Not that I'll be joining you."

"Why not?"

"Because I'm afraid." She looks at me like I'm dense. "Aren't you?"

I don't answer that. Just move away from the table to the closed door I somehow know opens not onto a closet or pantry or back stairwell up to the second floor, but down into the broad hole beneath the house.

Paula watches me grasp the handle and turn it. The sensation of her eyes on my back, pushing me forward to stand at the top of the stairs. Her finger stroking the ring of the coffee cup faster now so that the ceramic issues a wavering note of warning.

A light switch turns on a pair of bulbs below, though I can't see them yet from this height, only the two yellow aprons they cast upon the concrete floor. And then, halfway down the stairs, the one to the left goes out. Not the pop that comes from burnout, but the fizzle of being too loosely screwed into the socket. I could walk over through the dark and fix it with a single turn. Yet that's a less-inviting prospect than keeping my eye on the remaining circle of warmth to the right.

When my feet make it to the floor, I can take in some of the details the light offers. Worktables against the walls, cluttered with tools, shears, Mason jars full of lugnuts and screws. Antique paint cans stacked in teetering towers. Paper yard-waste bags piled in the far corner, their bottoms black from their slowly liquefying contents.

It is these bags that emit the smell. A decidedly organic rot, pervasive and strong. The back-of-the-throat tickle of burnt-sugar icing.

No Delia to be found. She could be in the dark to the left. But even if she sat on the floor knitting socks I wouldn't be able to see her. Only now does it occur to me that, prior to my turning on the light switch, she would have been in total darkness herself. If she's down here at all.

What was I thinking, trusting an old lady dirtied with blood and soil who'd just returned from a ten-day sojourn without knowing how she'd spent the time? An old woman with a gift for hearing things the rest of the world prays to never hear? A liar—because no coffee had touched that cup this morning. There was no smell of it in the kitchen, either, no pot on the stove.

I *wasn't* trusting her, of course. I have had to dispense with the deliberations that trust requires. There isn't time. The downside of the headlong advance, however, is skipping straight into a trap. And *this* is a trap. Paula is probably closing the door at the top of the stairs right now. Wasn't there a latch on the outside, silvery and new? She must be slipping the padlock through even as I back up and make the bottom step. Clicking it shut—

"Over here."

A voice like Paula's—but not Paula's—stops me. Lets me see that the door at the top of the cellar stairs remains half open just as I left it.

As I turn, there is a metallic scrape along the floor. And there she is. Delia Reyes. Pulling an overturned washtub into the range of light and sitting on its edge with a weary sigh.

"Good morning," I say.

"Morning. Is it? You take the sun away and you can lose track of time down here."

"You didn't turn the lights on."

"Didn't I? You live in a place long enough and I suppose some things you can see just fine in the dark."

At first, I'd taken her slouch and hooded eyes for fatigue, the posture that follows the completion of some physical task. Yet, with this last sentence, it strikes me that I am wrong. Despite her friendliness, her words are hollowed out by an immeasurable sadness, reedy and thin. I know because it's how I hear my own voice now, too.

"My name is David Ullman. I came to—"

"I heard," she interrupts, lifting her eyes to the ceiling. "*Half* heard."

"You must be delighted. About Paula."

She returns her eyes to me. "Are you real?"

"As far as I can tell."

"What have you done?"

"I'm sorry. Not sure that—"

"If you're here you must have . . ."

She lets the thought drift away. Draws a hand over her face as though to pull off a cobweb.

"You find it cold down here?" she asks.

"A little," I say, though in truth, within the last few moments, the cellar's temperature feels like it's dropped ten degrees or more.

Delia rubs her shoulders. "This was always a cold house. Even in the summer it never warmed up, never got all the way into the corners. Like the rooms themselves hated being touched by the sun."

She appears as though she is about to stand, then changes her mind. A mind that's been transported to a particular sliver of the past.

"Me and Paula always going around in long coats in August," she says. "And scarves' round our ears on Christmas morning!"

Her laugh is reminiscent of her sister's, but unlike the latter it signals loss rather than amusement.

"A good thing you had each other out here," I say.

"Maybe so. Or maybe there's such a thing as being too close to somebody."

"How's that?"

"Twins. You can lose grasp of what's what in a cold house for sixty years. And just another you to talk to. Another you to look at."

I take a step closer. It's what she seems to require. A hand on her elbow to help her to her feet. Someone to tell her it's all over, there's no need to dwell on some long-ago misgivings down here in the foul-smelling dark. Yet at my approach she lifts a finger to stop me. There's the curious feeling that she wants not only to finish her thought, but prevent me from coming too close.

"I prayed to heaven to take her away," she says. "It's a shameful thing, but it's true. Since I was a girl I've had days when I wished for my sister to get her arm caught in the thresher or fall asleep at the wheel on a drive back from town or get a chunk of stew caught in her throat and not find the air to spit it out. I could *see* the ways it might happen. So simple. Terrible things to wish for! But all of it seeming perfectly natural. Accidents."

167

She's crying now. A messy sound that remains separate from her voice, so that it's like she is performing an act of self-ventriloquism, sobbing and throwing her speaking voice at the same time.

"Why would you wish for an accident?"

"So I could be alone for once! Not one half of a whole, not what folks called us all our lives. Not the Terrible Twosome or the Reyes Twins or The Girls. Just myself." She swallows, but she goes on without clearing her throat, so that her voice is even quieter. "I prayed. But heaven never did a thing. So then I started praying the other way. This time, something answered."

"We should go now," I say.

"Go? Why?"

"Your sister came home. Remember?"

"I killed my sister."

"No, Delia. She's okay."

The old woman shakes her head. "I killed her."

"But I was just talking to her upstairs. Paula's not missing any-more. She's here."

"That . . . *thing*. That's not Paula."

"Who is it?"

"The one who answered my prayer."

The old woman lifts her hand to point at a place over my shoulder in the darkness behind me.

There is no choice in it. I can't let there be a choice in it.

I turn from her and move forward with my own shadow cast ahead of me as another layer of dark. I keep my hands raised so they might catch hold of the other bulb's string hanging down from its switch. Just when it feels like I've gone too far it tickles over my cheeks. My fingers follow it up to the bulb. Screw it in tight. The heat tells me it's back on before the revelation of its light.

The sisters sit side by side in the corner. Their backs against the far wall, at the edge of the light's reach, so that their faces are illuminated but only dimly so. It is enough to see that they are real. That the shotgun lying across Delia's lap, the dark, fresh wet against the bricks from the exit wound at the back of her head, the gaping mouth where the barrel had been placed, is real. That Paula's remains, speckled from the dirt that clings to her, the root-ends and pebbles from the ground she'd been dug up from, the skin purpled with bloat, is real.

There is a handful of seconds between the apprehension of this image and the first grappling with what it means. And it is in this time of the brain rushing to catch up that the rest of the body jumps ahead. It swings me around. Prevents me from being sick right here right now.

"Why did you bring her here?" I ask Delia, who now sits rubbing a knuckle under her glistening, running nose.

"It asked me to."

"Tell me its name."

"Doesn't have one."

"They'll think you did it."

"I did do it."

"It told you to."

"It told me I *could*."

"But everything you've said to me—the thing I spoke to upstairs, your prayers—nobody will ever know."

"You know."

Now it's the other bulb's turn to flicker and extinguish. The Delia I have been speaking to returns to darkness.

"You know you'll kill, too, don't you?" she says, much closer now.

"No . . ."

"That's what it wants. For you to know what it does. To show how you can do it, too. For you to believe. To kill."

The old woman is so close I can read the outline of her face inches from mine even in the darkness. The stained ivory of her smile.

"Someone close," she whispers.

I step backward and start up the stairs. Slowly at first, making sure of my footing on the narrow steps. Then running for the top, my breath a labored heave in my own ears. Bounding through the kitchen—the single coffee cup still there, the chair empty—and out the door to my car.

I peel out of the farmhouse's yard and gun it down the lane to the road, slapping at the wheel to make the turn and knocking against the REYES mailbox post with my bumper as I go. The mailbox pops its door open, so that when I glance back at it a couple hundred yards on it looks like a stooped figure lurching after me, its mouth wide in a scream.

I DRIVE SOUTH. IT SEEMS LIKE THE LEAST PREDICTABLE DIRECTION. East is where I'm from, the logical direction of retreat. And north is Canada. Not a desirable option for me. I left there a long time ago in the name of drawing a line between what I came from and what I could reinvent myself as being. I've got enough on my hands at the moment as far as spirits go without some long-buried ghosts wriggling up for a visit.

So farewell North Dakota, hello South Dakota. Just when I'm thinking there's never been a less necessary reason for a border, I roll into Nebraska, which looks more like North Dakota than North Dakota. Finally, Kansas. Not especially distinct from the previous states but with a whiff of fame about it, Dorothy and Toto and mobile home parks flattened by twisters. There is something, too, about the look of the fields (or the look of the day) that reminds me of the crop duster sequence from Hitchcock's *North by Northwest*. Cary Grant ducking from the plane's buzzing attacks, wondering what the hell he'd been dragged into. One of O'Brien's favorites.

And now, all at once, the thought of her clenches at my heart. How much I miss her. How a drive across the flats can double the loneliness of an already lonely journey.

How terribly, unshakably frightened I am.

THE ROAD CAN WIPE THE MIND CLEAN. IT CAN ALSO PULL UP MEMories at random, disordered and careless, throwing them against the windshield so hard you jump back in your seat at the impact.

Just now, for instance. My first camping trip with Tess.

Diane wasn't much for what she called the "out-of-doors." It left me alone to drive up into the Adirondacks with Tess when she was five so that I could teach her some of the skills I'd learned in my northern Ontario youth: building a fire, storing food up a tree to keep out of the reach of bears, the wrist-turn required for a smooth J-stroke.

On the drive we played I Spy and co-composed some of the naughty limericks Diane forbade at home (*There once was a girl named Dotty / Who tooted when she sat on the potty*). The truth is I was worried the whole way up. About rain, about mosquitoes, about *not having fun*. Tess being a born New Yorker, I didn't want her to be freaked out by all the discomforts encountered over a couple nights in the woods. More than this, I didn't want to fail. To return home with a kid blotchy with poison ivy and promises from her father to never try *that* again.

Instead, we had a great time. Butterflies that landed on Tess's shoes after she stood as still as a statue for almost an hour in a blueberry patch, pretending to be "a giant flower" until the Monarchs fluttered close, trusting her. Night swims in the lake, the movement of our bodies twisting the reflected moon over the still surface. Perfecting the stick rotation required for evenly roasted marshmallows.

Though all of this comes back to me later. After the memory that has me coughing for air as I drive through the endless fields.

After our second day, Tess asked that I wake her up in the middle of the night so that she could see what I described to her as "the real stars." She didn't believe my talk of the Milky Way, of skies where the needlepoint of light matched the dark. I set my watch for three AM. When the time came we unzipped the tent and stood in the middle of our campsite, tilting back our heads. The dome of sky ablaze.

Neither of us spoke. Just returned to the tent after a while, went back to sleep. And in the morning, we woke at the exact same time. Looked at each other and started to laugh. Not a laugh *at* or *about* anything. Not a silently shared thought. Just the two of us meeting the dawn with spontaneous gratitude.

This is what nearly pulls me over to get my breath back and stop my hands from shaking on the wheel: I remember, even as the moment was happening, having the clear thought that *This is the happiest you have ever been.*

And it was.

Still is.

AN HOUR OUTSIDE WICHITA I STOP AT A SERVICE STATION AND STEP into a phone booth that smells of mustard and fart.

"Look at me," O'Brien says when she picks up. "Sitting by the phone like a teenager without a date for the prom."

"Would you come to the prom with me, Elaine?"

"Not a chance. I'm never forgiving you."

"Why not?"

"You haven't called, nimrod."

"Been a while since I've been called that."

"Really? Then let's make up for lost time. Where are you, nimrod?"

"Kansas."

"Where in Kansas?"

"Just outside Wichita. Probably stay there tonight. I passed a bill-board for the Scotsman Inn a couple miles back. Figure I'll check out their haggis."

"Haggis in Kansas."

"Say *that* three times fast."

"How did things go in North Dakota?"

Fine, I guess. Spoke to a demon in the form of a dead old woman, followed by a conversation with her twin sister's ghost. Was the first to discover the remains of their real-life murder-suicide, then ran away without calling the authorities. Oh, and a hit man—or something like a hit man—is after me because he thinks I possess evidence incontrovertibly proving the existence of demons. Which I do.

"Weird," I say.

"Was more . . . revealed to you?"

"I think so, yes."

"Like what?"

Like the demon I'm trying to find needs me as a witness to his influence in human affairs. He needs me as an apostle.

"I'm not sure you'd understand," I say.

"Try me."

"I think Tess is trying to reach me as much as I'm trying to reach her."

"Okay. That's good, right?"

"Unless I can't get to her."

A silence as we both weigh the meaning of this.

"Anything else?" she asks finally.

"I think I've been shown how the presence—how the Unnamed—works. It looks for a door, a way into your heart. Sadness. Grief. Jealousy. Melancholy. It finds an opening and enters."

"Demons afflict the weak."

"Or the ones who ask for help without caring who's ready to give it."

"Then what?"

"It breaks down the wall between what you can imagine doing and what you would never do."

"You realize you've just described your own situation, don't you?"

"How you figure that?"

"A man in grief. Now doing something he would never normally do."

"Doesn't quite apply to my case."

"And the distinction is—"

"The Unnamed doesn't want to possess me. He wants me—or at least the better part of me—to remain myself."

"To what end?"

"That I don't entirely know yet."

"Okay," O'Brien says with an audible gulp of breath.

"There's something else."

"Shoot."

"I'm right."

"About what?"

"Everything. I'm even more certain that although the things happening around me are insane, *I'm* not insane."

"Delusions alone don't make you insane."

"Maybe not. But *I* thought I was. Until now." I take a breath. It brings the fatigue into my bones all at once, so that I plant my hand against the booth's glass for balance. "I'm not sure where I'm supposed to go next."

"You're waiting for a sign."

"You could at least try to hide your sarcasm."

"I'm not sarcastic. It's just hard to talk about this stuff without unintentionally *sounding* sarcastic."

A pause. When O'Brien speaks next her snappy banter is replaced by her doctor voice. If she can't make fun of me for even a full minute, I must be in worse shape than I thought.

"You sound broken, David."

"I *am* broken."

"Do you think it might be a good idea to hold off on this quest thing for a while? Get some rest? Regroup?"

"That might make sense if I had any regard whatsoever for my own well-being, but I don't. I'm holding on to the end of a frayed string out here. And I can't let go of it."

"Even if it leads you somewhere bad?"

"It already has."

Outside the phone booth, cars roll in and out of the lot. All of their drivers throwing glances my way. Me, a guy in need of a shave talking on a pay phone. Only five years ago I'd appear as a harried salesman putting in a long-distance call to his wife. Now, in the age of the cell, I'm a possibly-criminal curiosity. A middle-class crackhead looking to buy. A john arranging a date. A homegrown terrorist.

"There are things in this world most of us never see," I find

175

myself saying. "We've trained ourselves not to see them, or try to *pretend* we didn't if we do. But there's a reason why, no matter how sophisticated or primitive, every religion has demons. Some faiths may have angels, some may not. A God, gods, Jesus, prophets—the figure of ultimate authority is variable. There are many different kinds of creators. But the destroyer always takes the same essential form. Man's progress has, from the beginning, been thwarted by testers, liars, defilers. Authors of plague, madness, despair. The demonic is the one true universal across all human religious experience."

"That may be true, as far as anthropological observation goes."

"It's true because it's so pervasive. Why this one shared aspect of belief for so many, for so long? Why is demonology more common than reincarnation, more than sacrificial offerings, more than the way we pray or the houses of worship where we congregate or the form the apocalypse will take at the end of time? *Because demons exist.* Not as an idea but here, on the ground, in the everyday world."

My breath catches in my throat, and I realize I'm panting like I've just come up for air. And the whole time O'Brien says nothing. It's impossible to say if it's due to the digestion of what I've said, or alarm at recognizing how far gone I am. There is a quality to the silence that makes it clear I've either won her or lost her in the last minute.

"I've been thinking about you a lot," she says eventually.

"Likewise. How are you feeling?"

"Sore. A bit pukey. It's like a hangover more than anything. A chronic hangover without the fun of the night before."

"I'm so sorry, Elaine."

"Don't be sorry. Just listen to me."

"I'm listening."

"I'm not trying to guilt you or anything, but I don't know how much time I've got. And you're my best friend. We should be together."

"I know it."

"But you're in Wichita."

"Yes."

"Wichita's a long way away."

"I'm being a shitty friend. I'm aware of that. And you know I'd be with you if I could. But I have to—"

"You have to do this. I accept that. I'm done with trying to convince you otherwise. I just want to ask you something."

"Go ahead."

"Has it occurred to you that whatever forces you're convinced you're up against want to isolate you?"

"How do you mean?"

"You think you're doing the right thing by keeping me out. But it might not be doing you any favors. The distance between us—that might be part of the demon's plan. Think about it. If it was just about making you a believer, you could do that in New York. But you've been led far away from home. From me."

"What choice do I have?"

"Take me with you."

"I can't risk you getting hurt."

"I'm dying, for God's sake. Bit late for that."

"Elaine? Listen to me. I'm going to ask you to make me a promise."

"I promise."

"Don't ask about coming with me again. It's too hard for me to keep saying no. But I have to say no."

"My turn."

"Okay."

"Tell me this. What is it with men and feeling like they have to act like self-destructive superheroes whenever trouble shows up?"

"It's the only way we know how to love."

The cars come and go. It's as true a thing to say about America as any. They reverse, they park, they join the flow. It would be a comfort of a kind if one of the cars, somewhere miles away out there in the prairie's endless night, didn't contain the Pursuer.

"I should hang up now," I say.

"You're not going to tell me who's after you, are you?"

"Nope."

"But somebody *is* after you?"

"Yep."

"A real person. A human being."

"As real and human as they come."

"Is he *there?*"

"Not yet. But he's coming."

"Then go, David. And be safe," she says and, to my surprise, hangs up. It's a more effective proof that she believes me than any declaration she might make.

I get into the Mustang and drive on toward Wichita. Evening falling over the interstate with the abruptness of a pulled plug. I think of turning on the radio, but every time I do I hear something—a song, a used car commercial, a weather forecast—that reminds me of Tess.

Hell is a night drive looking for a missing child.

I FIND THE SCOTSMAN INN WITHOUT LOOKING FOR IT. SUITABLY without a view, without charm, without anything Scottish about it. It's perfect.

I pad around waiting for the Domino's I ordered to arrive, and, after chucking all but a single slice of it into the garbage, turn the TV on and off three times, the volume dial not turning low enough to avoid the grating shrieks and sobs of prime time. I'd give sleep a try, but Delia and Paula return whenever I close my eyes. And I don't think I can manage any more surprises from Tess's journal. Not tonight.

Eventually I go out to the car, pop the trunk, and grab my office copy of *Paradise Lost*. The paper plumped by years of penciled marginalia and lectern read-alouds. As close to a friend as I have in Kansas.

But it's not helping tonight. Every attempt to enter the familiar language only throws me out again, the words swimming, unmoored. It's as though the book itself has come alive, aligned with some new purpose. As I stare at the page the poem rewrites itself, taking the letters as though they were tiles in a Scrabble game and spelling random profanities and blasphemies.

I get up out of the chair and leave the book open on the seat. Crawl under the covers and wait for sleep to come. It doesn't take long.

Or perhaps I'm not asleep at all when I next look and see her.

Tess.

Sitting in the same chair I just vacated. My *Paradise Lost* held open in her hands.

She is looking straight at me. Her mouth parted, lips forming around words I can't hear, only read as she shapes them. Somehow it doesn't seem that it is speech, that she isn't attempting conversation with me. It's why she holds the book. Though she doesn't look down at it, she's reading aloud from its pages.

Tess . . .

The sound of my voice awakens me. It also makes her go away. The book spine-up on the chair just as I'd left it.

In the dream—if it was a dream—she looked at me. But her words came from the book in her hand.

My copy of *Paradise Lost* lies open on the chair by the door in the same place I'd laid it before getting into bed. But the page is different. Someone picked it up as I slept, only to put it down on page seventy-four.

I read the page myself and, almost instantly, come across the lines I could lip-read Tess reciting to me.

O sun, to tell thee how I hate thy beams
That bring to my remembrance from what state
I fell . . .

Satan's heartfelt complaint against sunlight, one of the many comforts he turned his back on when he pursued his ambitious rebellion against God and his creations. To feel light only reminds him of what he once had. A metaphor for grief. Indeed, the case may be made—by me, now, here in Room 12 of the Scotsman Inn in Wichita, Kansas—that the entire poem is the story of Satan's impossible rage against his own looming, unstoppable death.

But it was Tess who chose those lines. It isn't only Satan, but my daughter who lives in a place denied of sunlight. And it was she who, through unimaginable effort, came to my room in the night to pick up my book and speak to me in a code she hoped I might understand. Perhaps she was only doing as her captor instructed her. Perhaps it was the Unnamed assuming Tess's form. But I don't believe it. It hasn't yet pretended to be Tess. Why not? It doesn't wholly have her yet.

Moments ago, she held the book she had tried to read and abandoned many times, trying to see what I saw in it but frustrated by the density of the words, the compressed allusions and layered meanings. But perhaps she took more away from her attempts than I'd ever given her credit for. For she read those lines without looking at the page. She knew them by heart.

And she was here. That's what's important. She was *here*.

But can I find her again?

O sun.

The sun shines everywhere over the course of the day, no matter how clearly or veiled by cloud, no matter how long the night. There must be something to shape the concept of "sun" that I'm not seeing yet. Something that carries a "where" within it.

There *is* a "where" in the passage, of course. Satan falls not from heaven, but from a "state." A condition of being, but in my case, maybe, a location. Like North Dakota.

The sun state.

Or Florida.

The Sunshine State.

It's thin. But so were the conclusions I drew from being dropped off outside the Dakota, and that seemed to work well enough. And in any case, what else do I have to go on?

Sleep takes me for real this time. It brings no images, only the sensation of growing heat. Thickening over my body in waves like a kind of fluid, ungraspable blanket.

And then I'm awake.

A sheet-kicking panic. A nightmare I can't remember coming to its unthinkable end, the pillow spongy with a combination of perspiration and tears. It's late. 11:24. I've slept through the night and then some. Though I feel less rested than flattened.

It's why, when there's a single knock at the door, I open it without looking through the peep hole. Without asking who's there.

Whether it belongs to the living or the dead, I'm ready to hear what it wants.

"C OFFEE?"

I don't recognize her at first. The lost weight. Her skin pale as chalk. The change is so striking that, for the first second or two, I mistake O'Brien for the Thin Woman.

"You're here."

"In the sallow flesh."

"How did you find me?"

"How many Scotsman Inns you think there are in Wichita?"

"You *flew* out here?"

"A bus didn't seem the best use of time."

"My God! Elaine. You're *here!*"

"Yes, I am. And are you going to take this coffee or not? Because it's burning my damn hand."

I take the coffee. And it burns my damn hand.

But O'Brien is in my room. Closing the door behind her, flopping down on the bed and making a snow angel out of the damp sheets.

"Night sweats," she observes, sitting up. "Know them well."

"How are you doing?"

"How do I look?"

"Fine. As always."

"David, if I always looked like this I'd have done myself in a long time ago."

I sit beside her on the edge of the bed. Take her hand in mine.

"You're thinner," I say.

"And I *eat*, too. But there's a greedy little monster inside me, gobbling it up. It would be almost fascinating if it wasn't happening to me."

"Should you be here? Without your doctors, I mean?"

"I've already told you what I think of my doctors. And I've brought all that modern medicine can offer me right here." At this, she pulls a vial of pills from her jeans pocket. "Morphine. I'll share if you're really nice."

"This coffee's fine for the moment, thanks."

"That coffee tastes like boiled rat turds."

"So *that's* what it is."

I take another gulp. Nearly spew it back out when O'Brien starts to laugh and I join her in it. By the time we get control of ourselves again it's a minute later and I'm wiping the coffee that's come out of my nose, and O'Brien is showing a distressing pink in her cheeks from the wracking cough that took hold of her.

"Wait a second," I say. "You promised you wouldn't come."

"Not true. I promised I wouldn't ask if I *could* come."

"So you hopped on a red-eye—"

"—and rode through the night to your rescue."

"I don't need rescuing."

"That's arguable. But you sure as hell need *me*."

There's no debating this.

"You know what, O'Brien? I gotta tell you. I'm scared."

"Of what, specifically?"

"Losing Tess."

"But that's not the only thing, is it?"

"No, not the only thing. There are the things I've seen. The Unnamed I think I'm getting closer to. The guy following me."

"Something else, too, I bet."

"What?"

"That I'm right. That you've misplaced your marbles. That you're just a guy who needs serious help."

"Maybe. Maybe that, too."

"Let me worry about all of it for a little while, okay?"

"That's the thing. Now that you're here, I'm worried about you, too."

She goes to the window. Parts the curtains a half inch and peeks out at the lot, the robin's-egg sky.

"Let's get something straight," she says when she turns to me. In the near-darkness the disease is somehow more evident than in the direct light. It reveals how much of her has already dissolved into the surrounding shadow. "You listening?"

"I'm listening."

"This is the last trip I'm ever going to take. I don't know how long I'll last, but I can tell you this, I'm going to the very end with you. I can't entirely say why, but this is as important to me as it is to you."

"I want you to live. To get well—"

"But *I'm not going to*, David. And that's okay. I just need you to know that I'm not looking for sympathy, or for somebody to wipe my brow or listen to sunshiny memories of my childhood. I'm here for my own reasons. And so the more you spend time worrying about me and not keeping your mind on the matter at hand, it's only going to piss me off."

I go to her. Wrap her in my arms.

"I'm glad you're here," I say.

"Gentle now. I bruise."

"Sorry."

She pulls away from me. Blows her nose.

"We should get started," she says.

O'Brien starts for the door but I hold her by the elbow. The bone a smooth ball bearing held in my fingers.

"Why did you come?" I ask.

She meets my eyes.

185

"To help you," she says.

"Help me back to New York?"

She places both hands under my jaw. Pulls my face close, so that all I can see is her.

"Here's a promise," she says. "No more questions, no more doubt, no more therapy-speak. I'm *in*. You got that?"

"In for what?"

"Finding Tess. And when we find her, we're going to bring her home."

Tess.

Home.

Hearing these two words together in the same sentence, spoken by someone who seems to feel that it may be possible to connect them, that it's worth *trying* to connect them—it's enough to pull the plug on the last days' tubful of accumulated emotion. I'm crying. Crying like I have no memory of ever crying before. A messy, horking, red-cheeked breakdown while standing buckled over in the middle of Room 12 of the Scotsman Inn of Wichita.

It's quite a show. Not that O'Brien lets me indulge in it for long.

"Give me the keys," she says. "I'll drive."

AS O'BRIEN KEEPS HER EYES ON THE ROAD, I TELL HER EVERYTHING. Or pretty much everything—the exception being Tess's journal, which for some reason feels too private to share. But I recall for her the Thin Woman. The professor in the chair in Venice. The correct foretelling of the world's stock market results. The Pursuer. The Unnamed appearing in different forms, though always those of the already dead. The Dakota. The Sunshine State. Tess, silently calling for me.

How we only have two and a half days until the new moon.

The whole time O'Brien doesn't interrupt, doesn't ask a question. Just lets me ramble on and pile fact upon interpretation upon impossibility. When I finish, she drives on another few miles before she speaks.

"What do you think these clues are leading you toward?" she says.

"I don't really know. I suspect they're leading me closer to the Un-named."

"So it can do what? Destroy you?"

"It could've done that anytime, probably."

"You sure? That hitchhiker attacked you."

"Don't remind me," I say, involuntarily cupping myself.

"Then how are you so sure it doesn't want you dead?"

"It probably *does*. Eventually. Just not yet."

"Not yet. Not before *this*?" O'Brien sweeps her hand around the car's interior, littered with fast-food wrappers and coffee cups and the road atlas open across my lap. "Why do you have to follow bread crumbs across the country?"

I recall what the introductory voice said to me out of the man's mouth in Venice. How we weren't enemies, but conspirators.

"To ask me to be a part of something," I say.

"You're saying it has a purpose for you."

"Yes. Though it hasn't said what that is."

"The document. You have that. And if it's all you say it is, it's proof of something that has only existed in mankind's imagination before this. Just *absorb* that for a second."

"It's something, all right."

"It's *enormous*," she says, smacking the dash. "Demons are real and exist among us. Not metaphorically, but literally. It's *astounding*."

"I'd certainly have to rewrite all my lectures."

"Makes you wonder what they're up to."

"John the Revelator would say they are readying us."

"For what? The Big End?"

"That comes a bit later. First, the descent. The apocalypse. The Antichrist."

"Thanks a lot, Debbie Downer."

"It's the *Bible*, not Danielle Steel."

We drive on in silence for a time. Each of us trying to hide the shudders that our conclusions provoke.

"Okay, let's not speculate," O'Brien finally announces. "Let's just say that, in the immediate term, that document of yours potentially signifies the biggest development in religious and social history for at least the past two thousand years."

"This is hurting my brain."

"And I think that's part of it," she says, building steam. *"We can't handle this stuff.* It's like those UFOlogists or whatever they call themselves. The Area 51 conspiracy theorists."

"Roswell."

"Who knows? Maybe your clues will lead us there. Does 'Roswell' show up anywhere in Milton's *Collected Works*?"

"You were making a point?"

"The point is, what's the argument that the aliens-made-the-pyramids people always make? Why do they feel the comings and goings of extraterrestrials are a vast secret the government is refusing to let us in on?"

"It would blow our minds."

"That's it. Mass panic. Dow Jones goes to zero. Global anarchy and horror. Everybody disappears into their bomb shelters, everyone else rapes and pillages. It would be the End Times of our own making. Why condition any of our actions anymore? Why bother with morality or the law? They're *coming!* All of us waiting for the little green men to probe us or decimate us or turn us into shrubbery."

"You think it's the same with demons?"

"No. I don't think the government knows more about Satan and his cohorts than any Sunday school graduate."

"So what would the document mean?"

"Verification. Legitimacy. There are all sorts of religious texts out there, all manner of belief. But there's no *proof*. Nobody thinks there ever *could* be proof."

"That's why they call it faith."

"Exactly."

"Except now there *is* proof."

"There is, if David Ullman decides to open up his Manhattan bank deposit box. And if its implications are what we think they are, it makes video of an E.T. in a body bag look like a slow news day."

I lean forward to look into the passenger-door mirror. Checking the highway behind for the square grille of the Crown Victoria.

"That's why the Pursuer wants it," I say.

"And maybe the Unnamed wants the same thing."

"Why? It showed me what it wanted to. I didn't take anything, it *gave* it to me."

"That might be the point."

"If it is, I'm not getting it."

"We have to assume that the Unnamed, despite all its powers, has limitations."

"It can't take the shape of the living, only the dead."

"That's a big one. So if it has a message for this world, it requires a messenger."

"A disciple."

"Something like that. A demon can't go on TV and make a case on its own behalf any more than God can—or at least, neither have taken that route yet, as far as we know."

"And it sees me as a potential spokesperson."

"Why not? You're legit. A Columbia prof, specializing in this stuff. Smart guy. No ties to the government, no means of personal profit. I'd choose you, too."

I tell O'Brien about Professor Marco Ianno, the identity of the man in the chair. A man a lot like me.

"Maybe he was a candidate for the same job," O'Brien concludes.

"The Unnamed took something from Ianno—maybe his daughter, his wife, his lover—and he went after them just like me. But in the end, he wouldn't seal the deal."

"Or the ride got too rough for him."

"How do you mean?"

"Maybe all this—seeing ghosts, following signs, somebody hunting you down—maybe it's a test. To see if you have the right stuff."

"In the Old Testament, the Devil served God as a tester of man's faith," I say. "Kind of like the Heavenly Father's sergeant-at-arms."

"The Book of Job."

"That would be the leading example, yes. A good man who endures loss and afflictions to see if he can withstand them, and in withstanding them, prove his love of God."

"That's some seriously tough love."

"The point of those stories, though, isn't really about what Job or whoever puts up with. It's not really even about faith. From a demonological perspective, it's about Satan being taught a lesson, not the man."

"And what's the lesson?"

"That man can overcome evil through nothing more supernatural than love."

"Okay. So you're a new-century Job."

"Except in this case, it's not a plague of boils or the loss of my oxen and camels. It's a test to see if I can go all the way to Tess without breaking."

"And how do you think it's going?"

"The body is weak—"

"—but the heart is strong."

"I wouldn't go that far. But it's still beating. That's about all I'm asking for."

AFTER ANOTHER HALF HOUR OR SO, THE MORNING COFFEES WORK their magic and both of us need to pee. We pull over at the next rest stop, a cinderblock Men's and Women's set amid a grove of poplars. I finish before O'Brien and stand outside, waiting for her to come out, ready to take a shift at the wheel, when I hear the far-off sounds of struggle. The thud of limbs against tempered glass. A man's fiercely whispered commands. A woman's stifled screams.

The rest stop's parking lot is narrow and long, a snakeskin of pavement designed to unobtrusively weave through the trees. It makes it hard to know where the sound is coming from, left or right. It's a feeling more than a judgment that pulls me behind the washroom building to where the lot reaches into the bush and ends in an unoccupied clearing dotted with picnic tables. A sense that it is the old Dodge pickup, parked alone, where an assault is under way.

Even as I run the fifty yards between myself and the truck, the option of ignoring what I heard flirts with the front of my mind. *Whatever is happening inside the Dodge stands a good chance of being a crime of some kind. And crimes require reporting, statements to police, the beginnings of a record. Crimes slow you down.*

Though I have these thoughts, I don't hesitate. Someone is being hurt. Something is being *taken*.

The sounds are more distinct when I stop a few feet from the truck. Grunts. Tight-throated yips. Starving animals warring over the last meat from the kill.

Whoever is inside hasn't noticed my approach. It allows me to ease closer. Look in through the half-open passenger-side window.

A man and woman. The man older than she, judging from the striped button-down shirt he wears, the khaki slacks around his knees. The hair yielding to gray and in need of a cut, the trying-too-hard curls bouncing against the back of his neck. Beneath him, only the woman's pale arms can be seen, a spray of copper hair over the bench seat. Her freckled hands clenching his back in pain or resistance or urging.

It is, at first, impossible to determine the existence of consent. The sounds they make rise now to hyena screeches, thoughtless and cruel. I was wrong earlier when I thought I'd heard words of command. There is no speech, nothing recognizably human at all. Their two bodies fused in agony.

I come close enough to place my hands on the edge of the open window. Something must be done now. To linger any longer makes me complicit somehow. A voyeur.

At the same instant I open my mouth to speak, I recognize who they are.

Hey.

They stop at the sound of my voice. It's as though this is what they've been waiting for. Not the consummation of the act, because that's not possible for them ever again. They are dead. And they are here only for me.

The man's head turns without any motion from the rest of his body. His slicked face grinning at me over his shoulder in triumph.

"Poor David," Will Junger says. "Can you even fuck that sick bitch riding with you now?"

I want to pull away, but my hands refuse to let go of the door. I have to stay long enough to hear what I need to hear.

Yet the next voice doesn't come from Will Junger's ashen lips, but the girl who slides her face out into view from under him. The hitch-hiker. Raggedy Anne.

Live while ye may, Yet happy pair, she says. Shows her black-rooted teeth.

Now I let go. Ready to run. But the man who was once Will Junger begins to change, and I stay to see what he becomes. A subtle shift in the features of his face that doesn't wholly turn him into something else but reveals the thing within him nevertheless.

"Who are you?"

The Unnamed answers in the same tone of false erudition it spoke with before. The words clearly formed, but brittle, inanimate.

Not to know me argues yourselves unknown.

I start to back away. But the Unnamed's hand reaches out to grab mine. At the touch, thrumming pain passes through it and into me, electric and dizzying, a surge of distilled anguish. It's a glimpse of the enormity of its loss that holds me more than its strength.

It says the same thing Will Junger said, in precisely the same voice, the last time I saw him on the steps of Low Library on a warm spring day at the end of term.

Gonna be a hot one.

Through his touch, he shows me Tess.

The real world—the rest stop lot, the weedy picnic area, the stand of poplars, the clearing sky—all of it blackens as though a velvet curtain had been pulled across a stage. Then, from out of the black, a figure steps forward. Her hands out in front of her, feeling for a way out. To fend off an attack.

Tess!

My shout comes from a thousand miles off. But she hears it. Hears me and runs—

The black curtain is pulled away to reveal the world again. And now I'm the one who's running. Sidestepping away from the Dodge and then swinging around to lengthen my stride toward the Men's and

Women's. Toward O'Brien, who is limping my way, shouting something I can't hear.

When I reach her I put my arm around her, guiding her away from the truck. But she surprises me by the firmness of her stance.

"You see something?"

"In the pickup."

She starts away. Her hips obviously sore, knees stiff. But still faster than you'd guess.

"Elaine!"

She makes it to the truck and immediately thrusts her head into the cab. Throws herself halfway in before she can see what's waiting there.

Then I'm rushing up next to her, trying to pull her out. Not that I can see past her into the truck. Not that I can hear anything but O'Brien telling me to get my goddamn hands off her.

I let her go. And she comes sliding out to reveal an empty cab. Nothing on the bench but a crushed pack of cigarettes.

"They're gone," I say.

"I didn't see anyone get out."

"I don't know *how*. But they were here. And now they're not."

"Just like that."

"I didn't ask you to look. In fact, I haven't asked you for—"

"*HEY!* Who the *hell* are you?"

O'Brien and I both turn to face the speaker of this question. A middle-aged man in an undersized business suit emerging from the trees with a woman adjusting her skirt, gloss smeared outside the line of her lips. Both of them picking off the leaves that cling to their shirts and hair.

"We were—"

"What the *mother* do you think you're doing in my truck?"

"Just checking on something," O'Brien says.

"Yeah?"

"There were . . . *sounds*," I add. "Coming from inside."

"Sounds," the man repeats, taking an unconscious step away from the glossy-faced woman, who appears undecided whether she has an urgent need to laugh or relieve herself.

ANDREW PYPER

"Hold on a second," the man says. "*Hold* the *fuck* on. Do you work for my wife?"

"What?"

"She hire *investigators* or something?"

"No. No, no. This is all just a—"

"*Bitch!*"

O'Brien is already backing away. She hooks my elbow as she passes me, the two of us mouthing silent apologies. Then we turn and start as quickly away as a walking pace permits.

When we make it to the Mustang I start to explain what I saw back at the truck, but O'Brien is already opening the passenger door and throwing herself in.

"Drive," she says. "You can tell me without me worrying about some secretary screwer putting a bullet in my skinny ass."

We slip back onto the interstate. Me checking the rearview for the Dodge, O'Brien checking e-mail and voice messages on her phone.

"You expecting a call?"

"A nervous tic," she says. "I get anxious and start playing with the buttons on this thing."

"That's *everybody's* nervous tic."

O'Brien collects herself. Asks what I saw in the truck.

"Raggedy Anne. Remember the hitchhiker I told you about?"

"Yes. Unforgettable Anne. But she wasn't alone, was she?"

"You're not going to believe this."

"It's way too late for you to preface anything you might say with that."

"Anne was doing the nasty with someone. A particularly *nasty* nasty."

"I thought she was dead."

"She is. And I got the distinct feeling the man she was with was, too."

O'Brien is absorbed by her phone's screen. Then she sniffs and sits straight. Eyes blazing with a kind of mad excitement.

"Tell me who it was," she says.

"Will Junger."

194

She makes a sucking intake of breath so sharp I take it to be a flare of pain.

"Let me ask you something," she manages.

"Okay."

"Have you checked your phone today?"

"No. Besides, I've been sitting beside you all day. Have you seen me check it?"

"No."

"Why is this important?"

"That last e-mail I read came from Janice in the Psych Department at Columbia."

"What'd it say?"

"A car accident. Just last night. Solo crash into a bridge abutment on the Long Island Expressway," she says, sucking air again. "Will Junger died four hours ago, David."

18

TWO PROFESSIONAL TALKERS ON A LONG DRIVE WITH STRANGE news swirling around their Ivy League noggins and neither O'Brien nor I say much more than "You hungry?" and "Any more Dr. Pepper?" between Denton, Texas, and Alexandria, Louisiana. We may be trying to figure things out. We may be in shock. We may be wondering if we will ever go home again. The only certainty is the road rolling out before us, indifferent and shimmering. Along with the sun that drills through the windows, licks of clammy air around our necks. We welcome the South with brooding silence and incremental bump-ups to the A/C.

We decide to stop in Opelousas for the night. The Oaks Motel offers rooms for "less than a gimlet at the Algonquin," as O'Brien points out, so we take two with a pass-through door between them.

Sleep isn't possible. I know this without trying. So I open Tess's journal again. Find another entry that proves my daughter knew so much more of the world I have entered than I could ever imagine.

I know where bullies come from.

There's one in my class. Her name is Rose. Probably the most wrong name for a person in the world.

   Everyone is afraid of Rose. Even the boys. Not that she's so tough or anything like that. If you saw a picture of her you wouldn't think SCARY! But if she's in the room with you, you feel it. When she looks at you, you wish she'd stop.

   (Rose is a little on the fat side. She's getting boobs, too. The first in our class. And her nails are long and dirty, like she uses them to dig. She's an almost-fat girl with dirty nails and boobs.)

   She never bothers me. It's because I know why she is the way she is. I even whispered it in her ear one time.

You think you have a secret friend but it's not a friend

And after I did, she gave me this look. A How could you know that? *look.*

   Now she leaves me alone. Like she's the one scared of me.

   Miss Green taught a special class about bullies at the beginning of the year. She said they do bad things because they're just scared and alone. She was only half-right.

   Bullies are scared. But they're not alone.

   There's a secret friend inside them. Something that starts out saying nice things, keeping them company, promising to never go.

   And then it says other things. Gives you ideas.

   That's how I know about Rose. I can see her secret friend.

After another couple pages I come upon another disturbing passage. Disturbing in part because of what it says about the horrors she experienced. In part because what she wrote was meant for me to read now that she's gone.

They are all around us.

Open your mind to them and they're with you. Inside you. It's almost too easy once you do it a few times. And even if you don't like it, it's hard to stop.

What do they want? To show us things. What they know, or want us to think they know. The future. How to make the world ready for them.

They are all around us.

I reread the passage. And again. Even before the pity, before the guilt, is the certainty that she was right. *About all of it.* I've opened my mind and closed my eyes and now I, too, have seen some of the things they want to show us. Though there is much more that hasn't been revealed to me that had been to her. Even as we walked through Central Park to feed the ducks on the weekends, even as I read to her from *The Secret Garden* at bedtime, even as she kissed me good-bye and threw her bird-boned arms around my neck at the front doors of her school, *she knew.*

A knock on the pass-through door. When I open it after tucking the journal out of sight, O'Brien is standing there with her tongue hanging out in a pantomime of deathly thirst.

"Let's get a drink," she says.

We walk across the street to the Brass Rail and order Budweisers before sitting at a table in the corner. The beer has no taste, but it's fizzy and cold and performs the tongue-loosening magic of alcohol.

"He must have been on his way to or from visiting Diane," I begin.

"Probably right."

"Maybe I should call her."

"You want to?"

"No. For about eighteen different reasons, no, I don't."

"Then don't. Seems to me this isn't the best time for insincerity."

"I didn't wish the guy dead."

"Really?"

"Injured, maybe. Something to wipe that smirk off his face, sure. But not dead."

"Well, he sure as hell's dead now."

"And the first thing he does with his time on the other side is find me."

"Sounds like that wasn't his decision alone."

"The Unnamed."

"It chose Will to speak to you. What did it say?"

I don't repeat the cruelty about O'Brien's condition. But I once again make mental note of it. Not for its obscenity, but the fact that the Unnamed referred to O'Brien right off the top. It means we are being watched. But what's also significant is that O'Brien may have been right about me being lured out here, far from New York, to deny me the support of my friend. In any case, for the hundredth time today, I'm grateful she took the flight out to Wichita to join me.

"Anne spoke first, actually," I white-lie. *"Live while ye may, Yet happy pair."*

"Don't tell me. Milton."

"Who else?"

"Why that line? Was she referring to you and Tess?"

"No. You and me. But the tone was distinctly sarcastic."

"You and me," O'Brien echoes, hugging herself.

"It's from Book Four. Satan has arrived in Eden and is plotting Adam and Eve's ruin. He's hatefully jealous of all they have—enjoyment of their bodies, the natural world, God's favor. So he tells them to have fun while they still can, because it won't last long. *Live while ye may, / Yet happy pair; enjoy, till I return, / Short pleasures, for long woes are to succeed."*

"A threat."

"Certainly. As well as a joke. He's comparing us to Adam and Eve in the garden."

"And here we are in Louisiana. Middle-aged, one of us searching for a lost child, the other withering from a terminal disease. About as far from sinless joy as a pair can get."

"But there's something in this," I say, growing excited. "Something for us to use."

"What?"

"An indication of its sensibility."

"A comedian."

"An ironist. All along, it has been citing a canonical text, a masterpiece of the poetic form, but with ironic intent. It says something of its personality."

"Who cares about its personality?"

"I do. I have to."

O'Brien sits back in her chair and brings the bottle to her lips, surprised to find it empty. She waves it at the bartender and throws up two fingers for more. Then corrects herself by adding another two fingers.

"Just in case," she says.

When the beers arrive I tell O'Brien how when I asked the Unnamed who it was it answered with another Milton quote.

"Not to know me argues yourselves unknown."

"Okay, Professor," O'Brien says. "Unpack that."

"It's a Satan line again. When he's stopped by angels guarding the earth, and they demand to know his identity. He doesn't give them a direct answer. His pride is too great. The Devil feels they ought to know who he is for all his accomplishments, his fame, the fear he provokes."

"So our demon feels we should know who it is."

"It's more that he wants me to figure that out."

"Another test."

"I'd say so."

"Why does it *need* you to puzzle out its name?"

"I've wondered that, too. And I think it has to do with intimacy. If I am able to speak its name, it brings the two of us closer. And it needs us to be very close." *Not friends, perhaps*, I recall again its dead voice predicting from Tess's throat. *No, certainly not friends. But unquestionably close.*

"Maybe it *can't* be the first to say its name," O'Brien offers, slamming her beer down. "It *needs* you to say it, to give him greater authority. Anonymity is one of the demonic drawbacks. It denies them a degree of power. Think about it. 'My name is Legion.' Satan not introducing himself at Eden's gates."

"The exorcist's first step is to discover the name."

"Exactly! Names have power, and it can go both ways. In the case of demons—*our* demon—it doesn't say who it is because it's not able to. But if *you* are able to determine its name and say it aloud, it opens a channel for it somehow. Through you."

O'Brien puts her hand over mine. Her blood pulsing so strongly through her papery skin I can feel each beat.

"I think you may be right," I say. "Except I would go a step further."

"Step away."

"*Not to know me argues yourselves unknown.* It's a two-way street. We will be united only once I discover who it is *and* who I am."

"The line says 'yourselves,' David. Plural. I think I'm part of this self-discovery, too."

We drink some more. Start into our "just in case" third beers.

"So here's the million-dollar question," O'Brien says, wiping the sudden sweat from her forehead with the back of her wrist. "What's the Unnamed's name?"

"I'm not sure yet. But I think it's one of the Stygian Council who sit in Milton's version of Pandemonium."

"Definitely not Satan?"

"No. Though it covets its master's fame."

"Ambitious. Add that to its characteristics."

"And literary-minded. Using *Paradise Lost* as a kind of codebook."

"Language. It shares a passion for words with you, David."

"Seems that way," I admit. "And it seems like it would like to have a talk with me as much as I would with it."

O'Brien abruptly opens her mouth wide in a sudden yawn.

Even here, in a roadhouse lit only by neon beer signs and old pin-ball machines, O'Brien's illness is plainly drawn over her features. For stretches of time her humor and animation disguise the ongoing damage being done within her, and then, all at once, it pushes through to show itself. It's like the Unnamed doing his face-morphing trick with Will Junger in the truck, or the man in Venice becoming my father. Cancer is a kind of possession, too. And like a demon, before it claims you, it nibbles away at who you are, erases the face you have always presented to the world to show the unwanted thing inside.

"Let's get you to bed," I say, rising and offering O'Brien my hand.

"I might think you were coming on to me if you didn't have that worried-little-boy look on your face."

"I *am* a worried little boy."

"Here's something I've learned the hard way," she says, standing but leaving my hand untouched. "You all are."

WE RETURN TO THE MOTEL, BUT WHEN I GET TO MY DOOR O'BRIEN stands right behind me. I turn to face her and she pockets the key to her room.

"Is it okay if I stay with you tonight?"

"Sure," I say. "But there's only one bed in there."

"That's kind of why I'm asking."

Inside, she slips out of her jeans and sweater so that, in the single lamp's light, she stands in only a T-shirt and underwear. I don't mean to stare, but I do. Her lost weight confirmed by the bones nudging against her skin, replacing curved lines with knobs and ridges. But she is still beautiful despite this, still an elegant woman capable of invitation with her poise, the promises of her body's shape. Perhaps tomorrow the disease will steal this, too. But not yet. Tonight, she is a woman my eyes linger on with desire more than pity.

"I must look awful," she says. But she doesn't cover herself, doesn't hide beneath the sheets.

"On the contrary."

"Really? I'm not hideous?"

"I think you're lovely."

"Then make love to me."

"I don't—"

"I might not be able to tomorrow. You might not want to," she says, as though reading my mind's assessment of a moment ago.

"Are you sure about this?"

"Think about what we're after out here, David. What's after us. If we're anything at all, it's two people who have left being sure of things behind."

"Elaine—"

"Don't think about it. Don't *Elaine* me. Just come here."

She opens her arms and then I'm in them. Kissing her cheek. Holding her against me in an embrace she pushes away from because it's too much like what we've done before, the tender but polite contact with which we would conclude our evenings out in New York. She wants this to be different. So she unbuckles my belt, pops the button. Slides her hand down.

"Okay," she whispers. "Okay. That's *good*."

She clicks off the light and pulls me down onto the bed. Taking off my clothes more expertly than I could manage it myself. Then it's my turn.

Her skin cool and tasting of grass and, more faintly, lemon zest. She is a woman I know so well and yet now, instantly, not at all. A thrilling stranger. A tumbling discovery of new gestures, new ways of pleasing and being pleased.

She directs me onto my back and straddles my thighs, working her way up, stroking me with both her hands. Readying me.

All along we have been so close that there has been nothing to see but O'Brien's eyes, her face, her body. But now that she is sitting up, the room is partly visible again.

And there is something here that wasn't here before.

A darker shade of black than the rest of the room's shadow that surrounds O'Brien like an aura. Yet, without any light except whatever trickles in through the curtains and under the door, she could not possibly cast any shade herself. It's not a shadow, then, but something *made* of shadow. Standing at the foot of the bed directly behind her.

As she rises, it moves. Takes a single sideways step to show the profile of its face. A man looking down at something a short distance off, transfixed. Unmoving except for the recent exertions of his trembling arms. He could be calculating a loss, he could be awaiting further direction. The whites of his eyes casting their own dim illumination, revealing the water dripping off his chin, his matted hair. The mouth and nose recognizable, in their handed-down shape, as my own.

Dad?

I don't say this aloud. But I hear it. My voice at six years old, uttering the same word—spoken with the same immeasurable puzzlement—I did the day Lawrence drowned. My father, too late to save him, standing in the water just as he stands waist-deep in shadow in this room.

"David?"

O'Brien kneeling over me, her breath now slowed. Her look of concern becoming something else as she sees my own expression change. The horror I felt as a child when my father turned to me on the day my brother died and I saw a stranger.

Just as that stranger turns to me now.

NO!

I push O'Brien off me and she lands on her side, gripping the fitted sheet to stop her from falling over the edge.

"What's wrong?"

"Do you see him?" I ask, eyes closed but pointing to where my father stood.

"See who?" O'Brien flicks on the bedside lamp. "There's nobody there."

"My *father* was here," I tell her after opening my eyes to confirm he's gone.

"It's okay. We're safe now."

"No. I don't think so."

O'Brien puts her T-shirt back on. Stands in the same place my father stood a moment ago.

"Toss me that, would you?" she asks, pointing to my *Paradise Lost* on the table. I throw it to her and, as it flies, the pages flap like panicked wings. Even when she catches it the book seems agitated in her hands, the cover flapping open every moment it's not pressed shut, so that it appears like a mouth gasping for air.

O'Brien heads into the bathroom. As she goes she reaches her hand out against the wall for balance.

"You all right?"

"Fine," she says, not sounding fine. "Just need to pee."

"And you're taking that with you for some light reading?"

"Want to see what all the hype's about."

She swings the door closed behind her. Before it closes, I catch a glimpse of her in the mirror. I'm expecting to see disappointment at our failure. *My* failure. Or maybe frustration at where we've found ourselves, how she's let herself be talked into a situation that, if it wasn't me, and if her days weren't so sparsely numbered, she would have avoided. Instead, I see that she is scared. She doesn't need to go to the bathroom. It is her fear she doesn't want me to see.

Almost right away I hear her crying. I've never known O'Brien to make such sounds, and it takes a moment to confirm this is what she's doing. Snuffling gasps and little chokes like a drowning swimmer pulled from the water.

"How you doing in there?" I ask when I go to stand outside the door.

"Look at me. I'm like a girl who's lost her virginity at a rec-room party."

"Technically, we didn't do it."

"And technically I'm not a virgin."

"Ah. An analogy, then."

"Thought you might be familiar with those."

"Can I come in?"

"You bringing your dad with you?"

"Not as far as I can tell."

"Then sure."

O'Brien sits on the toilet but with the lid down. *Paradise Lost* laid open on her lap, her hands wiping at her cheeks and nose with starchy tissues. In the past three minutes she has aged twenty years. And yet, at the same time, she sits in the knee-to-knee, pigeon-toed posture of a child.

"I'm sorry about that in there," I say. "I was enjoying myself."

"Me, too."

"Seems like our friend doesn't want us to have any fun."

"That, or you've got some *serious* sexual guilt issues."

She coughs out a laugh. And keeps coughing. One hand gripped to the countertop and the other against the wall, holding her body up as it heaves against some new obstruction in her chest. In only a couple of seconds, her skin colors. Not pink, but blue.

I fall to my knees and get close to her, unsure how to help. The Heimlich? Mouth-to-mouth? Neither seems right.

All at once, O'Brien stops coughing. Stops *breathing*. Eyes wild, pleading. Her hand brought to my face so hard it almost knocks me onto my back.

She pulls in the little air she can in a long draw, forcing herself to be calm. It takes a long time. A sudden quiet except for the book that drops, flopped open, to the floor. Both hands braced against my shoulders.

Exhales.

Something comes loose within her rib cage with an audible click. The sour-milk breath from the deepest pockets of her lungs blows out at once. And with it, right at the end, a fine spray of blood. Warm dots landing on the tops of her legs, my chest, my face.

And then she's breathing again. Patting at my stains with the bath mat.

"God, I'm sorry. That was *awful*," she says.

"You scared me there for a second."

"*I* scared *you*? I was *drowning*."

My brother. The river. My father standing in the current, transformed. *Drowning*. Even this single word seems intentional. But I've never told O'Brien about Lawrence other than that he died accidentally when I was young. If she's drawing a connection to me, it's coming from some other source.

"We should go to a hospital. Get you checked out."

"No hospitals," she says. "Don't even *mention* hospitals again. Understand?"

I slide back from her as she stands before the mirror and washes her face. I'm about to rise, too, when I notice the copy of *Paradise Lost* sidled up to the edge of the tub. Open to page eighty-seven, where Satan decides upon his plan to ruin mankind by tempting Eve with knowledge.

Can it be sin to know,
Can it be death?

It's also the same page where *Live while ye may, / Yet happy pair* appears. Along with a single point of O'Brien's blood near the bottom of page eighty-six.

In the mist that blew forth from her chest, only one part of her landed on the book. A glistening asterisk next to "Jupiter."

Smiled with superior love, as Jupiter
On Juno smiles.

"O'Brien?"

She turns and I hand the open book up to her. I watch as her brain goes through the same interpretations mine just did.

"You don't use a red pen, do you?"

"No."

"So that's part of me there," she says. "Doesn't seem like an accident."

"Nothing does anymore."

"The Sunshine State."

"There's a Jupiter in Florida."

"Yes, there is."

After the briefest pause she's past me. Slipping into my bed and pulling the sheet up to her chin.

"An hour's sleep first," she says.

"Not sure I can sleep."

"Then get in here and keep me warm, for Chrissakes."

I hold her against me, somehow colder and bonier than she felt only moments ago. Each breath a small fight. Around me, the darkness mulling over what shape it will take next.

I WAS WRONG ABOUT BEING UNABLE TO SLEEP.

You have to be asleep to wake up and realize something's changed about the room. That the bed is empty now. That the sound that wakened me was the click of the door being pushed shut from inside.

"O'Brien?"

I can't see anything. Which means only that my eyes have yet to regain their focus in the dark, and not that nothing's there.

Because something is there.

The hush of a leather-soled shoe pressing down on carpet. A metallic glint floating higher. Closer.

"Don't scream," the Pursuer says.

The voice even, mistakable for kindly. A doctor warning of a brief discomfort as the needle goes in.

"It won't make any difference," he says, now setting a knee onto the mattress next to me.

His face coming into semi-visibility. Perfectly calm, distracted almost, his thoughts far away. The hunting knife hanging in the air, still as the light fixture over the table behind him.

"Please. Not yet," I think I say, though the storm of blood in my ears makes it impossible to tell. "I've gotten so close."

"That's why I'm here."

His back straightens. The foot still on the floor readies for the push forward as he brings the blade down.

Yet when the knife comes, he comes with it. A heavy collapse on top of me, so that I have to wriggle out from under him.

Once I'm standing I reach for the bedside lamp. But it's the one on the other side that comes on first. A single 60-watt bulb revealing a collection of elements I can't put together.

The hair at the Pursuer's crown seeping blood, leaving a wet halo around his head on the bedsheets.

The hunting knife, polished and dry, lying on a pillow where it landed.

O'Brien standing behind him, the ceramic lid of a toilet's water tank leaned against her toothpick legs. A half moon of blood at one end.

I meet her eyes but she doesn't see me. She's too occupied by lifting the heavy lid again, kicking the backs of the Pursuer's legs wider so she can step between them, and bringing it down on his skull once more.

Its weight brings her with it. For a long moment she lies on the Pursuer's back as though she'd fallen asleep in the middle of giving him a massage. But then she's sucking in air. Waving her hands until I realize I'm meant to take them.

O'Brien lifts away and the two of us tumble against the wall and slide to the floor. We watch the body, waiting for it to move. It doesn't.

"Can you carry me to the car?" O'Brien asks directly into my ear.

"Sure. Yeah."

The room is quiet. The yawning stillness that follows the abrupt discontinuation of noise. Yet the events of the past moments were conducted in near-silence. A violent shadow dance of whispers and shuffles and sighs.

"David?"

"Yeah?"

"I'm thinking *now*."

19

WE TAKE SHIFTS THROUGH THE NIGHT. ONE DOZING, THE OTHER cruise controlling, then pulling over, switching seats. We don't talk, not at first. Warm air blown off the Gulf spritzing the windows. The tires humming in search of some forgotten melody.

"That was him, wasn't it?" O'Brien eventually asks.

"Yes."

"He would've killed you."

"And you, too, once he was done with me."

"So can we have our own little trial here and now and call it self-defense?"

"We don't need a trial."

"Humor me."

"Okay. Case dismissed."

"Just promise me one thing."

"Anything."

"Don't ask me what it felt like. Doing it."

"Okay."

But then, after an AM listener request for "Hotel California" is over, she puts her hand on my own.

"The terrible thing is how easy it is," she says. "You give yourself a reason, and killing is goddamned easy."

She laughs a squeezed laugh through "Bad Moon Rising." Then cries for half of "Stairway to Heaven."

We don't speak of it again. Which means we've forgiven ourselves, recognized the necessity of our actions. That, or the demon we search for is already a greater part of us than we'd like to believe.

BY DAWN WE'RE DEEP INTO THE PANHANDLE, BREAKFASTING AT a Waffle House just outside Tallahassee. While I work through my icing-sugared French toast, O'Brien taps at my iPhone screen, searching for why Jupiter may be our intended destination.

"So we're looking for what, exactly?" she asks, sipping her coffee and shaking her head at the bitterness as it goes down. "Cult rituals? Babies born with claws?"

"Nothing that obvious. Just a story that doesn't add up."

"Seems like there's more and more of those out there. Always thought it was just the freak show-ization of the Internet."

"Maybe. Or maybe there *are* more and more of them out there."

O'Brien reads aloud some recent news stories she's pulled up from the east coast of central Florida, a good number of them amusingly bizarre. A cat that found its way home after being dumped at the side of the road ten miles away ("We're absolutely keeping her now," the owner was quoted as promising). A man who won two multimillion-dollar lottery jackpots in back-to-back weeks ("First thing? I'm paying off my damn truck!"). A shark that munched the foot off a visiting Australian tourist ("I knew something was wrong when I hopped out of the water and people started screaming."). But nothing that seems to bear the stamp of the Unnamed.

"We'll just have to sniff around once we get there," I say. But O'Brien's not listening to me. Absorbed by whatever she's now reading on the phone's screen. "Found something?"

O'Brien finishes reading the story as I wave the waitress over for more coffee.

"It happened just two days ago."

"That's when I was in Wichita," I say. "The day I got the *O sun, to tell thee how I hate thy beams* clue."

"Which means this was happening at the same time you were being drawn to it. A simultaneous connection."

"Are you going to give me the summary or do I have to read it myself?"

O'Brien picks up her glass of orange juice but, scowling at the pulp on its surface, lowers it again before it reaches her lips.

"By all accounts they were good kids," she begins. "Which only makes it more unbelievable. Only makes it worse."

An elementary school on the western edge of Jupiter known for community involvement, high standardized test results, as well as its close affiliation with local church groups. Kids who mostly knew each other since preschool. Upper-middle-class sons and daughters from "the heart of God-likes-us-best America," as O'Brien puts it.

Third grade. Eight years old. Goofing around in the playground behind the school before dinner, after the teachers had gone home, the older kids off to wherever they spent their twilight hours. Nothing remarkable about the afternoon in any respect. But sometime between 3:40 and 4:10 when the first adult arrived on the scene, all of the kids—all seven of them—attacked one of their playmates. A boy whose name has been withheld by the police. Someone that the school's parents and teachers and the attackers themselves attested that they liked, a boy without any racial or religious or demographic differentiation who grew up in Jupiter just like all of them. But using rocks and sycamore branches and their own fists and feet his friends spontaneously beat him into a coma.

Animals. This word comes up a lot in the reports. "They acted like animals," said this neighbor or that town councilor. But as a mother of one of the accused corrected, "Animals don't do that to each other without reason."

Investigators have looked into the possibilities of drug use, bullying, gangs. But they have been forced to conclude that the violence was unprovoked. At least one local crank has raised the specter of toxic poisoning of some kind, a cloud of gas that visited temporary insanity on a single playground, though there is, unsurprisingly, no evidence to support such a claim. The school board psychologist attests the event is outside her experience. It's an observation O'Brien agrees with.

"Eight-year-olds don't do that to other eight-year-olds," she says, now making herself gulp down some juice to fight off the cough that scratches at her throat.

"What about those two boys in England? The ones who murdered that toddler they lured out of a mall?"

"That was a dynamic between two kids. And the victim was a stranger, one they viewed as the subject of their experiment. We're talking about *seven* kids here—three boys and four girls—*all* in on it. And the victim was a friend."

"What are the kids saying about it?"

"Nobody remembers much except the doing of it. As to the why, they all offer the same explanation."

"Which is?"

"'Toby told me to do it.'"

The room spins. A greasy-spoon carousel of plasticky oranges and yellows.

Toby. The one who came to visit Tess from the Other Place. The one who has a message for me.

A boy who is no longer a boy.

"Who's Toby?" I manage after pretending to cough away something stuck in my throat.

"Good question. Nobody knows."

"What *do* they know about him?"

"All the kids say he was someone new in town, someone who didn't go to their school but who showed up that afternoon and talked to them. And within ten minutes, Toby had them all convinced they ought to rip their friend apart."

"Are the police looking for him?"

"Of course. But they have no leads. And do you think they will?"

"No."

"Because—"

"Because there is no Toby. Or at least no Toby anymore."

O'Brien and I stare at each other over the table, a silent recognition passing between us. If one of us was crazy before, we both are now.

"Did the kids offer any descriptions of Toby?" I ask, tossing down cash to cover the bill.

"Another odd thing. None could give sufficiently precise physical details, so the sketch artist has been unable to come up with a composite. But they were all quite sure about his voice. Coming from a kid but using grown-up words. *Sounding* like a grown-up."

"The kind of voice you can't say no to," I say. "Yeah, I've heard that one."

WE DRIVE ACROSS THE STATE ON I-10 TO JACKSONVILLE, FOUR LANES plumped up on piled gravel that keeps us from sinking into the swamp or tangled forest that rolls out on either side. Then south on I-95, past the countless exits to resort towns and retirement "opportunities" and Early Bird buffet deals.

We don't stop until Jupiter. Drive right through town until we're stopped by the ocean, a much-advertised but long-doubted fact folding brown waves onto the sand. We park and O'Brien wordlessly steps out of the Mustang, kicks her shoes off next to the car, and starts down toward the water in a stiff gait that I watch as I sit up on the hood. The air carries a savory cologne of saltwater and seaweed and, ever present, the distant whiff of fried food.

O'Brien starts into the water without taking off any of her clothes, without rolling up her pant legs. She just limps in like someone who has no intention of coming out. It occurs to me that I should go to her just in case she gets into trouble, snagged by the undertow or simply slipping beneath the surface. But then she stops, standing chest deep, each new wave picking her up and placing her feet back down on the bottom, the froth massaging around and past her.

It takes her some time to make her way back to the car. Soggy in the clothes that now hang off her, so that she appears like someone who'd just swum ashore after days of clinging to a piece of wreckage.

"That's the last time I'll ever feel the sea," she says once she sits next to me.

"Don't say that."

"I'm not being dramatic. I just listened to the water, and that's what it told me. It was comforting, actually. A farewell between old friends."

I want to deny this—that this is what is happening to her as we sun ourselves after a long drive, that she is dying even now in this very moment of almost forgotten pleasure—but she is right, and now is not the time for empty comfort. And then, just as I'm about to go around to the trunk to fish out a towel stolen following the hasty, incomplete wipe-up in the previous night's motel, O'Brien grabs hold of my wrist.

"Chances are we're going to fail. You know that, don't you?"

"It's never far from my mind."

"What I'm saying is, what we're up against—it's stronger than us, David. It is pre-ancient, near-omniscient. And what are we?"

"A pair of bookworms."

"Perfect for squashing."

"Is this supposed to be a pep talk? Because if it is, it's not really working."

In place of laughing, O'Brien squeezes my wrist even harder.

"I've been hearing a voice, too," she says. "It started after you came back from Venice, but over the last few days on the road with you— even the last twenty-four hours—it's become more clear."

"Is it—?"

"Not the Unnamed. It's something *good*, despite everything. And though I'm calling it a voice, it doesn't speak to me. It *enlightens* me. That sounds ridiculous, I know, but it's the only way to put it."

"So what's it telling you?"

"That anything can be endured if you're not alone."

She kisses me on the cheek. Wipes away the wet marks she leaves on my skin.

"The Devil—the one we're talking to, anyway—doesn't understand what you feel for Tess," O'Brien says, barely more than a whisper. "It *thinks* it comprehends love. It's learned all the lines, read all the poets. But it's only mimicry. That's our one—and very slight—advantage."

"That what that voice of yours told you?"

"More or less."

"Did it happen to mention how we might use this one, very slight advantage?"

"No," O'Brien says as she slides off the front of the car to shiver in the blazing heat. "So far it hasn't said a fucking peep about that."

JUPITER ELEMENTARY IS LOW-RISE, YELLOW-BRICKED, WITH THE Stars and Stripes wetly hanging from its pole in the drop-off zone ("5 MIN. LIMIT. VIOLATORS WILL BE TOWED"). The very picture of American normalcy. Also, increasingly, the backdrop to TV reporters' breathless accounts of unaccountable horror. The loner with the duffel bag. The bully victim good-bye note. The walk home abduction.

Here, something a little different. Something that makes even less sense.

There are a couple of local news vans parked on the street, though at first, as we pull to the curb, the cameras can't be seen. But then the bell sounds. At the same time the doors open and children scuff out, drained by a day full of grief counselors and somber gym assemblies, the competing TV crews appear from out of nowhere, slipping past parents anxiously waiting to collect their children and wagging microphones in front of faces.

What is the mood inside the school today?

How are you handling what happened?

Did you know the kids who did this?

And the half-stricken, half-overacted replies.

"It's like a movie."

217

"There's a lot of people really *hurting*."

"They were just normal kids."

As we cross the street and join the milling crowd, I start toward a girl who looks to be around eight or nine. I bend down in the baseball catcher's crouch that's meant to signal a friendly grown-up, the posture of the understanding cop. And she responds as if trained to. Walks right up to me like I've flashed a badge.

"My name's Officer Ullman," I say. "Just wanted to ask you a question or two."

She glances up at O'Brien, who smiles down at her.

"Okay," she says.

"Did you know those kids who beat up on that classmate of theirs?"

"Yeah."

"Could you remind me of the name of the injured child?"

"Remind you?"

"Yes," I say, slapping at my pockets in a pantomime of a misplaced notepad. "My memory's not what it used to be."

"Kevin."

"Kevin *what*, sweetheart?"

"Lilley."

"Right! Now, do you remember those kids in your class who hurt Kevin? Do you recall them talking about a boy named Toby?"

The girl links her hands together and holds them over her waist. A gesture of shame. "*Everybody* talked to Toby," she says.

"What was he like?"

"The same as us. But different."

"Different how?"

"He didn't belong to anybody. He didn't go to school. He did what he wanted."

"Anything else?"

She thinks about this. "He smelled a little funny."

"Oh yeah? Like what?"

"Like something in the ground."

Her nostrils flare at the odor's recollection.

"Did he tell you things?" I ask.

"Yes."

"Bad things?"

She squints. "No. But they made you *feel* bad."

"Can you remember one thing he would say to you?"

"Not really," she answers, her arms rigid with the effort to summon specific words to mind. "It's like he didn't talk. Or like it was you talking to yourself."

The girl looks up at O'Brien again. Starts to cry.

"Hey now. It's all right," I say, reaching out to the girl to hold her up. "It isn't—"

"Don't *touch* her!"

I turn to see a man striding across the school's lawn. A big, pissed-off guy in an XXXL Miami Dolphins shirt. The turquoise fabric billowing under his swinging arms.

"There's no need—" O'Brien starts, but leaves the sentence unfinished. How could it end? *There's no need to kick my friend's jaw off.*

The girl runs to her father. When he stops to pick her up, he looms over me. By now, some of the other parents and kids are looking our way, even inching closer to get a better look.

"Who are you?" he asks me.

"Reporters."

"With who?"

"The *Herald*," O'Brien offers.

The father turns to her, then back to me. "I already spoke to the guy from the *Herald*," he says. "Which makes you two a pair of dirty liars."

We don't argue with him on that. O'Brien is in no condition to prevent what's about to happen next, and I can think of no way of getting to my feet and out of range of his feet or fists fast enough to avoid their blows. The three of us paused in mutual acceptance of the inevitable.

And it's in this moment that I see I was wrong about the point of the man's rage. He's not angry at us for speaking to his kid. He's not, in fact, angry at all. He's scared shitless by what his daughter told him about Toby, the boy who doesn't exist. The boy who told her and her classmates to dream up the most awful thing they could do and then do it for real.

"My daughter is missing," I say to the man, low enough that only he and his child can hear. It holds him even more still than he was. "I'm looking for my little girl."

Something in his face shows that he not only believes me, but that he understands my search has something to do with Toby and the playground beating and the things he doesn't understand that have come crashing into his formerly not-too-bad Floridian world. He gets it without remotely comprehending it. Which is why he pulls his daughter even closer against his chest and steps away.

It allows me to start back toward the Mustang with O'Brien a half step behind me. The faces of the parents and kids and hairsprayed reporters absorbing our retreat with the gratitude of those who know that, no matter how lousy things are for us, it's not as bad as it is for *them*.

MAYBE IT'S BECAUSE O'BRIEN LOOKS MORE LIKE A PATIENT THAN most of the patients, but it turns out to be easy to walk up to the main-floor nurses' station of the Jupiter Medical Center, ask for Kevin Lilley's confidential room number, offer assurances that we're blood relations, and be given directions to the bed of central Florida's most famous ICU resident.

From there, it's up to the third floor, the two of us wondering on the elevator ride what we expect to find out from a kid in a coma.

"A mark, maybe," O'Brien suggests.

"Like 666? A pentagram?"

"I don't know, David. You're the one who brought us here. What are you looking for?"

Another sign. The last one.

"I'll know it when I see it," I say.

Our luck continues when we reach Kevin's room to find him without the hand-holding parents or hovering visitors I'd expected. A nurse changing his IV explains they'd all headed home for the night only moments ago.

"You're not with them?" she asks.

"We're up from Lauderdale," O'Brien says, as though this answers everything anyone could ever want to know about us.

A moment later we're left alone with Kevin and his assembled machines, beeping and puffing. A kid so swollen and discolored he looks like he's wearing a second skin, one he's grown out of and will soon shed completely, revealing the new kid beneath. His head is the most worrying aspect. The skull wrapped in complicated caps and gauze, protecting his brain from contact at the places where the bone has been torn away. But it's his eyelids that are the hardest to look at. Thick and shiny as linoleum.

"Kevin?"

O'Brien surprises me by addressing the boy first. The whole way over she felt it was of little use coming here, and she might be right. But her pity for the child triggers an attempt at contact. Reaching out to him in a place as distant and unknowable as wherever Tess is.

The machines beep. Kevin breathes, the tubes in his nostrils sucked at like straws in an empty glass. But he doesn't hear.

"Why?" O'Brien whispers, wiping at her cheeks.

To prove that they're with us. That they've always been with us.

"I don't know," I say.

"We were brought here to see this?"

The corruption of man. Their greatest achievement. A masterpiece-in-progress.

"I don't know."

O'Brien goes to look out the window. The late afternoon clouds collecting like confused thoughts on the ocean horizon. In a few hours the evening will come, the hospital overseen by the overnight skeleton crew. And Kevin will be here, alone with the cluster of Get Well Soon cards on the night table and a bouquet of flaccid balloons on the sill.

"You don't know me," I whisper to him, stepping around the side of the bed. "But Toby has spoken to me, too."

Some part of me—the foolish part, growing bolder in its childish, magical thinking—expects this to elicit a signal from the boy. That because this quest the Unnamed has set me on has me at its center, I am the key to every lock. But the truth is everyone loses someone they think they can't live without. All of us have a moment like this, when we believe our heavenward plea, our dark incantation, will trigger a miracle.

"Kevin? I'm the man that Toby has mentioned to you," I say, bending close to his ear, the skin smelling of disinfectant. "I have a little girl, not much older than you. Something bad happened to her, too. It's why I've come here from so far away to see you."

Nothing. Maybe even less than nothing. His breathing sounds more shallow here, so close to him. His connection to life an even quieter thing than it first appeared.

Then I touch him.

Place my hand over his and lift it up an inch. Hold it without squeezing. Lend his forearm the simple animation it's unlikely to ever perform on its own again.

But when I stop moving, the hand doesn't.

A finger. The index, extending half-straight to point at me.

I bend closer. My ear almost touching his lips. Close enough to hear Kevin's voice. So quiet only someone who had already long memorized the lines could hear them for what they are.

Even as he forms the words—tentative, a struggle to remember the precise sequence—I realize that Kevin has memorized them, too. It's something that Toby has asked of him and, to keep his hope of swimming up to the light alive, he is being the best student he can be.

A dungeon horrible, on all sides round
As one great furnace flamed, yet from those flames
No light, but rather darkness visible

His nose sucks at the tubes with a slightly stronger pull for a minute, a near-silent recovery from his efforts. Then he is asleep-but-not-asleep again.

O'Brien touches my shoulder. When I stand straight I see that she hasn't heard what I've heard.

"We should go," she says.

She starts for the door but I linger. Return to the bedside and whisper words from a different book into Kevin's ear.

Though a host encamp against me,
my heart shall not fear.

20

AFTER LEAVING THE HOSPITAL, O'BRIEN JUST TAKES THE WHEEL and we roll through the palm-lined streets of Jupiter, a world of convenient parking and jumbo signage. Few walk the streets. I try to catch someone getting into or out of their car, but never do. The traffic is the only living thing in evidence. Slowpoke seniors steering the last of Detroit's cruisers, looking for a deal, for something to do. Their human expressions reduced to the lame jokes of personalized license plates.

"I'm tired," O'Brien announces. She looks it. A tired more than tired, bone-deep. I look at her and realize that it is the new view she has of the world that draws the color from her skin even more than her illness.

"Let's go back to the motel," I say. "You should rest."

"There isn't time."

"Just lie down for half an hour. It'll be okay."

"What are you going to do?"

"Keep driving around."

After I drop O'Brien off I head straight for a destination I didn't have in mind. The playground. The place where seven children spilled the blood of another upon swing-set sand.

There's nobody here. It's the teeth-brushing hour. My favorite part of the day with Tess. The ritual of bath, pajamas, and book. A succession of comforts I could reliably deliver night after night. Through nothing more than these simple repetitions, I could make things better.

Not tonight. Wherever she is now lies beyond my reach. Beyond hearing of a whispered "Once upon a time . . ." or *You are my sunshine*.

Yet I sing for her anyway. Sit on one of the swings and fight to stay in tune. A broken lullabye in the twilight.

You make me happy when skies are gray . . .

A boy walking over the grass.

He is the same age as Kevin Lilley and his classmates. A good-looking kid in need of a haircut and wearing a junior-sized Rolling Stones T-shirt, the one with the big lips and tongue on a black background. Moving uncertainly, stiffly, as though recently risen after a long sleep in an uncomfortable position.

The boy sits on the swing next to mine. Looks down at his feet. It could almost be that he hasn't noticed I'm here.

"You're Toby," I say.

"I was."

"But you're dead now."

This seems to confuse him. Then, when he figures something out, his expression turns to one of piercing sorrow before he recovers, merely hopeless.

"I belong to him," he says.

"Who is he?"

"He doesn't have a name."

"Is there a girl with you, where you are?" I ask. "A girl named Tess?"

"There's a lot of us."

"That's what he's told you to say. You know more than that, though, don't you? Tell me the truth."

He shifts around, wincing, as though he'd swallowed a steak knife and is trying in vain to find the least agonizing position to sit in.

"Tess," he says. "Yes. I've talked to her."

"She's where you are?"

"No. But she's . . . close."

"Can you find her now?"

"No."

"Why not?"

"Because she's not *meant* to be found."

I pinch my eyes. Drag a wet sleeve over my face.

"What happened to you, Toby?" I ask him. "When you were alive."

He kicks at the sand with the toes of his shoes.

"There was a man who hurt me," he says.

"Who?"

"A friend . . . who wasn't a friend."

"A grown-up?"

"Yes."

"Hurt you how?"

"With his . . . hands. The things he did. The things he said he'd do if I told."

"I'm sorry."

"I had to make it stop, that's all. My mom had these pills. I had to make it *stop*."

He looks at me. Just a boy. Unspeakably afraid, broken before he had a chance to be whole.

Then, all at once, Toby's face goes slack. Without any other physical alteration, without the morphing I'd seen in the faces of others the Unnamed had taken possession of, the Toby part of the boy drains away, and there is only a shell. A once-human boy sitting on a swing, lifeless in a way beyond death.

Then it moves again.

The eyes swing up to fix on mine. When it speaks, it's with the voice I know so well now it's like a part of me, emanating from inside

227

my own head as they say fillings can pick up radio frequencies in your teeth.

"Hello, David," it says.

"I know who you are."

"But do you know my name?"

"Yes."

"Tell me."

"Say it yourself."

"Then it wouldn't be a test, would it?"

"You don't say it because you can't."

"It would be an error to presume to know what I can and cannot do."

"You *need* me to know you."

"Really? Why would that be?"

"For me to speak your name would lend you the substance of identity, however shallow. So when you are given a name, you might pretend to be more fully human."

The boy scowls at this. And though it is the expression of a petulant child, a look almost laughable in any other context, it is enough, from this boy, to race the heart.

"Tess is crying, David," it says. "Can't you hear her?"

"Yes."

"She's stopped believing you will ever come. Which means she will belong to me by the moon—"

"No!"

"SAY MY NAME!"

This time, the voice reveals the hatred that is its true character. The words passing through Toby's cracked lips in white bubbles of saliva.

"Belial."

This is me. The demon's name escapes my lips and flies out into the air like some winged creature that has been hiding within me, and now, in haste, it is returning to its keeper.

"I'm so pleased," the boy says. And it *is* pleased, the voice returned to what it was. A vacant smile pulling his mouth wide as though by invisible hooks. "When did you make your determination?"

"I think a part of me has known since I heard you speak through Tess in Venice. It's taken me this long to confirm it. Accept it."

"Intuition."

"No. It was your arrogance. Your pretensions of civility. A bogus sophistication."

The boy smiles again. Not in pleasure this time.

"That is all?"

"And your rhetoric," I continue. Unable to stop wanting to hold its attention. "You were the Stygian Council's great persuader.

On the other side up rose
Belial, in act more graceful and humane;
A fairer person lost not heaven; he seemed
For dignity composed and high exploit:
But all was false and hollow.

The elegant voice that calmed Moloch's raging call to arms, argued to wait until God's anger soothed before mounting a surprise attack on heaven. *Our supreme foe in time may much remit / His anger, and perhaps thus far removed / Not mind us not offending.* Lover of fame and empty erudition. *Yet he pleased the ear . . . his thoughts were low.* That is the meaning of your name, after all. Belial. *Without worth.*"

The boy's face is fixed again. Unchanging, unmoving. Though his feet push against the dusty earth beneath the swing. A slow back and forth, forcing me to turn my head to follow him. A dizzying pendulum.

"You and John have much in common," it says.

"I've studied Milton's work. That's all."

"Haven't you ever asked *why* you have been so drawn to it?"

"All art is worthy of study."

"But it is so much more than that! He is the author of history's most eloquent record of dissent. Rebellion! That is why, in his verse, John presents such a sympathetic case for my master. He is on our side, however secretly, unconsciously. Just as you are."

"You're wrong. I have never done harm to anyone."

"It's not about *harm*, David. Violence, crimes—these are the detritus of evil, minor matters compared to those of the spirit. And what you and John share is the spirit of resistance."

"Resistance to what?"

The boy doesn't answer. Swings back and forth without pumping his legs, without touching the ground, without moving his eyes from mine. The chains creaking in a repetition of an identically inflicted hurt.

"All your adult life you have studied religion, Christianity, the works of the apostles—and yet you do not believe in God," it carries on after a time, then pauses.

No, more than a pause. An opening gap in time. A falling away.

A moment ago the two of us sat on canvas swing seats in a suburban Florida playground. Now, as I raise my eyes, I see that while we remain on the swings, immediately beyond our small square of sand is forest. The trees barren, standing too close to each other, starving for lack of water to be drawn from the ash-powdered earth. I try to peer through the trunks but there are only more bent trees, the ground flat and without end. It is a vision of the woods on the far side of the river my brother and I feared as children. Untouched by air or birdsong or any voice but the boy's, whispering from scripture in my head.

And the Lord said unto Satan, "Whence comest thou?"

I can't see it, but I know that something watches from the trees. A density so great it bends the air, a kind of sideways gravity that pulls and distends everything around it. It communicates nothing in its swelling silence but want, timeless and insatiable. This is the territory it wanders, on and on. Ravenous with grief.

Then Satan answered the Lord, and said, "From going to and fro on the earth, and from walking up and down on it."

My eyes return to the playground's sand. Try to hold them there. Let nothing in but the boy's words, now spoken aloud.

"Why not?" it says, carrying on as though I had stopped time and now switched it back on. "Because you cannot accept the notion of his absolute goodness! You have suffered too much, in your way—in your melancholy—to serve unquestioningly before an ever-loving, ever-tyrannical Lord. His goodness is another name for Authority, a written command from an absent father. Your critical mind gives you no choice but to see this. And in this, you remind me of John."

The boy looks skyward. At first I'm grateful to have his eyes off me. But then he speaks in another's voice—his true voice, a wet and hateful hiss—and I know that this, not his stare, is what I will never forget. This voice, quoting the poet, will be the narrator for what remains of the nightmares of my life.

To do aught good never will be our task,
But ever to do ill our sole delight,
As being the contrary to his high will
Whom we resist.

When it's done, the boy looks at me again. The voice once again the one he's chosen to speak to me with.

"Brave resistance. It's what binds us, David."

"I am not with you."

"But you are!" The boy jumps in before my last word is out. "You have always known it. John was with us from the beginning, just as you have been."

"That's a lie."

"Is it? His best friend from childhood dies at sea. His first wife leaves him soon after marriage. Suspended from Cambridge for arguing with his tutor. A stay in prison for his dissenting views. He was, like you and I—like my master, his most magnificently drawn hero—resistant to servitude. A rebel, sensitive to all the losses and unfairness of his life. *Paradise Lost* is the most wonderful misrepresentation, don't you think? Purporting to justify the ways of God to men, but in fact a justification for independence, for freedom. It was, for its time, the finest piece of what one may call demonic propaganda. My masterpiece."

"*Your* masterpiece?"

"Every poet has his muse. And I was John's. Or even something more than that. I gave the words to him. He merely signed his name to them."

"Your arrogance has made you blind."

"Blind! *John* was blind when he wrote his poem! Have you forgotten? That's when he asked for help. He begged the darkness enclosing upon him for inspiration. And I came! *Yes!* I came and whispered my sweet nothings in his ear."

The Devil lies, David.

"Bullshit."

"Don't be crude, Professor. Profanity is one contest you will not win with me."

At the edge of the swing set's square of sand, a pair of seagulls fight over what looks at first to be a pile of chicken bones. The little rib cage, the little skull. Not there before. Not chicken bones.

The birds pecking out each other's eyes, biting the backs of each other's necks, pulling and ripping at feathers, at flesh. The trees crowding closer to see the first spits of blood.

Toby raises his hand and brushes the air. The seagulls flap away. Their screeches joined by others from within the forest.

"I know what you're thinking," the boy says. "If I was the voice in John's ear, why would he depict us so unfavorably? You know the answer, Professor. He was limited by his times. To praise Satan and his fallen angels outright would have been illegal, impossible. So he named us the antagonists of the poem while clearly standing with us in his sympathies. Answer me this: Who is the real hero of the poem? God? Adam?"

"Satan."

"As you have repeatedly and passionately argued yourself, in your admirable essays."

"An academic argument only."

"You don't believe that! Why else devote your life to this position?

Why bother convincing your colleagues and indoctrinating your students in what, in John's time, would be called blasphemy? It is because you stand with us, David. And you are far from alone."

His speech—the snaking logic of his rhetoric—is so disorienting I keep glancing down to make sure my feet remain on the ground, holding me in place. But what is "ground" here? What is "remain"? I've only to look at the boy again and the sensation of movement returns. A dry-land seasickness.

"Why Tess?" I say with a dry swallow. "Why me?"

"I keep her with me to give you focus. Every poet—every storyteller—requires motivation."

"That's how you see me?"

"What you call the document is proof of our existence. But you, David, are my messenger. And the message is your testimony. All you've seen, all you've felt."

It's not me swinging that makes me feel so dizzy. It's the whole world, the withered garden, spinning.

"Will you let me see her? Talk to her?"

"This is not yet the end of your journey, David."

"So tell me where to go."

"You already know."

"Tell me what to do."

"Leave the woman behind. Complete your wandering."

"For wanderers eventually find their way to you."

"It is not surrender I seek! I am not your enslaver but your liberator. Don't you see? I am your muse as much as I was John's."

Part of me knows there is weakness in his argument. But I can gain no traction on the substance of what he says, as though a food I have ingested now sits, heavy and unnourishing, in my gut. It leaves me no choice but to keep speaking, keep asking. Try not to think of the hungry thing in the woods that, without looking up, I know has stepped out to show itself. Moving closer.

"Propaganda," I say. "That is how you see the document, isn't it? How you see me. I can help you make a case where you cannot make it yourself."

"The war on heaven has never been waged in hell, nor on Earth. The battleground lies within every human mind."

"The mind is its own place, and in itself / Can make a heaven of hell, a hell of heaven."

"John saw that. As did the other John."

"The Book of Revelation."

"A book not to be taken too literally."

"What is your interpretation?"

"The Antichrist will come bearing weapons of persuasion, not destruction," the boy says, growing louder, firmer. "The Beast will rise not from the sea, but within you. Each of you, one at a time. And in a manner suited to your own misgivings, frustrations. Your grief."

"You're waging a campaign."

"A crusade!"

The boy opens his mouth as though to laugh, but nothing comes out. It is a skill the original Toby would have possessed, but that the one who occupies his body now has never known.

"Revelation is a vision of the future of man," I say, reasoning on the fly. "But Matthew offers a vision of *your* future. *What have you to do with us, O Son of God? Art thou come hither to torment us before the time?* Your crusade will fail. It is foretold. *The time.* You are destined to die in the lake of fire."

The boy blinks at this. And then, a sudden darkening under his eyes, as though he might weep. For the first time, he looks like an actual boy.

"There is so much to do before that," it says.

"But it will happen. You don't deny that."

"Who can deny the will of the Heavenly Father?" the boy spits.

"You will lose."

"I will die! It is what I have in common with you, with all humankind. We all bear the knowledge of our own deaths. But God? Of course *he* goes on! Eternal. Indifferent. Pure goodness is cold, David. It's why I embrace death. Embrace you."

For an awful moment I fear he is about to pull me against him. I try to stand and move out of his reach, but I sit frozen on the swing's seat, hands clenched white around the chains.

Yet the boy doesn't try to hold me. He only tries his empty smile once more.

"I hoped you appreciated my gift."

"I don't know what you mean," I say, though instantly, I do.

"The man who was enjoying your wife in a way you have never known. Not to worry. Professor Junger won't be bringing anyone pleasure ever again."

The boy grins.

Gonna be a hot one, he says in Will Junger's voice.

Somewhere, not far off, there is the thud and scratch of something heavy moving through the deadfall. Perhaps many things, though of one mind.

"Let me understand," I say, hoping a new question might wipe away the terrible shape of the boy's gaping mouth. "You see me as a crusader? For you? Your master?"

"It is a different time since John wrote his poem," the boy whispers in nostalgic regret. "We are living in the Documentary Age. People demand veracity. The unmediated truth. It is no longer time for the poem to make our case, but evidence. Yet this alone is not enough. We need you, David. The personal account. A human voice, speaking for us."

"Saying that real demons exist in the world."

"It is an old story," he says, jumping off the swing. "It is also true."

The boy starts away. The space between us hardened by the cold he leaves in his wake.

"I'll do it! Please! Just let her go!"

I lift my eyes and the dark forest is gone. It is only a playground bordered by chain-link fence and, beyond it, downmarket townhouses with their curtains drawn. Air conditioners throatily humming like a Gregorian choir.

The boy turns. Though nothing has visibly changed in his expression, the potency of his hatred can be felt even more acutely now, a short distance off, the veil of his charm lowered to show something closer to his actual nature. The bright agony of a blade splitting the nerve. A rank odor of decay.

Like something in the ground.

"You have one last discovery to make. One last truth. Your truth, David."

The boy walks on. Watching me even with his back turned. A child whose shadow stretches as long as a towering beast's across the grass.

It isn't until we cross the state line from Florida into Georgia that O'Brien ventures to ask why I'm so sure Toby has pointed us to Canada.

"It wasn't Toby," I tell her.

"Then how do you know?"

"Kevin Lilley told me."

"David, that's not *possible*."

"Why not?"

"That boy can't speak."

"He spoke to me."

"Well, I didn't hear it."

"You weren't supposed to."

For a moment, a jealous frown pulls against O'Brien's features. She tries to hide it from me by looking out the passenger window but I catch it nevertheless. You don't get to win the scholarships and grants and research chairs she's won without being competitive.

"Belial had Kevin memorize something. Something he managed to whisper to me," I say, hoping to draw O'Brien back with the lure of an implied question. It works.

"*Paradise Lost,*" she says. "What lines?"

"*A dungeon horrible, on all sides round / As one great furnace flamed—*"

"*—yet from those flames / No light, but rather darkness visible.*"

"Them's the ones."

"I don't get it. We're going to a dungeon? A furnace?"

"It ain't the penthouse suite."

I explain how I didn't understand it at first, either. There was no word that jumped out as a destination, no city or state veiled by poetry. Though I had a good idea that no matter what it was, it had something to do with me. Which turned out to be an idea confirmed by Toby's farewell.

Your truth, David.

"If it's personal for you, then it must be personal for me, too," O'Brien muses. "*Not to know me argues yourselves unknown.* Remember?"

"I remember."

"How can our two lives lead to the same truth?"

"I don't know. But I think I know where it's going to happen."

The lines Kevin recited tell of Satan surveying hell, his home. Also his prison. A dungeon in name, though not necessarily in substance, as it is a place just as often described as a lake of fire.

"Once I thought of this, I knew I had it," I say.

"Great. But I still need some help."

"Lake. Fire. We lived in a cabin for a couple years when I was a kid. One of my father's many stretches of whisky-inspired unemployment."

"A *lakeside* cabin," O'Brien says, pounding her fist on the dash. "Let me guess. One that burned down."

"Half right. A cabin by a river. A river that feeds into Fireweed Lake."

"The river where your brother drowned."

"I never told you he drowned."

"But I'm right, aren't I?"

"Yes."

"Okay," she says, her voice retreating to a cracked whisper. "Consider me convinced."

I ASK O'BRIEN TO DRIVE FOR A WHILE AND PRETEND TO SLEEP IN the backseat. Instead, I open Tess's journal to where I left off last time. Reading her words as much for the shape of the letters she made as what she expressed. *Her* hand, working over *these* pages. The trace of a presence I can almost touch, almost summon into being.

Dad always tells me things about when I was a kid. Things I don't really remember because I was too young. But they seem like my *memories now, I've heard the stories so many times.*

Like this one:

When I wasn't even two yet, I would climb into bed with my mom and dad early in the mornings. My dad was always first to wake up. He'd try to let my mom sleep, so he was usually the one to take me to the bathroom and pour my cereal, etc., etc. He says it was his favorite part of the day. But I've heard him say the same thing about reading bedtime stories. And seeing my face when he picked me up from kindergarten. And the two of us sitting at the diner counter and having tuna sandwiches. And brushing my hair after a bath.

Anyway, he would wake up first and I'd be there LOOKING at him. Three inches from his face. (Dad always says it was close enough to taste my breath. What did it taste like? Warm bread, he says.)

I would ask him the same question every day:

"Are you happy, Daddy?"

"I'm happy now," he'd say every time.

The funny part about it is I still want to ask my dad the same thing. Even now. Not just because I'm interested in the answer. I want to be able to make him happy by asking. To be breathing near him and for him to feel it and for that to be enough.

And then, along with the entries like these, something odd.

Insertions that don't line up with what precedes or follows them. A second voice more powerful than the first, cutting through.

Dad thinks he can run from what follows him. Maybe he doesn't even see it, or tells himself he doesn't. IT DOESN'T MATTER. It's coming for him just the same. Like it's coming for me.

I saw a nature documentary about grizzly bears once. It said that if you encounter a bear in the wild, you should never run, but stand your ground. Talk to it. Running marks you as prey. As food.

The ones that run never get away.

But maybe, if you face it, you can show you're not scared. You can get a little more time. Find a way to escape for good.

When the time comes, I won't run. I'll look at it STRAIGHT ON. Maybe it'll be enough to give Dad a chance.

Because if the bear doesn't take one of us, it will take us both.

How did Tess know all this? How could she see what I had hidden so well I couldn't see myself? I was always aware of our closeness, the amount of unspoken information we could pass in a look over the dinner table or in a rearview mirror glance. Yet I thought we were no more special than the luckiest of similarly hardwired fathers and daughters.

Turns out she could read far deeper signals than that. How we shared the unwanted gift of melancholy, the burden of the Black Crown which, for us, was what opened a doorway through which other things could come and go. The entities that usually go by the name of spirits but feel heavier and more willfully destructive than the wispy apparitions that word implies. Beings long ago separated from their bodies but so fierce in their search for new skins they are indifferent to the harm they cause, indeed take pleasure in that harm, as they slip inside the living again for a time. What they leave behind is never the same again, the ones who walk among us but whose stares go emptily through us.

It makes me think of my father. How whatever marks Tess and me marked him as well. A man who grieved before he ever lost anything, who suffered without any obvious grounds for suffering. Through his distance from us, his family, through moving from town to town, through alcohol, he tried to run from the bear that stalked him. And in the end, Tess was right. The ones who run never get away.

Maybe I'd been running since then, too. But not anymore.

I CALL MY WIFE FROM A KFC MEN'S ROOM STALL.

Not that there's anything to say—that is, there's too much that cannot be said—but there is the unavoidable compulsion to try. That I make the attempt sitting on a closed-lid john while absently reading some of the filthiest graffiti I've ever seen strikes me as oddly appropriate.

Then, Diane's voice. She hasn't changed the recording since before Venice, so that there's a lightness in it still, an almost flirtatious promise. It would be different now.

You have reached the voice mail of Diane Ingram. Please leave a message.

"Hey, Diane. It's me. I don't know if I'll be able to call again after—"

After what? Something final, whatever it is. So I should say good-bye at least. Or maybe it's already too late for that.

"I'm sorry. *Shit!* If you had a nickel for every time you heard me say that, right? There's just no other way to put it, I guess. It covers all the bases. Tess. You and me. Will. I heard about the accident and, believe it or not, I'm sorry about that, too."

The bathroom's door opens and someone comes in to wash their hands. The faucet turned on full blast, raining spots onto the floor I can see from under the stall door.

"Diane. Listen, there's—" I start, lowering my voice. But the idea of someone hearing what even I don't know I'm about to say stops me. I wait for whoever stands at the sink to finish. But he doesn't. The water pounding into the sink. The drops pooling together into puddles on the tiles.

"I just hope you find a way to be happy again," I whisper. "I hope I haven't taken that away, too."

Too? What did I mean by that? I've taken her happiness as well as the wasted years of our marriage? As well as her daughter?

The hand-washer clears his throat. Draws a wheezing breath. Begins to laugh.

I yank the stall door open. The water still on full, plumes of steam graying the mirror. But nobody there.

Next I'm plowing out into the hallway to hug the wall, to feel its cool reality against my cheek. Visible to those sitting at plastic tables, digging chicken out of buckets, some of whom look back at me. Their thoughts of *Drugs* or *Crazy* or *Stay the hell away* written on their faces as they chew.

I check the phone and hang up. An almost three-minute message. The first half a stuttered apology, the second a torrent of running water, concluding with the laughter of something dead. *What would Diane make of it? She'd probably come to a similar conclusion to the drumstick-holders staring at me now. There's no helping someone like that.*

The funny part is I'd meant to be comforting. I'd meant to sound sane.

WE PASS INTO TENNESSEE WITH O'BRIEN SINGING THE FEW BARS of "Chattanooga Choo Choo" she can recall. The actual Chattanooga slipping past as yet another cluster of highwayside motels, padlocked factories, and self-storage barracks. There is a real town beyond this ass-end of streets. Neighborhoods with families buoyed by the same affections or shattered by the same crimes as other neighborhoods, the ones we have lived in and therefore deem more real. People who, for all I know, are conducting similarly impossible searches. Talking to the dead and praying to whoever will listen.

There's gonna be
A certain party at the station . . .

Soon the asphalt ribbon switchbacks up into the Appalachians, though nobody slows, a collective denial of charging eighteen-wheelers and yawning cliffsides. And nobody more indifferent than us. Tag-teaming the wheel through the night, gnawing on tacos and reconstituted chicken products, washing it all down with coffee near-solid with Sweet'N Low.

From time to time, O'Brien asks about my father. It prompts me to remember more than I tell her.

Because I was so young when he died, I can summon only snap-shots, the taste left behind in the air by his darkening moods in the months leading up to my brother's accident. Behavior that, considered in light of my own experiences of late, takes on a greater resonance. How he, never a religious man, began reading the Bible cover to cover, then starting again when he was done. The lengthy silences when he would stop whatever he was doing—mowing the lawn, spooning in-stant coffee into his mug—and appear to listen to instructions none of us could hear. And his *looks*. These more than anything else. How I would catch him looking at me, his son, not with pride or affection but a strange appetite.

I keep what I tell O'Brien to the surface things. His depression, his drinking. The lost jobs. His urging me to not be like him. And until recently, I thought I'd succeeded.

"But there's more of him in you than you figured," O'Brien says. "It's why we're going to him."

"Even though he's dead."

"Doesn't seem to be stopping him from coming back, does it?"

"He's not the only one."

I HAVEN'T TOLD O'BRIEN EVERYTHING.

Not because I worry she won't believe me. I haven't told her be-cause it's just between me and Tess. To reveal it runs the risk of breaking the thin thread that still connects us. To speak of it aloud might let Belial know that such a thread exists.

For instance, I didn't tell O'Brien all the reasons I know we have to go to the old cottage by the river. I didn't tell her about the entry in Tess's journal where she spoke of the dream-that's-not-a-dream.

Standing on the bank of a river of fire.

Tess taken to the far bank where my brother and I never ventured as

243

kids. We didn't speak of it, but we knew it was a bad place all the same. The trees there growing aslant, their leaves never quite returning in the summer, so that the forest appeared hungry.

The same place Belial had shown me on the swing in Jupiter. The playground surrounded by dark forest. An emerging beast.

The line between this place and the Other Place.

And my daughter on the wrong side. Hearing me searching for her, calling her name. Watching my brother's body float past.

Arms pulling me back. Skin that tastes like dirt.

Tess begging me to find her.

Not words from my mouth through the air, but from my heart through the earth, so only the two of us could hear it.

I hadn't known that's what it was. That the sound I can sometimes recognize beneath the ringing tinnitus and talk-radio blather and exhaust-tainted air blasting past the open window, is her.

WE MAKE OHIO AND SWITCH TO I-90 AT TOLEDO, SO THAT WE NOW speed along the underbelly of Lake Erie, flat as aluminum foil in the night. The irony of a sign for Eden draws us off the interstate to park at the rear corner of a Red Lobster lot for a half hour of sleep, though only O'Brien cranks her seat back and closes her eyes.

As O'Brien gasps and whistles her way through the slumber of the unwell, I flick through Burton's *Anatomy of Melancholy*. I'm drawing my thumb across the pages and letting them flip and blur when the book opens to a bookmark I didn't know was there. A photograph. Curled at the edges, white borders turned yellow with time. A photo of me.

This is who I take it to be at first, anyway. Though in the next second I see it is my father. The only picture I have of him. I know this because I had long believed I'd destroyed all the others. The shock of the similarity leaves me slightly breathless, fighting for air just as O'Brien does next to me.

He would have been almost exactly the same age I am now when he went out into the woods with the Mossberg 12-gauge his father had given him, slipped the barrel past his lips far enough to reach the trigger with his free hand, and fired. In the photo, taken only weeks before my brother's accident, his expression might appear as one of fatherly satisfaction. The underslept smile of the dad who's been pulled away from his work by his wife, who has sat him down here, in an easy chair before a fire, to snap a portrait of the breadwinner in the prime of his life.

But the more studied appraisal reveals the efforts of both the subject and photographer: the glassy, mirthless eyes, the shoulders and clasped hands angled in a "relaxed" pose. An overlookable sort of man whose near-desperate sadness was evident in his details, from dimpled half-moons under his eyes to the psoriasis-reddened knuckles.

I'm thinking about opening the car door and letting it slip out onto the concrete when I notice the only underlined section on either page the photo had been stuck between.

The Devil he is a spirit, and hath means and opportunities to mingle himself with our spirits, and sometimes more slyly, sometimes more abruptly and openly, to suggest such devilish thoughts into our hearts. He insults and domineers in melancholy, distempered phantasies especially.

Why that passage? I don't remember it having any particular significance in my research, and I've never cited it in any of my lectures. But it must have leapt out at me nevertheless. And I'd placed the only photograph of my father between the pages to mark it though I'd never returned to it over the years.

A foreknowledge. That's what it must have been. I'd read those words—*melancholy, distempered phantasies, Devil*—and sent a message to my future self I couldn't have understood at the time. I'd recognized my father diagnosed by Burton's observation. A man of reasonable promise, blessed by better luck than most, but nevertheless a ruin, a witness to a child's death, a violent suicide.

How did Robert Burton know so much about such things? A cloistered academic in the earliest days of the seventeenth century?

Here's an answer: the same way I know so much about it now, a cloistered academic four centuries on. Personal experience.

O'Brien coughs herself awake. I slip the photograph between the pages and slap the book shut.

"You want me to drive?" she asks, reading the clouds gathered in my eyes.

"No. Just rest," I answer, roaring the Mustang to life. "I'll take us the rest of the way."

I CAN'T SAY IF O'BRIEN'S THOUGHTS HAVE TURNED TO THE PURSUER or not, but mine certainly have. Neither of us have mentioned him, in any case. I suppose it's because there's little point. O'Brien saved my life by doing what, only days ago, would be an unthinkable thing. She'd gotten out of bed at the sound of his fiddling with the lock and found the only weapon a motel room could offer, then hidden with it against the wall by the door, hoping not to be noticed when he opened it. Then, when he'd pulled out the knife, she'd done what she'd done.

It's hard to guess at how this act weighs upon her. Perhaps she worries about who they will send after us now. Or perhaps, like me, she only calculates how little time there is left.

WE CROSS THE BORDER AT NIAGARA FALLS IN DARKNESS. AT O'BRIEN'S insistence we park the car and take a couple minutes to walk to the water's edge and look over the rail. A smooth collapse of broad river falling away into an exploding cloud of mist, though its gray reach upward lends it the restlessness of smoke more than water.

"That's us, isn't it?" O'Brien says, staring at the drop. "Going over the falls in a barrel."

"Minus the barrel."

O'Brien takes hold of my hand.

"Whatever we find, wherever we're going, I'm ready," she says. "Not reckless but . . . clear."

"You're always clear."

"I'm not talking about the mind. I'm talking about everything else."

"That makes two of us."

"Not true. You have Tess."

"Yes. Except for Tess. She's the only thing that's clear for me." I pull O'Brien against me. "And you, too."

When the mist finds its way through our clothes to chill our skin we head back to the Mustang and find the highway again. Drive around the western end of Lake Ontario, through the peach orchards and vineyards of the peninsula, then into the growing density of the outlying towns and industrial cities before Toronto. A glimpse of its towers, then the turn north again. The new suburbs looking old. The rolling croplands.

A couple hours later the multiple lanes shrink to an uncertain road, tightening through the wooded curves, the sudden overhangs of blasted rock. We're past the Muskoka lakes with their multimillion-dollar summer compounds and private golf courses, and past now, too, the smaller, cheaper lakes that follow. Soon we are making one after another of the thousand turns through the unpeopled land. A thread of blacktop teased out over a landscape of endless forest so that there is no decision but to advance or retreat. Which, in our case, means no decision at all.

It's dawn by the time we pull over onto the shoulder and I get out, stiff-kneed, to haul open the metal gate at Fireweed Lake Lane. Though "lane" hardly suits: an unmaintained trail through the brush, two wheel ruts in the earth and branches shaking hands across the gap. The cover of trees so thick it darkens the way in greenish night.

"How far?" O'Brien asks when I return to the car.

"About a half mile in. Maybe a bit more."

O'Brien leans over. At first I think it's to whisper something in my ear but instead she kisses me. A real one, almost warm, on the lips.

"Time to see what he wants us to see," she says.

Over even the last few hours her skin has been pulled tighter over her cheeks, her chin. Core pounds lost despite the steady cheeseburger and vanilla shake diet. Yet she is still here. The essence of Elaine O'Brien, the last of her, meeting my eyes.

"I—"

"I told you. I know already," she says and returns to sit straight in her seat, staring into the shadowed trees. "Now, let's go."

22

THE MUSTANG ROLLS OFF THE SHOULDER AND WE ARE INSTANTLY swallowed up by the green.

I remember doing this drive in the backseat of my father's Buick station wagon, a wood-paneled monster that handily managed to jostle through the mud slicks and over the larger rocks on the juicy suspension of yesteryear. The Mustang, however, lets us feel every knock and worry over every tire-spinning hesitation.

We break through a final veil of scrub to have the old Ullman cabin revealed to us. Not that it was ever really ours. Not that it's really a cabin.

An aluminum-sided bungalow with a pair of squinty, curtained windows, one on each side of the front door. The kind of hastily constructed kit home you find in the downmarket neighborhoods of factory towns, yet in this case plopped in the northern Ontario woods, as though lifted by a tornado and long forgotten about.

We get out of the car and lean against it a moment, breathing the surprisingly cold air and getting our legs back. No other tire tracks in the leaf-littered yard. No sign that anyone has been here for weeks, or probably longer.

"What do we do now?" O'Brien asks.

"Look around, I guess."

"What should we be looking for?"

"Doesn't matter. It'll find us."

The front screen door, hinged only at its bottom, swings open in a curl of breeze and utters a rusty yelp. I find myself walking toward it without any clear intention of opening the door behind it. But that's what I'm trying to do. Hauling on the handle, shouldering into it in case it's merely stuck in its frame.

"Locked," I say.

"There a back door?"

"It's probably locked, too."

"Let's have a look-see anyway."

I follow O'Brien around the corner and the river is suddenly before us, seventy yards down a sapling-dotted slope of waving grass. The current looking stronger than I remember it, whirlpools spinning about at the midpoint, stray branches racing by the shore. Not a wide crossing—maybe a hundred feet or so—but I wouldn't want to try it. I'm not sure anyone ever did.

On the far side, the dark forest. Gnarled and dry.

"You're right," O'Brien announces off to my left, rattling at the rear door at the top of a deck blackened by mold. "Locked tight."

There's a football-sized rock on the ground not far from where I stand. I pick it up with both hands and join O'Brien.

"We'll just have to pick it," I say, and swing the rock down on the handle, shearing it off. The door swings open half a foot.

O'Brien is the first in. She pulls the curtains open and lets the available light spill onto the floor. Tries the light switches, but none work. Pokes her head into the bathroom I know to be just around the corner from the kitchen. All before I take a step inside.

"This look familiar to you?"

"I was just a kid the last time I was here," I answer.

"That doesn't answer my question."

"It's all different. In the details. But yes, it's familiar, all right."

"So why don't you come inside?"

"Because it smells like the past."

"Just smells bad to me."

"Bingo."

But I do go inside. And it does smell bad. Damp wood and pine needles that, together, obscure something rank, a once living creature now trapped or poisoned beneath the floorboards or behind the wall. A nasty surprise for whenever the current owners decide to return, if they ever do.

And the kitchen's turquoise walls. The original color of loss.

"I'm going outside," O'Brien says as she passes me, looking even more ill than earlier.

"You okay?"

"It's just hard to breathe."

"I know. It's a bit foul in here."

"Not just inside, but out." She grips both hands around my forearms. "There's something *wrong* about this place, David."

There always was, I almost say. But before I can help her O'Brien releases me and shuffles out the back door where I hear her pull in a couple gasps as she stands on the deck, hands clutched on her knees.

Now that I'm here I breathe it in. And the life I'd buried fills my lungs in an instant, so that I'm remembering from the inside out.

The first thing that appears is my brother. Lawrence. Standing just beyond reach and looking at me with the same mixture of affection and obligation as he did in life. Two years older than me and always tall for his age, which meant he was often mistaken for being more mature, more able to "manage it," as my father put it, where the thing to be managed was himself.

He would sometimes call him Larry but I never did. He was no more a Larry than I was a Dave, both of us too serious, too brooding and reserved to properly wear a shortened name. Not that Lawrence was a fearful kid. As we moved from school to school he protected me from every bully, shielded me from the taunts of every clique,

251

sacrificing his own opportunities for inclusion (he was an athletic kid, and had invitations) in the name of preventing me from being alone.

Who knows how happy he would have gone on to be—how happy either of us might have been—if we'd had a different father. One who didn't drink so prodigiously, even proudly, as if someone had challenged him to a self-destructive competition and he was damned if he was going to lose. Other than whisky, his main interest lay in pursuing cheaper and cheaper rents in ever more remote places, dedicating himself to lowering our already poverty-level expenses in the way other fathers dedicated themselves to finding better jobs in better towns.

My mother stayed because she loved him. Over the seventeen years that followed before she died, too, of natural causes (what they still called smoking-related emphysema at the time), she offered no alternative reason to me. Though perhaps self-pity held her in its grip, too, a taste for the tragic, the delicious heartbreaks of the could-have-been.

As for our father, while he could never find his way to love us—he was too busy for that, too distracted by the avoidance of collectors, the hustle for advance payment on odd jobs—he was not especially cruel, either. No slaps, no belt thrashes, no time in locked rooms. No punishments at all, really, other than our not having him present in our lives. A mobile emptiness that occupied the space of the living room chairs and head of the kitchen tables and laid upon the bathroom floors we paid a couple months for, then were asked to leave for the months we didn't.

Nobody called depression a disease then. Nobody called it depression. People were said to have "nerves," or be "under the weather," or allowed themselves to waste away in the name of a "broken heart." Our father, who still hauled a half dozen boxes of books he'd acquired over his earlier years of training and brief career as a schoolteacher and fancied himself a man of underestimated learning, preferred the term *melancholy* on the rare occasions he spoke of it. His drinking was justified on the grounds it was the only way he knew how to hold it within manageable boundaries. I never realized until this moment that I learned the word from him.

Outside, I find O'Brien sitting on the edge of the deck, her feet swinging through the grass.

"Feeling better?"

"That's probably too much to ask," she says.

"Would you rather wait in the car?"

"I'm fine here. I just need to pull my shit together."

"You need me, just squeak."

"Where you going?" O'Brien looks up at me.

"Just going to head down to the river. Take a look around," I say.

"Don't."

"What's wrong?"

"The river."

"What about it?"

"I can hear it. Voices. A thousand voices." She reaches up an unsteady hand and grasps the tips of my fingers. "They're in *pain*, David."

My toes touch the river and it sings with pain.

Tess heard it, too. And though I don't, I believe O'Brien does. Which means that's the way I have to go. A conclusion O'Brien comes to even before I do, as she releases my fingers without me having to pull them away. Returns her gaze to her own swinging feet.

The walk down reveals the slope to be steeper than it looked by the cabin. It has the effect of drawing you closer to the water faster than you want to go, an invisible undertow. This part of the property has been cleared and re-cleared over the years, so that while the forest is halfway to reclaiming it with trees, it's still a patch of unshaded ground. It blinds me all the way down to the bank's edge. The river alive with the light of the sun's rage, so that its surface appears to reach out to me, the water ablaze.

Yet it is only a river. Containing memories and voices only to the extent we contain them.

"The mind is its own place," I say aloud.

Magic words that bring my brother back. Or if not him, the memory of his scream.

I had walked down the slope I just walked down and stood where I stand now when I was six. Looking for Lawrence, whom my mother had permitted to leave the breakfast table before me. I knew he'd be down here. Fishing maybe, or collecting frogs in a jar. The river was where we'd come to be free of our parents, from the sounds and smells of home that are a comfort in other kids' lives.

Lawrence could have gone left or right from here. A narrow trail followed the bank for what might have been miles past our lot on both sides, and we had favorite, secret spots along its route. The six-year-old me had stood here, wiping the crumbs from his chin, trying to guess which way to try first. And I'd heard Lawrence's scream in the eastward distance. Just as I hear it now.

I run with my head down, beneath the arching willow boughs, the tails whipping my back. Twice I almost slip off the moistened path into the water but manage to windmill my arms and regain a lurching balance. And as I go, the same rushing question I'd had the first time.

Do you scream like that when you're drowning?

I'd doubted it then. Not that my brother might have slipped into the water or suffered an accident that had put him in jeopardy, but that he would make that sound if he had. Because his scream had the tremor of shock more than the summoning for help. The horror of something other than the river taking him down.

An answer comes to me now. One I didn't know enough to recognize as a boy.

You only scream like that when you're being *drowned.*

Lawrence watches me emerge from the trees and stop on a flat table of rock. Holding on for me. Wildly kicking against the rocks a foot beneath the surface, straining his neck to keep his mouth from breathing the cold current into his chest. A moment that, at the time of its first happening would have taken a second or less. Yet now in its return engagement has been slowed. Revealing a truth that passed too swiftly at the time, and I too young to read them. A pair of truths.

Lawrence meets my eyes from the far side of the river. The Other

Place we never crossed to. The side we feared and where Tess had stood in her real dream.

The second thing I see is that my father stands over Lawrence. One of his big hands on the small of my brother's back, the other tight around his neck.

Not trying to pull him up. Pushing him under.

And then he does.

My father has been waiting for me, too. To be a witness. To leave his mark on my soul.

Lawrence thrashes in the shallows. Held down lengthwise as though unsuccessfully learning to swim and my father his inattentive teacher. It is a configuration that led to my misunderstanding at the time. My father unable to get a grip to pull him up, my brother's struggle hindering his rescue. Confusing enough to build an alternative history around. A lie to tell myself from that point until today.

But when Lawrence goes still and my father looks up to me there is no question what his goggled eyes say. A triumphant hatred. The self-congratulation that comes with three lives taken at once.

It is my father who holds Lawrence down, but my father in body only. Even as I watch, his face alters to show the presence inside of him. A sharp-edged skull. Needle chinned. The cheeks—too wide, too high—bulging against his skin. What the Unnamed actually looks like. Belial's face.

The demon's malice was not satisfied even with this.

It released my father from its hold, and I watched him return to himself. Look down at what he'd done. Then look at me.

My father. Not Belial anymore, not a spirit. It was my father who had looked into his youngest son's eyes and spoken the truth in his heart.

It should have been you.

From out of the darkness, O'Brien's voice. A far-off shriek.

"David!"

I'm running back the way I came. No more than a couple hundred yards, though it feels longer on the return, the river slopping over the

255

bank and squelching underfoot. My heart a knot of pain finding its way out between my ribs.

Her voice again. Weaker this time. Not really a shout at all, but a hollow echo.

"Run!"

Is she urging me to come faster, or warning me away? Not that it matters. Belial is here. I know that. I've *seen* it. But the sound of O'Brien's desperation has, for this moment at least, swept his influence away.

When I come out from the willows and start up the slope I notice the van first. White, new. A rental. Ontario plates at the front. YOURS TO DISCOVER. Just visible around the corner of the cabin and parked in front of the Mustang.

Then I see O'Brien. Lying in the cabin's rear doorframe, her head uncomfortably propped against the wood and the rest of her splayed out. Her legs leaping in spastic jolts. Her tongue repeatedly licking her blanched lips as though in futile preparation to deliver a speech.

I see the wounds last, so that I'm kneeling next to her at the same time I notice how whatever had been used to cut her had left the pattern of a cross in her chest. The blood coloring through the fabric of her shirt.

"You have to go," she says. Her voice a series of small cracks.

"I'm not going anywhere. We have to get you to a hospital."

"No hospitals."

"This is different."

"I'm saying I won't make it even if you try."

She takes a breath and with it the wounds open wide, pulsing out. I cover her with my hands but there are too many entry points. Her body warm but turning instantly cool in its exposure to the air.

Yet she is calm. Her eyes rolled back to a line staring somewhere just above my head. Not afraid, no evidence of pain. One last squeeze of adrenaline. A final insight or vision, true or false.

"I can see her, David."

"See who?" I ask, though I already know.

"She's . . . waiting for you."

"Elaine—"

"She's holding on. But it . . . *hurts*. She—"

"*Elaine*. Don't—"

"—needs you to believe, too."

O'Brien's gaze lowers and she takes me in. It is the only way to put it. Her eyes hold me as though she'd lifted me into her arms and pressed me close to feel the last knocks of her heart. She doesn't have the strength to raise her hand let alone offer her embrace, so she manages it with her eyes. A dimming smile.

By the time I lower myself against her, she's gone.

It's quiet. Not in the sense that the birds have stopped singing or the breeze stopped blowing, but quiet in the way it has been quiet all along. There is only the river behind me. The water passing over the stones in continuous applause.

I lean against the doorframe opposite O'Brien. The sky a collection of clouds of the kind you might see animals or faces in, though none show themselves to me. There is the idea that something should be felt now, something clear. Sadness. Rage. But there is just the flat erasure of exhaustion.

And the knowledge that whoever did this to O'Brien is still here.

As if appearing by the power of my thoughts, there's a figure I hadn't noticed before ankle-deep at the river's edge. Bent over, hands in the water. Busying himself with a task I can't see from here.

For the briefest moment the thought of attempting escape occurs to me. It might be possible to rise unnoticed, slip around the cabin, and get to the Mustang, be the first one to start back along the trail to the road. But he knows I'm here. Knows I'm entertaining these very thoughts and is no more bothered by them than an untied shoelace.

The Pursuer only turns once I've walked down the slope to stand a dozen feet behind him. Close enough to see the soiled bandage he'd tied around his head. To see that he's washing a knife. The blade long, rubber-handled. The knife we'd left next to him on the motel pillow.

He glances over his shoulder and, at seeing me, grins in welcome.

Though there is no warmth in it. It is the look an animal gives another animal to lull it into calmness before doing it harm.

Slowly, he shifts his body around so that all of him faces me. His feet still in the water. Its movement carrying away discolored plumes washed from the knife blade, his pant legs, dripped from the ends of his fingers.

"You came down here just to wash that off or to give me a chance to leave?"

"You're not going anywhere," he says. "I pulled the plugs from your car."

"I could run."

"You wouldn't get far."

"There's still your van."

"Yeah," he says, and pulls his keys from his pocket. Dangles them tauntingly in the air. "There is."

All at once the fullness of his intentions burns up from my legs, and though I try, I can't prevent myself from shaking. The Pursuer sees it. Grins his not-grin again.

He pulls one of his feet out of the water and onto the bank.

"Why a van?" I ask, seeing that talking is better than not talking.

"Disposal."

"I would've thought this place was ideal for making a couple bodies go away."

"Burying isn't the way to do it," he says, shaking his head as though still disappointed to hear people make this mistake. "And you know what? I don't *like* it here."

The Pursuer brings his other foot out of the water and stands straight. For the first time I notice the blood on his jacket. Not the spray that came from O'Brien—though this is on every part of him, too, his cheeks, the tip of his nose—but a gash in his side, just above his hip. An oval seeping wider through the cotton.

He follows my line of sight. Nods at the hole in his body as if it's a mildly inconvenient task he'll have to tend to later. A dry cleaning pickup. An ATM withdrawal.

"Your girlfriend put up quite a fight for a sick lady," he says.

"You like killing women?"

"There's no liking or not liking about it."

"Your employers," I say. "What are they afraid of?"

"They don't have to justify their decisions to me."

"Guess."

"I'd say you're too close to something," he says, and shuffles up to the top of the bank. He stands below me still, but has swallowed up half the distance between us in a single stride.

"Wouldn't the Church approve of something like the document becoming public?" I say, my mind spinning around, looking for a plan that isn't there. "Might win a few million converts on the panic factor alone."

"They're not in the changing-minds business. It's about maintaining what they've already got. Keeping balance. If it ain't broke, don't let some stupid fucker fuck it up sort of thing."

"Something you're happy to help them with."

"I'm a hired man," he says with a weariness that seems to surprise himself. "I've done this quite a few times."

"A murderer for the Church. That ever trouble the conscience of an altar boy from Astoria?"

"You Catholic, David?"

"My parents were. In name."

"Still. You know what it is to follow holy orders."

"Thou shalt not kill."

"The most frequent exception. But hey, you're the expert, right?"

His laugh at this is genuine, cut short only by a burning flare in his side that bends him over a moment before he straightens again.

"You could tell them I got away," I say.

There is nothing in his expression that shows he's even heard this. Just another sliding step closer. And another.

He expects me to run. His arms held slightly out from his sides, knees bent, ready to get a jump when I start up the slope. He probably figures he'll be all over me before I have a chance to take a single step.

It's why he's startled when I run at him.

Not even thinking about the knife. Not thinking about anything but speed. Reaching him before his trained responses have a chance of booting up.

It almost works. The flats of my hands slamming into the top of his chest as he raises the knife, so that it passes over instead of into me. Cuts a flap through my shirt. A red line from shoulder to shoulder.

He's bringing the blade up again—unhesitating, unlike me, who pauses in this quarter-second to uselessly *think*—as I push into him once more. It's little more than a nudge, the roughness of contact you might have riding the subway at rush hour. But it's enough for him to wheel back slightly, for one of his feet to try to find firmer ground just behind him. Instead, the foot uproots a clump of turf and slides away. And I run into him again.

We both fall. An awkward embrace neither of us can release the other from. It keeps him below and me on top. Stays that way when we hit the water.

An insane thrashing. Sideways fists. Watery puke.

There is no fight, only the reflex to keep our heads above the surface. Beneath me, I can feel the Pursuer's fear as acutely as my own. Instead of creating a hesitation in me, his terror gives me a focus. I want him to experience *more* of it. The promise of this moves everything faster.

My knee comes to rest on his elbow so that while the swings of his knife can't connect with my gut or chest, he can reach my hands that are now clasped around his throat. Finding the windpipe. Pressing down with the weight of my body, arms locked straight. The click of something soft giving way in his neck. But he keeps swinging the knife at me until the blade lands on the base of my thumb. Gains purchase with the first gouge, the exclamation of blood. Then he starts to cut. A steady sawing through tissue. Then bone. Even as his face turns from crimson to purple to near-black he keeps methodically sawing. But I don't let go. The pain screeches like an animal locked inside me, biting itself, using its claws to get out. But I don't let go. With a jerk the Pursuer's knife cuts through to the other side and my thumb drops into the current. It floats away, bobbing playfully, leaving an oily stain upon the surface. I watch it. Feel the life now draining from me as it has just stopped draining from the man whose head I now plunge underwater. Hold there. Watching his nostrils and lips for bubbles that roar up, then slow. Then stop.

The white of unconsciousness veils over my sight. I don't let go. Even as I'm slipping forward or back or down, slipping away.

I don't let go.

THROUGH EDEN

23

WHITE.

THEN, PIECE BY PIECE, THE WORLD AGAIN.

Sitting in a car by a river. A van just ahead of me with Ontario plates. YOURS TO DISCOVER.

Blood.

It's the sight of the blood that quickens the rush of particulars—the steering wheel with FORD signatured on the horn, the iPhone on the dash, the hunting knife wetly nested atop the empty coffee cups in the footwell—along with the pain. Adding character as it grows. Improvising.

Your thumb's been cut off. Tie that up.

A voice in my head. Helpful but urgent.

Stop the bleeding or you'll black out again and never come back.

Tess's voice. Never known to be a first-aid expert, never good with the gross stuff. But right now, she seems to know what she's talking about.

I look into the backseat and find my overnight bag wide open, underwear and cotton T-shirts and an uncapped tube of toothpaste oozing blue gel over a bundle of socks. I grab one of the shirts and loop it tight around the stump. Watch the blood seep through. A map of enlarging islands.

I reach for the iPhone and dial 9-1-1 with the other hand. It replies with the little beeping song that signals failure. *No connection.*

Something has me opening a different window on the phone's screen. Entering the dictaphone feature, where there is a table of recordings. Find a selection. Hit play.

A roar of air. Driving fast with the windows down. And then a voice. Cutting through the background noise as though in command of it.

Do you believe in God?

The voice is young, female, but it doesn't belong to a girl. A voice made up of absences—no inflection, no hesitations. That there is nothing telling about it is what makes it inhuman.

I don't know if there's a God or not. I've never seen him if there is.

Me talking. The familiarly sharp edge that is the corrosion of grief. Along with something new. The dry catch of fear.

But I've seen the Devil. And I promise you, he is most definitely real.

The keys dangle from the ignition and I give them a twist, but the engine doesn't turn over. The spark plugs. He wasn't bluffing about that.

I knee the driver's-side door open and test my feet on the ground. There is something here I can't leave behind. Something I need to learn.

It goes well for the first three strides. Then my knees slip forward and I'm down, my cheek digging a trough into the gravel. But I'm on my feet again before I'm aware of trying. Around the corner to find the body at the back door.

My friend.

Her face so composed it suggests a communication of what she felt at the end. Something like bliss. Though this may be only another misreading. For isn't there something potentially mocking in her wide-open eyes, staring into the sun? Couldn't her smile be what's left of a cruel laughter? Amusement at the thought of what awaits me at the river's edge?

Because that's where my feet are taking me now. Thrashing through the grass to the gray current. The water slurping and curling around the rocks that poke through the surface like bleached skulls.

> *. . . yet from those flames*
> *No light, but rather darkness visible*

The dead man lies only a few yards downstream. Legs lolling right to left and back again in the passing water as though cooling themselves from the heat.

I kneel close to the body. Take the keys from his pocket, then put my hand to the unmoving chest. Feel for a heartbeat I know won't be there. Though I know just as certainly that he will speak to me.

The dead man's eyes open.

A slow slide of the wet lids that I refuse to accept is happening even as it happens. His lips, too. Parting with the sound of stuck-together book pages.

I bend and put my ear close. Hear the wet rattle that draws breath with the sound of sand dropped down a well.

He speaks to me. Not the man's voice anymore. A liar's voice I have no choice but to believe.

Pandemonium . . .

I'M HEADING BACK SOUTH IN THE PURSUER'S VAN. THINKING ONLY about staying on the road. Not letting the white take me again.

The closest hospital sign directs me off at Parry Sound and I stagger into Emergency with a horror show of a hand and a tale of an amateur home reno gone wrong. There are some demands for details, and I offer a vague reply about a lost grip on a rotary saw. The doctor notes the wound looks too "chewy" for that but I just beg for morphine, get a laugh for my remark about how you don't know chewy until you see how the wife is going to react when she hears about this.

They ask about the thumb's whereabouts and I catch myself before saying *It's probably floated downstream into the lake by now*. Admit to not remembering. No good to anyone at this point, is it? What's gone is gone. It's just a thumb. Wasn't one much for texting anyway.

I'm stitched and patched up when the doctor suggests I should be admitted, just for the night, as I've lost a fair amount of blood. I invent a brother who lives near town. He's on his way to pick me up as we speak. Okay if I stay with him instead?

Twenty minutes later and I'm walking out to the parking lot to the Pursuer's van, hoping none of the eyes from inside watch me hop into the cab and drive off.

For the time it takes me to find the highway ramp I'm expecting to hear the whoop of a police cruiser pulling me over, but the streets are empty. Then I'm roaring down toward the city again and, beyond it, the border. If I make it that far.

Because there will be more people after me soon. Not because somebody will come upon O'Brien's or the Pursuer's body overnight (or even in the morning, and possibly not until hunting season in the fall), but because the Pursuer's employers will be expecting a call saying the job is done. When they don't hear from him, they'll send somebody to check. And when they find what they find, they'll turn to Plan B and look for me with whatever means lie at their disposal. Which will include the police. And worse.

They will know, by the discoveries at the cabin, that I am close to doing what the demon has asked of me. I've likely gotten further than anyone has before. And though they wanted me followed at first to find out what my quest was for, now it's a matter of taking me down.

I could hide. Try to wait it out. But that has a few rather obvious drawbacks. One, they'll find me. Two, the people the Pursuer worked for want the document now with a desperation that will redouble their efforts for every hour I remain at large.

And three, if I have any chance of getting Tess back, it has to be now. Because at 6:51:48 PM this evening, she'll be gone.

Which means getting to New York as fast as I can.

Pandemonium.

I might be able to make the airport in Toronto and slip out on the next flight to LaGuardia. But airports are tougher border crossings than bridges. Cameras, passport checks, customs. When you're on the run—no matter from whom—airports are a bad idea.

Which leaves me to stay on the road. Though right now I'm riding in a dead man's vehicle. A man I killed.

I skirt around central Toronto and leave the bank towers and toothpick condos in the rearview when I smooth onto the QEW. Twice I pass O.P.P. cruisers on the shoulder, clocking speeders, but they don't come after me. It's good luck far less likely to hold if I try to cross the Rainbow Bridge into the States driving a rental van under George Barone's name, or whatever alias he registered it under. And I don't think they let you just walk over. Particularly not a guy in a bloodstained jacket and with a recently severed thumb.

At Grimsby, I stop at a 7-Eleven and buy Tylenol, a six-pack of Red Bull, sunglasses, a pre-made egg salad sandwich and, in the clothing section that is a single rack next to the tiers of gum, a Red Sox ball cap, a GO! LEAFS! GO! T-shirt, and a Goodyear Racing Team windbreaker. All useful. But there's still the van to be replaced.

Past St. Catherines I exit at a rural crossroads and take a few random turns. Drive off the road and into the middle of a cherry orchard, ditching the van next to an irrigation creek. Cover the roof as best I can with fallen branches. Then I'm creeping out of the rows at a farmhouse with a beat-up Toyota sedan out front. Tip-toeing to the side door while sending up a silent prayer (addressed to O'Brien, I find halfway through).

It works. The door squeaks open and I'm in a mud room of dropped coats and boots, kids' mittens, hockey sticks leaning against the wall.

Farmers like to own dogs, don't they? If this one does, it's only a matter of seconds before I set it off. I'll have no choice but to attempt to run the two miles to the highway and then—what? Hitch-hike over the border?

Another prayer goes up to O'Brien.

There's no key in any of the pockets. Which forces me up the half flight of stairs to the kitchen. Looking in the fruit bowl, the candy dish littered with change next to the phone, feeling around the dark corners of the countertop.

Upstairs, a large body rolls over in bed. An equally large body shifts to be spooned by the first. Or perhaps wriggles close enough to whisper *Did you hear that?*

The fridge.

This comes to me sudden and sure. But who keeps valuables in the fridge?

Nobody. Sometimes, though, they've stuck a plastic line of hooks to the door where they hang their keys.

Outside again, the car starts and I ease it away.

By the time I reach the road at the end of the property's lane I hear no woofs or shotgun blasts when I lower the window. Not wanting to give another breaking-and-entering a try, I tell myself I have to assume this one has been successful, at least for the next couple hours, when Mr. and Mrs. Cherry Orchard will awaken to find their 2002 Camry has slipped away.

Usually, there's a lineup at the bridge before it's your turn to approach the customs official in the booth, hand over your passport, endure the scrutinizing stare that makes you feel like you've sewed bags of heroin into the car seats instead of trying to get away with stashing a bottle or two in the trunk. I'm counting on the delay to get my story straight, prepare some replies to the most likely questions.

"This isn't your car, sir."

I work at the cherry orchard. They sent me to run an errand before we started work.

"An errand to the United States?"

Yes.

"For what?"

Ladders. For picking the cherries.

"You don't have ladders in Canada?"

Of course we do! They're just not as good as American ladders.

I don't even bother praying this time.

When I drive up there's no line at all. I'm lowering the window to look up at a fifty-something guy with the newspapery skin of a chain smoker. In addition to suspicious, he appears deeply unhappy.

"Citizenship?"

"American. And Canadian. I'm dual."

"Yeah?" He blinks. "What happened to your thumb?"

He leans over the edge of the door to his booth with interest in my bandaged hand.

"Cut the bugger off," I say.

"How'd you manage that?"

"Cherry picking."

He nods, instantly bored again. As though this very conversation is exactly the same conversation he has a dozen times a night.

"Take care now," he says sadly, and closes his window against the chill.

I OPT AGAINST I-90 AND TAKE THE UPSTATE BACKROADS TOWARD Gotham instead. Abandon the Toyota behind a Pizza Hut in Batavia. A used-car lot up the street is just opening when I walk in wearing my disguise—sunglassed and ball-capped, Goodyear racing striped collar standing straight up—and put my credit card down to take the red Charger they're showing off on the grass. Ten minutes later I'm throwing a state map into the backseat and accelerating onto I-90, figuring I'm more likely to become lost somewhere in the thatch of meandering secondary roads of upstate New York than pulled over on the most direct route to Manhattan.

The bad news comes at a service center outside Schenectady, where I stop to google my own name on my phone.

The first result triggers a howl from my guts: "Columbia Professor Person of Interest in Grisly Killings." I consider clicking the story open but realize I already know it better than anyone.

271

I get out of the Charger and walk away.

Used-car lots are out of the question now, as my Visa will light up the moment it comes close to an authorization terminal. It leaves me to walk into the closest residential neighborhood and open the front door of the first house I come to without bothering to even peep in the window to see if anyone's up and around. Keys right there on the dining room table. A toilet flush in the basement tells me I have a second, maybe two.

It's all I need.

Less than an hour and a half later I'm close enough to New York to ditch this car, too, and board a Hudson Line commuter train into the city. Joining the other midday trenchcoats and business suits finding their seats and hiding behind their *Times* or smart phones, rattling toward their work cubicles and windowed boxes.

I keep my collar up and cap brim low. Stare out the window so my face is something only those few pedestrians the train speeds past might see.

With every mile I am closer to you, Tess.

And, with a shaking cold that takes hold like a virus, closer to the one who keeps you, too.

24

GRAND CENTRAL AT FIVE O'CLOCK RUSH HOUR AND I'M SQUEEZING up the hot tunnels in a solid congestion of humanity, half of us looking for cabs that, when we make it to the sun-dazzled street, are nowhere to be found. A pair of cops by the station's doors keep to the shade of the metal awning, scrutinizing passersby in a ritual performance of vigilance. This afternoon, do their priorities include keeping an eye out for a David Ullman, last seen wearing a ridiculous 7-Eleven wardrobe and missing the primary digit of his right hand? If so, these guys are lousy at their jobs. They catch me looking at them and return a brief New York cop *keep-it-movin'-buddy* stare, then continue murmuring a dirty joke between themselves, their eyes alert for terrorists and miniskirts.

Even so, I doubt I have much time to continue undetected. Every minute now that I shuffle along the baked concrete toward the Chase Bank on 48th without someone shouting "I saw that guy on the news!" or being tackled by men spilling out of black Suburbans wearing fluorescent FBI vests is a minute I can't count on. And instead of keeping to the shade of the buildings' walls, I'm leaping off the curb every half block, waving for a cab, exposing myself to every police cruiser that passes. Eventually I decide the dangers of trying to hail a taxi are greater than just walking straight to the bank, camouflaging myself among moving packs of similarly attired tourists as best I can. The day's heat cooking me inside the nylon jacket, but I keep it on, fearing exposure if the raised collar stops shielding my jawline from view.

Entering the bank, I notice every black-domed security camera in the ceiling, every security guard with a wire whispering into his ear. And then, at the Client Services counter, new butterflies at having to give my name and ask to remove the contents of my deposit box. The assistant manager emerges to shake my hand (a bit of excruciating public-relations theater) and wishes for me to "Stay cool out there." But as she returns to her office down the hall, does she glance back at me and the teller who guides me to the vault? When she pauses to speak with a guy at an external desk, does he look up at me by coincidence or direction?

There's no retreat now, anyway. It's coming on close to six. *Less than an hour before—before what?* I try not to ponder this, just move to the next step. And right now, that's getting the document.

The teller brings me the oversized box and closes the privacy door, letting me pull out the briefcase. I double-check it to confirm the laptop and digital camera are still there. Two pieces of equipment that half a dozen electronic stores within two blocks of where I stand would sell for a couple grand, all in. Formerly recording little more of value than students' term papers and footage of Tess in a tutu at her spring ballet recital. Now containing a new history for the world.

I snap the briefcase closed and walk out with only the briefest nod at the teller. Keep my eyes on the revolving doors opening onto the heat-shimmered street. If I look at nothing but the doors, I won't be stopped.

And I'm not. Not yet.

A taxi pulls to the curb directly out front and I'm in the backseat through the street-side door before the current customer is finished paying. Then I'm slouched down so that only my ball cap is visible to the surrounding traffic. My eyes studying my shoes to avoid the driver in the mirror.

"Grand Central," I tell him as we ease into the bumper-to-bumper current. Realize the last time I gave a taxi driver this destination I ended up at the Dakota.

But not this time. We're not going anywhere. Jammed in the gridlock, the downtown traffic of 5th Avenue a narrow parking lot of black Town Cars, yellow cabs, moving vans.

"Try another route," I tell the driver.

"*What* other route?"

I push a fifty through the plexiglass window to cover the nine-dollar fare. Get out and sidestep past the bumpers to the curb. When I check both ways and can't spot any police, I run.

A heaving sprint east along 46th Street to Park Avenue. People on the sidewalk glancing up from their phones just in time to jump out of the way. Some mildly amused ("Ho-ho!") or vaguely impressed in seen-everything New Yorker fashion ("Mother*fucker!*"), others startled into fist-raised anger ("Com'ere, asshole!"). But none try to stop a hundred and ninety pounds of raging, unshaved madman.

I take the corner without slowing and a nurse screams as I nearly take out both her and the elderly man in the wheelchair she pushes. As I pass, his eyes seem to brighten, as though he'd been looking forward to the sight of me, wild-eyed and arm-pumping, all day.

I don't slow until I make it through the doors of the station. It's only once I'm inside that I realize I left my wallet in the cab. Credit cards, ID, every last dollar I have. And it's too late to run back to see if the taxi's still there. Not that it matters. What use do I have for any of that now? I'm about to enter another place altogether. One where money has no purpose. Where even my name has no meaning.

Down the stone slope and into the main concourse along with all the others seeking the gate to their train or a snapshot of themselves with the giant Stars and Stripes hanging from the ceiling in the background. None aware that, somewhere among them, there is an ancient spirit occupying the skin of the dead. And that a living man has traveled seven thousand miles to meet it.

I come to stand near the center of the floor, turning around and, first, scanning the upper level of bars and restaurants to see if Belial stands at a railing waiting for me. *But what am I looking for? What form has it chosen to take?* I keep an eye out for a repeat performance. Will Junger. Toby. One of the Reyes girls. Raggedy Anne. Yet no one familiar to me presents themselves, whether among the living or otherwise.

With a sudden wave of nausea the thought arrives that *I am wrong*.

The "clues" were never clues, the "trail" only a wandering of my own making. The demon, if it was ever real at all, merely delighted in watching me run around in this continental circle. A man lost in every meaning of the word.

Which would mean Tess is lost, too.

Soon the police will come. And they will find me here. Weeping in the crowd on the terminal floor, cursing the painted stars on the ceiling and whatever cruel architect screwed them into the sky, inviting those on Earth to look for patterns that were never there to begin with.

So farewell hope, and with hope farewell fear.

He stands beneath the gold clock in the same spot O'Brien would stand when I'd come here to meet her. Watching me with an expression of contentment he seemed incapable of while alive.

My father. Belial's final joke.

I approach and feel the malicious triumph radiating from him, a fouling of the air that passes into my lungs without taste, but repugnant nonetheless. Yet the setting of his face remains the same. A mask of fatherly pleasure at seeing his son after a long separation. The prodigal returned.

"You cannot know how long I have waited for someone like you," my father says in his own voice, though the inflections, however lifelessly flattened, belong to the demon. "Others have come close but lacked the strength to endure. But you, David, are a man of uncommon commitment. A true disciple."

"I'm not your disciple," I say, the words barely audible.

"When you were called did you not answer? Are you not a witness to miracles?" He looks directly down at the briefcase at my side. "Are you not in possession of a new gospel?"

I don't move. It's the fight against blacking out. Dots of shadow swarming around my father's head. A Black Crown.

"Give it to me," he says.

I take an unconscious step back from his hand, now outstretched.

"I thought you wanted me to make it public," I say. "To speak for you."

"You *will* speak for me! But the document will precede you. And then, when the time is right, you will tell your story. You will personalize the document, give people a way to accept it."

"The police are after me. Others, too."

"Submit to me, David, and I will protect you."

"Submit? How?"

"*Let me in.*"

My father takes a half step closer but somehow more than makes up the distance of my retreat, so that he is now all I can see, all I can hear.

"How our story is presented is as important as what that story is," he says. "The narrator must have a compelling tale of his own, and there is nothing more compelling than self-sacrifice. Milton was jailed, too. Socrates, Luther, Wilde. And of course, no one more than Christ himself understood how delivering your message from chains makes the message easier to hear."

"You want me to be a martyr."

"That is the way we will win our war, David. Not from the position of dominance, but resistance! We will win the hearts of women and men by showing them how God has suppressed their quest for knowledge since the beginning. The forbidden fruit."

"*Hence I will excite their minds / With more desire to know, and to reject / Envious commands.*"

"Yes! You will feed man's desire to know the truth of my kind, our unjust fall, the cruelty of God, and the emancipation that Satan offers. Equality. Is this not the most noble cause? Democracy! This is what I bring. Not a plague, not arbitrary suffering. Truth!"

My father smiles at me with a warmth so alien to the muscles of his face it causes a trembling in his cheeks.

"*Courage never to submit or yield.*"

"Quite so!" it says, mouth wide. "Our Lord Satan's pledge."

"But you forget the preceding lines. *All is not lost; th' unconquerable will, / And study of revenge, immortal hate.*"

"As I've told you," my father's voice says, though now without the empty humor of moments ago. "John was obliged to disguise his true sympathies."

"That is no disguise. Revenge. Hate. Those are your sole motivations. *All good to me is lost. Evil be thou my good.*"

"A play on words."

"That's all you do! Turn words inside out. You can't let them stand for what you feel because you feel nothing. Good for evil, evil for good. It's a distinction that lies beyond your grasp."

"David—"

"Belial. *Without worth.* The greatest lie you tell is that you are a creature sympathetic to humanity. It's why who delivers the document is as important as the document itself."

My father steps closer still. The power and size of his frame as evident now as when I was a child. Yet I cannot stop the words I speak to him. Convictions I'm arriving at as they pass my lips.

"All along I thought I was chosen for my expertise. But that's just window dressing. You chose me because mine is the story of a man who loves his child. And yours is the story of nothing. No child. No love. No friend. In all of the ways that matter, *you don't exist.*"

"Be *careful.*"

"Why? You can't return Tess to me. That was a lie from the start. I figured out your name, brought the document here before the new moon. None of it matters."

"David—"

"You have the power to destroy, but not to create, not to unite. No matter where she is now, you can't bring her back."

"How can you be sure?"

"Because I'm here for a different reason than helping you."

"Really?" he says, suddenly sure of itself again, knowing with this turn it has won. "Then *tell* me."

I can't answer that. It leaves me to look around the seething space of the great hall. Hear, as if for the first time, not its cacophony, but a chorus of human voices. Who among them would miss me if the serpent were to succeed? What would the end mean without Tess? Without her, I, too, am without worth.

Yet, though I am alone, those passing around me aren't. The young mother pushing a stroller with one hand and gripping the wrist of a toddler singing the alphabet with the other. An elderly couple kissing farewell, the man's crooked fingers drawn across the lines of his wife's cheek. Two women in burkas walking past a pair of Hasidim, the current of the crowd joining them for a moment as though in a secret meeting of the city's all-in-black devout. A man clipping by in heels and a red cocktail dress, his Marilyn wig in need of straightening.

Strangers set upon their own courses, crossing the terminal floor. But to see them as only this would be to take the demon's view. An erasure of their names, their own reasons for sacrifice.

"This isn't yours," I say, gripping the briefcase's handle with both hands.

"Your daughter—"

"I won't—"

"Your daughter is in PAIN!"

A head-splitting shriek. The echo of it shattering off the stone walls of the great hall. But nobody around us seems to hear. Just as nobody hears what he screams next.

"She is BURNING, David!"

I take a step closer to my dead father's face. Stare at the presence inside him through his eyes.

"If Tess is in hell, tell her I'll be there soon."

He is about to reply with force of some unpredictable kind. The coiled readiness of violence. Shoulders raised, fingers splayed out like claws. But something other than my defiance holds him back. His head turning as though at a shouted warning.

I take another step back and my father watches me go. His hate as pure as necessity, as a starving animal swallowing its young.

I turn and Belial's shriek follows me as I go. Grinding, metallic. Unheard by all but me.

If I keep looking at him I will be lost. Not because he will hunt me down, but because I will go to him. I can feel that as a weight greater than the briefcase sliding down against the back of my legs, its contents suddenly heavy as a slab of granite.

So I walk. Turn my back on my father and feel enveloped by the suffocating grief that is partly his, partly the thing inside him.

I'm halfway to the escalators when I spot the police. Two pairs of uniforms entering from the tunnel that leads up from the Oyster Bar. And then, a second later, coming down the stairs at the hall's opposite end, three men in suits who speak to each other under their breath, giving orders of deployment.

None of them seem to have seen me yet. Which means I have to move.

But I only remain standing where I am. Frozen by Belial's tormented cry. Its surface the sound of chaos. Yet beneath it, his knowing voice inside my head.

Come, David.

Sounding more fatherly than my father ever did. More falsely kind, falsely loving.

Come to me.

There is no choice anymore, no more refusal. I'm turning to go back to my father, still standing beneath the gold clock, when I see a woman who looks like someone I know. Someone I knew.

It's only her back. Only a glimpse. But in the next second it's enough to see that it is O'Brien. Not the woman with the frail, stooped posture of O'Brien at the end, but the tall and athletic Connecticut girl who never stopped, in her brainy, teasing, A-type way, being the tall and athletic Connecticut girl.

She doesn't look my way. Just goes to the ticket windows, her back to me. Cutting through the streams of travelers in a gray overcoat, her gait straight and unslowed.

I start after her. Which turns Belial's screech into a thundering howl.

The woman who looks like O'Brien purchases a ticket and then slips back into the crowd, heading toward the gates. It forces me to change course to follow, cutting across the sightline of the uniformed police who now jump up to scan across the heads rolling out before them like a rippled lake. I make no effort to conceal myself, judging a duck-and-run a greater risk of attracting notice than late-for-a-meeting swiftness. Trying to keep the dark-haired woman in view.

As I get closer, Belial's wailing suddenly lifts up several octaves before splitting in two, throwing part of its noise to a register lower than thunder, a nauseating sub-bass. So loud it feels like it will bring the stars on the ceiling down on us all. It spurs the reflex to look up.

And when I return my eyes to the crowd, O'Brien is gone.

At least, she isn't where she was a moment ago. Yet almost instantly I spot her again, maybe thirty feet to the left of where she'd been. *How could she have covered that ground in a second or two at most?* There is no time for the weighing of what is possible. I'm already following her again, now pushing people aside with murmured *Pardon me*s as she somehow carves through the same bodies without touching them.

When I catch up to her it hits me too late to pull my hand back from the woman's shoulder.

The animal smell of the barnyard. The mold of wet straw.

She turns. That is, her head swivels evenly upon its neck, though every other part of her seems frozen, a wax statue come to partial life. It's as though her face naturally looks backward, and she has merely parted her hair to show her bulging eyes to me, the pushed-out bones of cheek and chin, the black-rooted teeth.

"Shall we go, Professor?" the Thin Woman says.

I start to back away from her before realizing she holds my wrist. A grip as cold as the ring of a handcuff. With every pull against it there is a flare of pain at my elbow and shoulder that makes it clear the bones there are separating, the ligaments stretched to strands of gum.

"They hand in hand with wand'ring steps and slow," the Thin Woman recites, her voice calm as she slides me back toward the gold clock where Belial stands. *"Through Eden took their solitary way."*

I'm moving without stepping, as though dancing with my feet clamped atop my partner's. Over her shoulder, through a widening gap in the crowd, my father waits for me. His anguished screams now shaping into something else. A thousand children laughing at the spectacle of a chosen victim's pain.

I try to think of a prayer. A holy name. A line of scripture. But no words feel they could be uttered and believed at the same time. None but her name.

Tess.

It's only a thought at first. Then I say it. A whisper even I can barely hear. Yet it gives the Thin Woman pause, slows her floating progress. Lets me grip my arm with my free hand and jerk it back while kicking against the front of her legs with my feet.

Something pops at the base of my neck. *That's the collarbone* someone says, before I realize it's me. Followed by the pain, doubling and hot.

But I'm free.

Finding my footing on the stone floor again and backing away, the Thin Woman appearing puzzled for a moment before her lifeless half smile returns. She looks up at the clock that stands over Belial's head. The minute hand nudging to fifty.

Two minutes until the moon. Until she's his.

Come, my father offers again. *It's time, David.*

I turn my back to them both to catch sight of the other O'Brien as she disappears through the archway toward Gate Four. It turns my walk to a jog. And with it, Belial's screech returns. Louder even than before.

If I make it to the gate I will be out of view. Nothing matters but getting close to her. Because with every new foot I put between my father and myself—and every foot I come closer to the gate—the demon's howl diminishes. Losing its hold as though yielding it to another.

Quiet.

Instant and total. I make it off the main terminal floor and onto the platform with the others finishing their calls or tossing soda cans in the bins before boarding and finding a good seat. And I can hear the living world again, too. Their shoes upon the stone floor, their *I'll be home soons.*

She's not here. The woman I thought was O'Brien—but who wasn't, who *couldn't* have been—is gone. A look-alike I'd imagined. A summoned memory of how she'd appeared the times we'd been here together on our dates-that-weren't-dates.

As useful as the illusion was, it's no help now. There's no going back. If I have a chance of escape, it's not out there in the station, but on the train. But I don't have a ticket—have no way to *buy* a ticket—which means they will eject me at the first stop, or call security. Yet I'll be out of here. Away, for a few moments, from the police. From the thing that I can feel still waiting for me beneath the clock.

A hand on my shoulder. Firm and sure.

"Love the outfit, Professor."

I spin around to find her standing inches from me. Looking rested and well. More than that. Amused.

"Elaine. Jesus *Christ.*"

"What? He's here, *too?*"

I want to put my arms around her but all at once a cold wave washes over me and it nearly pulls me under.

"Please. Tell me you're not—"

"Don't worry," she says, pinching the skin of her face. "There's nobody in here but me."

"But you *can't* be here."

"I have a decisive rebuttal to that." She leans in close enough for me to smell the perfume at her neck. "I quite obviously *am* here."

"Are you—?"

"They don't give you wings or a halo or anything like that. But yes, as far as I can tell. I'd say yes."

A hundred questions compete for attention in my head, and O'Brien reads all of them and casts them away with a shake of her head.

"Get off at the Manitou station," she says, handing me the ticket she bought. "There'll be a white Lincoln in the lot with keys just under the left front tire."

"The document. I need time to put it somewhere safe. Or destroy it."

"That choice is yours."

"They'll still get me."

"*North by Northwest.*"

"I don't—"

"You're Cary Grant, remember? A good man caught up in a bad business. Mistaken identity. The Pursuer is known to police, the things he's done. You? You're a professor who's never gotten as much as a speeding ticket. You defended yourself the only way you knew how."

"That'll work?"

"Reasonable doubt. Works for the guilty often enough. You've got to figure the odds are even better for the innocent."

She puts her hands on either side of my face.

"You've done so well," she says. "Not just since Venice. Your whole life. I knew that, I think, but now I can *see* it. You've fought since you were a child."

"Fought for what?"

"To do the hard things most of us pretend are easy. To be good. You never let go. You were tested and you *passed*, David."

There isn't time for an embrace, I can see that in the flinch of her smile. But she holds me anyway. A coiled strength that passes through me, lightening the weight of the briefcase in my hands.

"You have to get on this train," she says, abruptly releasing me. "*This* train. Right now."

"I—"

"Yeah, yeah. I *know*."

I do as she says. Step through the nearest doors and hear them slide closed behind me. The train already pulling away.

The rear car I'm on is full, and I make my way up the aisle bending to steal glances out the window at the platform, but O'Brien is no longer there. By the archway a cop watches the train slip away into the tunnel and he sniffs after it, as though trying to detect a telltale trace in the platform's stale air.

Nothing to do now but find a seat. I pass through to the next car and find it only a quarter full. Stop to look over the rows, the backs of heads, trying to judge which position is least likely to attract a talkative passenger to join me farther down the line.

Choke on the air in my throat.

Halfway up the car, sitting alone by the window, staring out at the dark of the passing tunnel wall. A Riesling-colored braid just visible in the gap between the seats.

It takes what feels like a long time to make my way to sit next to her. For a longer time, neither of us move. The familiar orangey smell of her skin, now mixed with diminishing traces of wet hay, of animals kept in an unclean pen.

Her stillness suggestive of sleep. But in the window's reflection Tess's eyes are open. Taking both of us in. Chalky phantoms in the glass. The breath of her voice drawing a fog over us both.

"Daddy?"

"Yes."

"If I turn to look, will you still be here?"

"I'm here if you are."

The train speeds through the earth, under an island of millions. Soon we will rise on the other side of the river.

She turns and I see it's her.

It's her, and I believe.

3 1161 00880 5072

ACKNOWLEDGMENTS

Many thanks to Sarah Knight, Marysue Rucci, Jonathan Karp, Richard Rhorer, Kate Gales, Jessica Abell, Kate Mills, Jemima Forrester, Kevin Hanson, Alison Clarke, Amy Cormier, Felicia Quon, Max Arambulo, Dominick Montalto, Jonathan Evans, Jackie Seow, Molly Lindley, Esther Paradelo, Chris Herschdorfer, Jackie Levine, Anne McDermid, Monica Pacheco, Martha Magor, Chris Bucci, Stephanie Cabot, Peter Robinson, Sally Riley, Liv Stones, Howard Sanders, Jason Richman, and to my ring of angels, Heidi, Maude, and Ford.

ABOUT THE AUTHOR

ANDREW PYPER is the author of five acclaimed novels, including *Lost Girls*, which was an international bestseller and a *New York Times* Notable Book, and *The Killing Circle* (a *New York Times* Crime Novel of the Year). A number of his books are in active development to become feature films, including *The Demonologist*, which is being produced by Robert Zemeckis's company, ImageMovers, and Universal Pictures. He lives in Toronto.

DID YOU LOVE THE DEMONOLOGIST?
DISCOVER MORE NOVELS FROM ANDREW PYPER . . .

Praise for **The Guardians**

"Initially employing a quiet, confiding tone, Pyper reveals his skill with pacing as the story takes on the speed of a midnight dash through a graveyard. . . . This is a page-turner that will make your heart pound. You've been warned."

—*The Globe & Mail*

"Everything you could ask for in a thriller. It's psychologically un-nerving, moves like a bullet, and is fraught with so much tension you might crack a tooth reading it. Outstanding in every way."

—Dennis Lehane, author of *Mystic River*

"Ambitious . . . With a well-executed dual narrative, both past and present, strong characterizations, and some truly arresting images, *The Guardians* is a compelling and genuinely creepy read."

—*The Guardian* (U.K.)

"A perfect haunted-house story, a crisp, eerie, October night of a book that had me in its clutches from page one."

—Joanne Harris, author of *Chocolat*

"A master of psychological suspense. Andrew Pyper knows just how to lure you in to all the deep dark places of the human heart and then . . . twist."

—Lisa Gardner

"A splendidly eerie haunted house story, and a superb evocation of small town life. *The Guardians* gripped me from its opening line and never let go."

—John Connolly, author of *Every Dead Thing* and *The Lovers*

Praise for **The Killing Circle**

"If Andrew Pyper scripted our collective nightmares, we'd all be dreaming and screaming like the narrator of his gorgeously written and thoroughly unnerving suspense thriller, *The Killing Circle*. . . . Taken as either a classy ghost story or the chronicle of one man's mental breakdown, this is a terrific yarn. But in examining the universal need to define one's self through narrative, it also explores the darker side of storytelling."

—*The New York Times Book Review*

"Extraordinary . . . Powered by an ingeniously nonlinear narrative and suffused with a tone thick with dread, this is easily Pyper's most ambitious—and absorbing—work to date."

—*Publishers Weekly* (starred review)

"Pyper is a true prose-master . . . caustic and sharp-witted observations. An uncozy, fright-filled thriller."

—*The Globe and Mail* (editor's recommendation)

"The villain leaps off the page . . . Pyper does an impressive job building suspense, offering enough narrative twists and turns to keep the reader nicely off balance. Basing the experience of the novel in Rush's first-person perspective, he is able to capture not only the depths of the haunting and gradually mounting terror, but also the more routine aspects of the character's life. . . . A strong and compelling read."

—*The Vancouver Sun*

"A deliciously vicious thriller."

—*Toronto Life*

Praise for **Lost Girls**

"Exquisite . . . Pyper's writing moves fluidly from caustic wit to moments of striking insight and beauty. . . . *Lost Girls* itself inhabits, more than anything, Atwood country (with added passion)—a smart, wry, controlled tone narrating a northwood Gothic. A satisfying, old-style morality tale set in a ripping good—and complex—story brimming over with 90's style pockmarked souls and bruised psyches."

—*The Globe and Mail* (editor's choice)

"What sets *Lost Girls* apart is its brilliant evocation of place and mood. . . . For readers who relish metaphor with their narrative meat, *Lost Girls* is a rich meal."

—*Maclean's*

"Exceptional . . . Reads as though it were the secret love child of Alice Munro and Stephen King."

—*The Montreal Gazette*

"Everything about this dark, disquieting story confounds expectations. . . . It's hard to know exactly what kind of tale Pyper has told, but there's no doubt that he has told it brilliantly."

—*The New York Times*

"Pyper's spell-binding debut succeeds on so many levels—as a mystery, a legal thriller, a literary character study—that it's obvious why it was a #1 bestseller last year in Canada. . . . Compulsively appealing."
—*Publishers Weekly* (starred review)

"Most memorable . . . is the character of narrator Crane, who undergoes one of the most complete yet credible moral metamorphoses in recent fiction. A debut to remember and a real treat for crime fiction fans."
—*Booklist* (starred review; selected as Best First Mystery for 2000)

Hammond Public Library
Hammond, Ind.